PRAISE FOR VALERIE WOLZIEN AND HER NOVELS

"Valerie Wolzien is a consummate crime writer. Her heroines sparkle as they sift through clues and stir up evidence in the darker, deadly side of suburbia."
—MARY DAHEIM

"Wit is Wolzien's strong suit. . . . Her portrayal of small-town life will prompt those of us in similar situations to agree that we too have been there and done that."
—The Mystery Review

"Domestic mysteries, with their emphasis on everyday people and everyday events, are very popular and the Susan Henshaw stories are some of the best in this subgenre."
—Romantic Times

By Valerie Wolzien
Published by Fawcett Books:

Susan Henshaw mysteries:
MURDER AT THE PTA LUNCHEON
THE FORTIETH BIRTHDAY BODY
WE WISH YOU A MERRY MURDER
AN OLD FAITHFUL MURDER
ALL HALLOWS' EVIL
A STAR-SPANGLED MURDER
A GOOD YEAR FOR A CORPSE
'TIS THE SEASON TO BE MURDERED
REMODELED TO DEATH
ELECTED FOR DEATH
WEDDINGS ARE MURDER
THE STUDENT BODY
DEATH AT A DISCOUNT
AN ANNIVERSARY TO DIE FOR

Josie Pigeon mysteries:
SHORE TO DIE
PERMIT FOR MURDER
DECK THE HALLS WITH MURDER
THIS OLD MURDER
MURDER IN THE FORECAST

AN ANNIVERSARY
TO DIE FOR

VALERIE WOLZIEN

FAWCETT BOOKS • NEW YORK

A Fawcett Book
Published by The Ballantine Publishing Group
Copyright © 2002 by Valerie Wolzien

www.ballantinebooks.com

ISBN 0-449-00717-0

Manufactured in the United States of America

First Edition: August 2002

OPM   10   9   8   7   6   5   4   3   2   1

For my aunt, Betty Patrick.
And for her children, and her children's children.

ONE

MARRIED FOR THIRTY YEARS, THE HENSHAWS WERE GIV-
ing a party to celebrate this remarkable fact with their many
friends and neighbors. Susan had reserved the venue, the
historic Landing Inn in Oxford Landing, Connecticut, seven
months in advance. She had agonized over every detail of
the decorations and planned a menu that included family
favorites as well as selections for guests who insisted on
dieting or eating vegetarian. She had ordered six cases of
Napa Valley Merlot, six cases of French Sauvignon Blanc,
and five cases of Dom Perignon. She had taken ten minutes
to buy Jed a new tie and had spent three days shopping in
New York City before choosing the silver silk shift she
wore. Her hair and makeup had been done by professionals
just this morning. She had gone on a diet and actually lost
seven pounds.

So why, she wondered, wasn't anyone paying any attention to her?

"Susan, honey? Is something wrong?"

She smiled as Jed slipped his arm around her shoulder.
"Why? Do I look like something's wrong?" She brushed a
sweep of hair off her forehead.

Jed knew exactly what she was thinking. "Your hair is

fine. You look wonderful. Just a bit distracted. You were staring over the shoulder of that last couple we greeted."

"I was just wondering what's happening on the deck. Do you think they thought I was being rude?"

"Nope. I think they were too anxious to find the bar. Who were they, anyway?"

"Jed! After all the time we spent going over the guest list! That was the Freedmans. You know them. He was Chad's orthodontist, and she was the leader of Chrissy's Brownie troop for two years."

"Sue, that was over a decade ago. And I hope they weren't quite so anxious to get to the alcohol in those days."

"They're lovely people," Susan protested. "I did hear that he had been drinking a bit too much for the last few years, but Chad's teeth look wonderful. And Chrissy . . . Well, Chrissy was a bit too artistic for that troop. I remember when they were making little Christmas trees out of felt, glitter, and wire coat hangers, and Chrissy . . ."

"Susan, how many people did you invite to this party?" Jed interrupted his wife. "There's another large group coming in the door. . . . Ben! Good to see you!" Jed interrupted himself to greet an old friend and golfing partner.

For the next fifteen minutes, they were busy with the second wave of guests, many of them friends from the Hancock Field Club.

"Do you think we should check out there?" Susan asked when they were finally alone.

"Out where?"

"On the deck behind the inn."

"Why?" Jed asked, mystified.

"That's what I've been saying, Jed. All of our guests have been heading there as soon as they finish saying hello to us."

"Maybe we should have had the bar set up in here," Jed suggested. He and Susan were greeting their guests in the low-ceilinged living room of one of the oldest inns in Connecticut. A half dozen massive bouquets of summer flowers had been placed around the long, L-shaped room to brighten up its dark paneling. When the inn was built, glass was expensive and homes were heated with wood, so the windows were small and few. Dozens of golden beeswax candles stood in rows on the three fireplace mantels, their glow augmented by dim—and inauthentic—lamplight.

"It's a beautiful room," Susan said, "but much more cheerful outside. I'm so glad it didn't rain."

"It wouldn't have dared rain on our party," Jed said, taking her hand.

She smiled up at him. "It did before. Don't you remember?"

"When?"

"Oh, Jed, it rained the first night of our honeymoon. I was wearing a silk dress—my very first silk dress—and I was afraid it would water spot when we ran from the car to the inn. Don't you remember?" she repeated.

"What I remember is snuggling in bed and watching the rain on the little porch outside our room. . . . Wait a second. I thought we were going to stay in the same room tonight as we did thirty years ago."

"That was what I planned to do, but the inn has been remodeled since then, and that nice little private balcony was turned into a deck which connects all the rooms at the back of the inn. I thought we'd prefer something a little more private."

Jed grinned down at her, and for a moment, she recognized the sexy college junior she'd fallen for almost thirty-two years ago.

"Susan! Jed, sweetie. Why are you still out here? The place is jammed. Certainly you're not expecting more guests." Jed's mother swept into the room. Claire was wearing a sensational yellow dress that appeared to have been made from hundreds of little fabric petals. It fluttered as she walked and barely skimmed her knees. Susan thought she looked wonderful and said so.

"Oh, Susan, you're so sweet! I knew you'd recognize it!"

Jed glanced over at his wife. "Well I don't, Mother. Did you wear it to our last New Year's Eve party?"

"Oh, Jed, of course not! Just like a man, right, Susan?"

"Well . . ."

"This is a summer dress, Jed," Claire continued. "A very special summer dress. Can't you guess? Don't help him, Susan."

Susan couldn't help her husband. She didn't think she'd ever seen this dress before, unless . . .

"Our wedding!" Susan cried, suddenly recognizing it. "You wore that dress to our wedding!"

"Exactly! Remember, you told me you were going to carry daisies, and I knew this was the perfect mother-of-the-groom dress the moment I saw it at Bergdorf's."

Susan felt her smile stiffening. Not only had Claire's dress been three times as expensive as her own cotton wedding gown, but Claire could still fit into it while it would have taken major alterations for Susan, despite her recent diet, to squeeze into her wedding gown.

But Jed, having drained his glass, didn't have fashion on his mind. "I gather you don't think we need to stay in here anymore?"

"Of course not. Come and join your guests out back. There's still a bit of sunlight, and the air is lovely. Everyone is having a wonderful time."

"I'd like to touch up my makeup first," Susan said.

Claire squinted at her daughter-in-law. "Excellent idea," she said. "Where's the ladies' room?"

"I was going to go up to our room," Susan explained. "Do you want to join me?"

"I think I'll spend a few minutes with your husband, if you don't mind." Claire tucked her hand under her son's arm and led Jed away as though he were still three years old.

Susan smiled as a young waiter entered the room carrying a silver platter covered with appetizers. He smiled back and held out the tray.

"Crab cakes with cilantro tartar sauce or grilled shrimp with pepper mole?"

"Both. I'm starving." Susan piled seafood on a cocktail napkin, thanked him, and trotted up the creaking stairway to the rooms above. She pulled an old-fashioned metal key from her pocket, unlocked the door, and entered the room.

There was nothing chic about the bedrooms at the Landing Inn, where antiques casually mixed with reproductions. The quilt on the bed had been made recently in China. The watercolors that hung on the flowered wallpaper had been painted by someone with little skill, no talent, and lots of enthusiasm for deep, rich colors. Susan particularly liked the orange line around the eyes of a hideously misshapen kitten playing with what appeared to be a dirty old rag; that painting hung on the wall over the antique spool bed she and Jed would share that night.

Susan and Jed had worn jeans and T-shirts to the inn, and these clothes were draped over the room's two chairs. Susan tripped over one of Jed's scuffed loafers on the way to the lovely chestnut dresser where she had left her makeup bag.

"Damn." She kicked the shoe out of her way, dumped the bag's contents on the dresser top, and peered in the mirror on the wall. A professional had applied her makeup this morning, and Susan kept wondering if she actually looked better or just made-up. Unable to decide, she shrugged at her reflection, ran a comb through her hair, stopped in the bathroom for a few minutes, and hurried back to join her guests.

The Landing Inn was known for its food, and the original dining area had doubled many times over the years. Now Susan walked through the lobby to the oldest area of the dining room, smiling as the sounds of her party increased. For a moment, she stood in the doorway and watched. Everyone—everything—looked wonderful.

"You certainly do know how to give a fabulous party!" Susan's best friend, Kathleen Gordon, appeared by her side. "And I love that dress!" Kathleen continued.

"You should. You helped me pick it out! But tell me the truth," Susan continued. "Is everything okay?"

"More than okay. The decorations are sensational. The food is better than sensational. Everyone is having a super time." The smile on Kathleen's face dimmed just a bit. "Well, almost everyone."

"Who isn't? What's wrong?"

"Susan, don't panic. It's just that . . . Well, were you expecting Doug and Ashley Marks to show up? I mean, I know you had to invite them, but . . ."

"Don't tell me they're fighting. . . ."

"No, in fact, they're acting as though they're on their second honeymoon. I don't think he's let go of her hand all evening."

Susan laughed. "Maybe he's afraid if he does, she'll slip something into his drink."

"That's just the problem. Everyone's watching them to see . . . Well, frankly, to see if something like that happens."

"So it wasn't the placement of the bar," Susan muttered.

"What?"

"I wondered why everyone was rushing to the back of the inn."

"To see the Markses. They've been standing under that huge elm tree in the middle of the deck ever since they arrived. It's almost as though they're in a second receiving line."

Susan nodded. "Jed and I didn't have much of a chance to talk to them. They came early. In fact, a lot of our guests arrived just as the party began."

Kathleen nodded. "This is a great place, but if you don't arrive early, parking can be difficult."

But Susan wasn't interested in parking problems. "So I spend months and months arranging this party, and my guests are more interested in the Markses than in the Henshaws."

"Well, Susan, it isn't every day that you get to rub shoulders at the very same time with a woman who was just acquitted of attempted murder as well as with the man whom she supposedly tried to kill," Kathleen continued. "And it doesn't help that this is their very first public appearance since Ashley's trial ended."

TWO

"SUSAN, YOUR MOTHER'S LOOKING FOR YOU."

"Thanks, Deb. Did she say what she needed?"

"Susan, your son just told the funniest story. . . ."

"I hope it was clean."

"Wonderful party, Susan—as always."

"Thanks, Ben."

"Thirty years, Susan! Amazing!"

"I guess I have more stamina than anyone gave me credit for." Susan smiled to show she was joking and continued through the crowd toward the elm tree. She wanted to see for herself what Kathleen had described as the Markses' receiving line.

The Landing Inn, like many early Connecticut landmarks, was located on a river, and a large, multilevel deck extended from the back wall of the colonial building out over the rushing water. A half dozen trees grew up through holes in the decking, and Doug and Ashley were standing underneath the largest elm. Susan wondered if either of them knew it was known as the hanging tree. According to legend, a man had been hung from one of its strong branches after being convicted of murdering his wife. If they knew the story, it wasn't bothering them. Ashley was smiling and chatting with one of Susan's neighbors.

Susan, moving closer, heard Ashley's signature phrase. "Well, I have to tell you . . ."

Ashley, Susan reflected, always had to tell someone something—frequently something no one wanted to hear. This time, apparently, Ashley was talking about herself. Susan, along with many people nearby, moved just a bit closer.

"From the very first, our lawyer assured me I'd be freed. He says the police department in Hancock should be sued for conducting such a sloppy investigation. Of course I knew I was completely innocent, so I didn't worry. Not while I was in jail, at least. But just last night I woke up around three A.M. absolutely terrified."

"Why?" The question was asked in a breathless voice.

"Because of what our lawyer said. Are we safe in our beds if our police department is completely incompetent? I mean, really!"

Whether the general murmuring that followed could be taken as general assent was arguable, but Susan spied someone on the edge of the group who certainly would not agree with what Ashley was saying. She walked over to Hancock's handsome chief of police with her arms stretched out. "Brett, I didn't see you come in!"

"That's because I just got here a few minutes ago. We got lost on the way here," Brett Fortesque explained, kissing Susan on the cheek. "Jed said you were upstairs primping—and I must say, whatever you did worked. You look wonderful. If you weren't married already, I'd ask for your hand myself."

"Wouldn't Erika have something to say about that?" Brett had recently married Erika Deakin, an event that had thrilled all their friends.

"Only if she found out—which she's not likely to do this week. She's been working late in the city each night, and

what with the trial keeping me busy, we haven't been seeing very much of each other."

Susan glanced over at the Markses. "I guess the results
of the trial didn't make you very happy," she said quietly.

"Actually, I wasn't surprised. I didn't think there was a
case there. Not that that makes me happy. Someone poisoned Doug Marks, and just because he didn't die . . ."
Brett stopped midsentence, and Susan realized he was
looking over her shoulder at something. She turned and
found herself face-to-face with the man they had been talking about. Doug Marks looked furious, his face so red that
Susan wondered if he was in danger of having a heart
attack or a stroke. She opened her mouth, realized she had
no idea what to say, and shut it again.

"Don't worry, Susan. This is your party, and I certainly
wouldn't ruin it by punching out this bastard in front of
your guests."

"Doug, I—"

"Not that I wouldn't like to. How anyone could possibly
think that my wife would want to kill me . . ."

Susan tried again. "Doug, I—"

But this time Brett interrupted her. "Mr. Marks, as you
say, this is Susan and Jed's moment. If you have anything
to say to me, perhaps we should find someplace more
private."

"I wouldn't even consider going off with you to someplace more private. In fact, until you find the person who is
trying to kill me, I will not leave my wife's side." This last
was said loudly enough to draw the attention of most of the
people around them, and for a few minutes it was quiet
enough to hear the river rushing over the rocks below. Then
everyone jumped back into the conversation at the same

time. Doug glared at Brett, actually spun on his heel, and stomped off.

Brett watched him go, then turned his attention to Susan, a concerned expression on his face. "I'm so sorry. Perhaps I shouldn't have come."

"Don't be silly," she answered, suddenly annoyed with the entire situation. "You and Erika have been our good friends for years. Doug and Ashley must have known you'd be here. If they were uncomfortable about meeting you under these circumstances, they could have stayed at home." Susan smiled at her guests and moved toward a quiet corner of the deck. Brett followed, picking two glasses of champagne off a waiter's tray on the way.

"I had to invite them—after all, they're our next-door neighbors—but I never thought they'd actually be here," Susan continued, accepting one of the glasses he carried. "Frankly, I was surprised the trial ended so quickly."

"Don't tell anyone I said so, but our new DA really screwed this one up," Brett said. "He built the case against Ashley Marks on conjecture and wishful thinking. It was a kindness that Judge Hill didn't throw it out on the first day in court."

"Does that mean you're going to start the investigation again?"

"It never stopped completely. But that's not something we want everyone to know." Brett glanced around, and Susan wondered briefly who among her guests he suspected of attempted murder. "But let's change the subject. If Erika finds me talking business to you at this party, she'll kill me. You and I can talk tomorrow."

"Tomorrow! But I—"

"There you are, Brett. Hogging the hostess." Erika

appeared at her husband's side, a big smile on her face. "Susan, you look wonderful. I love that dress."

"Erika, I'm so glad you're here. Here." Susan plucked the untouched glass of champagne from Brett's grasp and handed it over to his bride. "And I love your outfit," she added. "As always."

Erika was wearing a slim olive green silk sheath with crystals portraying a burst of fireworks edging up the left side. "Thanks. I bought it in Paris."

"And I win the award for sensitive husband for going shopping with my wife on our honeymoon," Brett said, slipping his arm around Erika's shoulder.

"He came into the store for about three minutes, then headed for the nearest bistro, where he drank wine and chatted up the waitresses," Erika explained, hugging him back.

"Untrue. I drank café au lait and accepted condolences from waiters who were well aware of my wife's occupation."

"You two really sound like an old married couple," Susan said.

"In fact, it's our anniversary, too," Erika said. "We were married one month ago today."

"That deserves a toast." Susan lifted her glass to the couple. "Much as I'd like to talk, I think I'd better circulate."

"Tomorrow—" Brett began.

"That's what I started to tell you. Jed and I are spending the night here at the inn," Susan explained. "We won't be home until late."

"Don't worry. I won't come over without calling. Well, look who's coming. I didn't know the Hallards were in town."

"We wouldn't miss this party for the world. Hello, Susan." Dan Hallard folded her in a warm bear hug. "My gorgeous wife is around here somewhere. I think she wanted to get the latest dirt on the couple who bought our house."

Dan and Martha Hallard had lived next door to the Henshaws for decades. Dan, a doctor, had delivered Susan's second child. They'd moved to Arizona over a year ago, and Susan hadn't seen them since they left. Indirectly, Susan realized, they had caused this commotion at her party: If the Hallards had stayed in Hancock, they wouldn't have sold their home to the Markses. And then Ashley—or whoever—would have poisoned Doug in another location.

But Dan, never a man one would describe as pithy, was still speaking. ". . . can't tell you I was surprised when I heard The man struck me as a Milquetoast when we met. He didn't even bargain over the price of the house."

Susan nodded. "I remember Martha telling me about that."

"How are they as neighbors?"

The first word that popped into Susan's head was *annoying*. But she had been well brought up. "They're fine. But we miss you all so much," she added quickly.

Dan Hallard hadn't spent over thirty years treating women without learning how to recognize a polite lie—and how to respond. "Really? I was afraid Ashley Marks would be a real pain in the ass. In fact, the very first thing Martha and I said when we read about her arrest was that she had struck us more like a victim than a murderer. We thought she might be one of those people who seem to go through life collecting enemies."

"You read about the case in a paper in Arizona?" Brett asked.

"We keep up our subscription to the *Hancock Herald*. It arrives a few days late, but we read it from cover to cover."

"Dan, it almost sounds as though you're homesick," Susan said, glad to find an opportunity to change the subject.

"We miss good friends like you and Jed, but we don't miss shoveling snow seven months of the year. In fact, my dear, I've played golf every single week since we left Connecticut."

"Sounds good to me," Jed said, joining the group.

"Why don't you come on out for a visit one of these days? You and Susan have an open invitation."

"Maybe we will," Jed answered. "But right now—"

"We should circulate," Susan finished his sentence.

"No, we should go stand in front of the fireplace. There's going to be a toast, remember?"

"Not until it's time for dinner," Susan protested. "Jed, you know that! We must have gone over the schedule at least a dozen times."

"Didn't I buy you a very expensive antique Rolex for your birthday a few years ago?"

"Yes, and I love it."

"So why aren't you wearing it?"

"Well, the dress is silver and the watch is gold, and I wanted to wear the diamond bracelet you gave me this year and it's set in platinum, so . . . What time is it?" Susan asked, suddenly realizing why her husband was paying an unusual amount of attention to her wardrobe.

"Eight-ten."

"Why didn't you tell me? We're ten minutes behind schedule!"

"I just told you."

"Jed, we don't have time to stand around talking. We're late!" Susan grabbed her husband's hand and pulled him away.

Her mother was waiting for them by the fireplace, Susan having made the mistake of reviewing the schedule with all the members of her family. "Susan, the kitchen staff is waiting to lay out the meal. . . ."

"I know, Mother. We're—"

"And I must say your choice of appetizers was very nice, but just a bit rich, don't you think, dear?"

Susan decided this was no time to discuss diet. "Where is Jerry? He's supposed to be here to give the toast."

"I'm right behind you." Jerry Gordon, Kathleen's husband and Jed's best friend, tapped Susan on the shoulder.

"And . . . ?"

"And the waiters have made sure everyone has a full glass of champagne. Here's a glass for Jed. Now put smiles on your faces and prepare to graciously accept numerous compliments." Jerry grabbed a large copper cowbell from over the fireplace and shook it energetically. All those guests who didn't spill their drinks when startled by the resulting clanking were now ready to toast the happy couple.

Susan had no memory of much of her wedding service. All she actually remembered was looking over the minister's shoulder at the large bouquet of summer flowers on the church organ. Now, as Jerry spoke, she found her attention wandering around the room to the smiling crowd. But not everyone was smiling.

The Twigg sisters were standing at the top of the stairs, almost identical scowls on their faces. But they weren't guests; they had many responsibilities, Susan reminded herself, hoping nothing disastrous had happened in the kitchen.

Alvena and Constance Twigg owned the Landing Inn. It had been in their family for decades, and Susan remembered Alvena from their first visit to the inn thirty years ago. It had been Alvena who had guided them to their room and who had, unnecessarily, Susan thought, shown them around, turning back the bedspread and explaining how the plumbing worked. Alvena had been younger then, of course, but her long hair was still the same flaming shade of red. As Susan watched, Alvena whispered something to her sister and began to giggle, and Constance merely smiled. Susan decided all was well and turned her attention back to Jerry's speech.

Jerry's audience had erupted into laughter. Susan smiled, hoping he had said nothing to embarrass her, and applauded along with the group. Perhaps she'd better listen more carefully. She didn't want to miss the toast. Her timing was perfect. Jerry paused, took a deep breath, and held his glass up in the air.

"And, so I ask you all to raise your glasses and join me in congratulating the happiest married couple I know: Susan and Jed Henshaw."

Susan clinked glasses with Jed and Jerry, then sipped. There was a happy buzz in the room until someone cried out loudly.

"Oh, my God, I've been poisoned!"

THREE

"Just kidding." Douglas Marks didn't speak loudly, but his words were easy to hear in the now silent room.

Susan, who had gasped along with most of her guests, found herself speechless.

Fortunately, Jerry had no such affliction. "Good joke, Doug," he called out. "Now back to that toast. To Susan and Jed—a couple who deserves more than one toast if anyone does."

"Jed and Susan. Jed and Susan."

Susan knew she didn't imagine the relief in her guests' voices now that things were back on schedule. She could have killed Doug Marks all by herself—she might just do that, in fact—but now it was time for dinner, and she was the hostess. "There's a buffet laid out right down those stairs." She pointed as she spoke. "And the band will be starting up in about an hour for anyone who is interested in dancing. And—"

"And have a good time and thanks for coming, everyone. Now I don't know about the etiquette in these things, but I think my good wife and I should get our dinner first. After all, we've been standing in the lobby greeting everyone while you all sucked up the best appetizers." Jed pulled

Susan away as their guests chuckled at his words. She smiled vaguely and followed him to the food.

Kathleen grabbed her arm as they passed by. "The Markses are leaving. I was standing right behind them when Doug made that stupid joke, and I heard Ashley say that she just 'couldn't take any more.'"

"*She* couldn't take any more. . . ."

"I know, Susan, and I can imagine how you feel; but they are leaving. This is a great party. Don't let one stupid joke ruin it for you or your guests."

"You're right. But when I get home tomorrow night the first thing I'm going to do is order a big fence put up between the Markses' house and ours."

"I'm the new head of the zoning board, and I'll make sure your request for a variance is approved immediately," one of Susan's friends offered as she walked by.

"See, these are your friends. They all want you and Jed to have a sensational party," Kathleen reminded her.

"I know. And you know what? We really did miss most of the appetizers; I'm starving."

"Then let's fill those plates, find the perfect table, and dig in," Jed suggested enthusiastically.

"Good idea," Jerry agreed.

"I married a genius," Susan said.

"And I married the most beautiful woman in this room."

Susan, deciding that this wasn't the time to comment on Jed's ability to lie convincingly, accepted the large dinner plate she was offered by an attentive waiter.

Filling that plate with fabulous food kept her busy for the next ten minutes, and by the time the two couples were seated at a table with room for both of Susan's parents as well as Jed's mother and her date, the atmosphere in the inn had regained its festive air.

"Nothing like an unlimited amount of champagne," Susan's father said, draining his flute.

"Well, I can't imagine what that awful man was thinking. Imagine making a joke like that," Susan's mother said, shaking her head at a waiter standing behind her husband with an open bottle, ready to refill his glass.

"The man is an idiot," Susan's father said shortly, looking back over his shoulder and countermanding his wife's orders. "Someone said he and that murdering wife of his had left the party. I sure hope that's true." He took a sip from his newly filled flute.

"Well, I must agree with *that*," Susan's mother admitted.

Kathleen jumped into the conversation. "I love your suit."

Kathleen had volunteered to make sure Susan's parents had a nice time at the party, and Susan knew that she could depend on her to do just that. She turned her attention to Claire's date. "I don't believe we've met," Susan said, realizing as the words came out of her mouth that her statement was not true. How could she have forgotten.

"Kernel Jack. At your service, Mrs. Henshaw." The grin on Jack Stokes's face probably meant he was enjoying this lapse in Susan's memory.

"Of course. Just one of those . . . uh, senior moments," she stammered, reaching for her glass. How could she ever have forgotten this man? A self-made multimillionaire, Jack had started out in corn—"just spell *Kernel* with a *K*, you sweet thing"—moved into real estate, and ended up in oil. He had told the story at least three times during dinner last Thanksgiving. Susan had fled into the kitchen, preferring cleaning up to listening to this bore. "It's nice to see you again. And such a . . . a surprise."

"You didn't think I'd forget your kind invitation last November now, did you?"

"My invitation?"

"Yes, Susan," Claire said. "You remember how we were all talking after dinner, and you said you had talked Jed into agreeing to give this party. And when Jack said he'd never known anyone married for thirty years . . ."

"To the same person, Claire honey. I said I'd never known anyone married to the same person for thirty years. I've known people to be married for forever, but not to the same person. Most of my friends are more interested in . . . ah . . . variety."

"When Jack was talking about that you . . . or Jed . . . said he must come to your party next summer. Don't you remember?"

It was a party, so Susan didn't blurt out the truth: that any invitation to this man would have been issued out of politeness, not from any true desire to have him here tonight—and any semisensitive person would have realized that. And she certainly had not sent him an invitation. But she had excellent manners. "I'm just glad you could make it." She smiled at Kernel Jack.

"Wouldn't have missed your party for the world."

"I thought you were here to see me," Claire jumped in.

"Why, honey, I'm not here just to see you. I'm courting. Never go to a wedding or an anniversary party with someone you're not courting. That's my motto."

Susan looked up from her foie gras, noted the embarrassed expression on Claire's face, and smiled. Could her strong-willed, independent mother-in-law have met her match here? She started to speak when a familiar arm slipped around her shoulder.

"Great party, Mom! I haven't seen most of these people since my wedding."

Susan smiled up at her daughter. Chrissy, always a gorgeous young woman, was glowing. "You could come home more often, you know."

"I know, but I'm so busy at the gallery six days a week, and I don't want to miss my evening classes. And Stephen studies all the time. He thinks he'll be able to get his MBA a semester early. He's already getting job offers."

"Chrissy, that's wonderful! Are any of them in New York?"

Her daughter laughed. "Oh, Mother. You never give up, do you? We'll talk tomorrow. I have lots of news." And, gracefully, Chrissy floated away, waving to an acquaintance somewhere else in the room.

Susan looked over at her husband. "Has anyone seen Chad?"

"Yes, he was standing by the bar set up on the deck. I don't think he was as interested in the alcohol as in the attractive young woman tending bar," Jed added quickly.

"Ah, to be young and single," Jerry said. "Susan, this food is sensational. How come you never told us about this place?"

"To tell the truth, we hadn't been here for thirty years. I don't know why," Jed answered for his wife.

"I suppose we spend so much time at the Hancock Inn that we don't search out other inns." Susan turned to her husband. "Did you see Charles during the toast?" she asked, referring to the owner of the Hancock Inn.

"Yes, he looked like he was having a sensational time. He's with one of the best-looking women in the room."

"She's beautiful. I didn't catch her name when he introduced us, but she looks familiar."

"She works for him. She's probably served us a hundred times and we didn't even notice her."

"Just shows what a low-cut dress will do for you."

"Guess so. Uh-oh, it looks like Constance Twigg is heading over here. I hope nothing's wrong."

But Constance had a smile on her face. "Mr. and Mrs. Henshaw, I don't mean to interrupt your evening, but I wanted to make absolutely sure everything is to your satisfaction."

"Everything is a lot better than satisfactory," Jed answered. "Everything is wonderful. I don't know about our guests, but I'm having a sensational time."

"A man should enjoy his second honeymoon," Constance Twigg said and then blushed.

From behind her came a twitter. Alvena peered around her sister, eyebrows raised above pale blue eyes, a blush on her wrinkled face. "Oh, Constance, the things you say."

Constance stood up even straighter. "Don't be silly, Alvena. I was speaking of the party, of course."

Jed stood up and took the situation in hand. "In fact, I'm having a wonderful time. The food is delicious, and the inn is beautiful."

"Oh, well then you can just write that very thing on our guest satisfaction survey. You'll find a copy in your room. We do depend on our guests to help us improve our service. And we love getting compliments," Alvena said, smiling happily.

"But I'm afraid we can't take all the credit for this party. Your wife picked out the menu and the decorations," Constance said.

"But you hired the chef and, of course, dear Mother designed the deck," Alvena said.

"Your mother designed this?" Susan asked. "I wondered who was responsible. It's just fabulous—all the different levels. And it's fantastic that it was built around the trees."

"Dear Mother loved trees," Alvena said quietly. "She

used to take us for long walks in the woods around here and . . ."

"The Henshaws are not interested in tales of our quaint childhood," Constance interrupted. "And if you don't have anything else to say . . ."

"I do," Alvena insisted. "I'm here to ask the Henshaws what they would like us to do with their gifts."

"Oh, just put them in our room. I don't think we should open them in front of our guests," Susan answered.

"Good idea," Jed said. "We'll open them later. I was wondering what we were going to do after our guests left."

Alvena squealed and scurried off.

"She's turned into such a foolish old woman. Suppose it's because she never married," Constance said, watching her sister's back. Then she turned toward Jed and Susan. "I'd better check on the desserts. If you need me for anything, I'll be in the kitchen."

"Thank you," Susan said. After the sisters had gone, she turned to her husband. "You knew that would embarrass her!"

"Sorry, I couldn't resist."

"I thought your invitation specifically said no gifts." Susan's mother was working hard to ignore any sexual undercurrent to the conversation.

"Yes, but you know how people are," Claire said.

"I hope you don't mind gifts. Kath shopped for weeks to pick out ours," Jerry said, wiping his mouth.

"And it's waiting at your house," Kathleen added. "I didn't want you to worry about getting it home."

"To say nothing of us worrying about getting it here," Jerry said.

"What is it?"

"You'll find out tomorrow."

"I did notice a few people carrying packages," Jed said.

"More than a few. Those nutty old women . . ."

"They're not nutty old women. They're the owners of the inn," Susan's mother corrected her father.

"That doesn't make them less nutty or less old. Anyway, I saw them earlier piling up the gifts in the TV room. That was hours ago, before all these people arrived, and it was quite a pile already."

"Perhaps Jerry and Kath can take some home for us," Jed suggested.

"Oh, there probably won't be that many," Susan's mother said.

"Besides, if Kathleen and Jerry take them home, what will we have to do once the party's over?" Susan asked, looking over at her husband and smiling.

FOUR

But by the time Susan and Jed had said good-bye to the last of their guests, tipped the staff, and reassured the Twigg sisters that everything truly had been wonderful, they were so exhausted that they could barely make it up the stairs.

"I have the key here somewhere." Jed reached in his pocket.

"It was a wonderful party, wasn't it? I had a wonderful time. I think everyone had a wonderful time." Susan's statement ended in a yawn.

"And now you're going to get a wonderful night's sleep." Jed turned the key and pushed open the door. "But not in this room."

"What do you mean?" Susan peered through the doorway. "I don't believe it."

"I saw some people arrive with gifts, but I had no idea there would be this many," Jed said. The room was filled with beautifully wrapped presents. Pastel-covered squares and rectangles stood on the dresser and filled the wing chair by the window. What looked like a canoe paddle leaned precariously against the wall. Their queen-size bed was piled high with wrapped gifts. "What are you doing?" he asked his wife, who had preceded him into their room.

"I just thought I'd open one or two." Susan picked up a tiny, silver box bound with narrow, embroidered silk ribbon. "This is from Dan and Martha. You don't suppose it's from Arizona—maybe something from one of those fabulous art galleries Martha is always writing about." She tugged on the ribbon.

"Susan, it's late. You can start opening gifts if you want, but I'm going to see about another room."

"Another room! But this is our room, Jed. Besides, the inn is completely booked. Unless you can convince one of our friends to share a room, this is where we're spending the night." She yawned again.

Jed smiled at his wife. "You're exhausted. I saw you packing your favorite bath oil. Why don't you take a bath, and I'll move things around so we can sleep?"

"You don't think you'll need my help?"

"I know you around wrapped presents. You'll be shaking and guessing what's inside until you convince me to help you spend the night opening them. You take a bath. I'll move this stuff. It's the only way we'll get any sleep tonight."

"There should be a chilled bottle of champagne here somewhere." Susan looked around.

"When I find it, I'll pour out a glass and bring it to you. Now go."

She went. Their bathroom had been tucked under the eaves and contained many pieces of whitewashed wicker, apparently to make up for the lack of headroom. Susan had unpacked all the necessities earlier, and she poured green-tea oil under the less-than-gushing faucet before getting undressed.

She was tired, happy and tired. And the water was warm

and soothing—so much so that she fell asleep almost immediately.

She didn't know how long she dozed, but by the time she woke up, the water had cooled off. She looked around and smiled. No champagne. Jed must have drifted off, too. Well, they weren't as young as they once were. She got out of the tub and dried off, splashing on her favorite cologne before slipping into a silk kimono. Then she opened the door, prepared to kid Jed about how they had both fallen asleep.

For just a moment, she thought she had walked in on a joke. There was a strange woman asleep in the middle of their bed. Then she realized that the woman wasn't asleep. And she wasn't strange.

"Well, at least she's not a stranger," Susan said, walking over to her husband. Jed was standing by the bed, his cell phone to his ear. "Who are you calling?"

"Brett. He must not have arrived home yet, though. I left a message on his machine."

"She's dead, isn't she?"

"Yes. I held a mirror up under her nose. I think she was poisoned," he continued.

Susan leaned down to look more closely. A trickle of drool was drying on the dead woman's chin. "I see what you mean."

"I thought—" Jed's phone rang, interrupting his explanation. "Hello? Oh, Brett, thank God. . . . Well, it's simple. We found Ashley Marks in our bed. . . . Oh, dead. I should have explained that first. . . . Poisoned. At least that's what we think. . . . Got it." He pressed the button to hang up and looked over at his wife. "He's on his way."

"Did he say what we should do?"

"Don't tell anybody. Don't touch anything. . . . He said not to touch anything, hon."

"I don't think he was talking about the champagne, Jed. I'm thirsty, and it is our anniversary." She handed him the bottle. "Would you open it?"

Jed glanced at the dead woman, then did as his wife asked. "I hope no one comes in. It might look as though we were celebrating her death."

"I suppose someone is," Susan mused.

"Why do you say that?"

"Someone killed her."

Susan and Jed hadn't been married for thirty years without learning the art of silent communion. They had both turned and were looking out the small window to the silent street below, their backs to the bed. "I wonder where Doug is right now," Susan said, sipping her drink and putting it down on the only available space—the narrow windowsill.

"Good question."

"Everyone is going to assume that he killed her," Susan said.

"I don't see that."

"Well, Jed, think about it. She tried to kill him."

"She was acquitted."

"Yes, although Brett said that was because the district attorney didn't have much of a case."

"But Brett didn't say he believed Ashley was the poisoner."

"She must be! I mean, who's in a better position to poison someone than the person who cooks for him?" Susan asked.

"According to the story in the *Hancock Herald*, Ashley's attorney claimed that Doug did most of the cooking."

"But Ashley made their cocktails every night. And you know the evidence was that the poison could have been in drinks as well as any other food. I know, you don't think she's guilty."

"I said all along that Ashley is one of the most competent women I know. If she set out to kill someone, they'd be dead."

"Apparently the same could be said about whoever killed her. . . . Jed, where are you going?"

"To get a glass. I don't need more champagne, but I'm thirsty."

"You don't think the dinner was too salty, do you?" Susan asked, again the concerned hostess.

"Susan, the dinner was wonderful, but I suspect it's going to be a long night. I wonder if you could go down to the kitchen and get us some coffee. There must be people around. I can't imagine that the cleanup crew is done already."

Susan frowned. "I guess I'd better get dressed."

"You look fine," Jed said. "I would go down, but then you'd have to be alone with—" He looked over at the bed. "—with her."

"I'll get three cups. Brett might want some, too," Susan said quickly, wrapping her robe tightly around her and heading for the door.

The hallway was dark, lit only by electrified sconces burning tiny and ineffective flame-shaped bulbs. She ran smack into a large chestnut blanket chest. "Ow!"

"Who's out there?" The voice seemed to be coming from the room across the hall. Susan decided there was no reason to answer and, rubbing her sore hip, scurried off to the stairs.

The dining room was deserted, already prepared for

tomorrow's buffet breakfast, with tables set, coffeemakers out, and trays in place to hold the doughnuts and pastries for which the inn was famous. Susan stopped a moment, taking in the peaceful, orderly scene. It really had been a wonderful party. . . .

An extraordinarily loud crash brought her back to reality, and she wiggled between the tables toward the kitchen. One shove, and the padded swinging doors opened to reveal bedlam. A radio blaring rock and roll was competing with the roar of the commercial dishwasher as a half dozen young people dealt with mountains of dirty pans and baskets of filthy silverware. As Susan watched, a deafening alarm indicated the end of the wash cycle, and the stainless steel doors were opened. A whoosh of steam filled the room, causing many of the workers to complain of the increasing heat. Cans of soda were lifted in the air and brows wiped of sweat.

"Excuse me."

No one heard her.

"Excuse me," she repeated, more loudly this time. "I'm looking for coffee."

A young man with a scarf tied around his forehead looked up from his mop. "God, lady, breakfast isn't for hours. Give us a break, okay? We just finished working this huge, fancy-schmancy party and—"

"Is there anything I can do for you, Mrs. Henshaw?" The head of the kitchen staff, a young woman who had helped Susan plan the party, rushed up to her.

"I . . . we . . . is there any way to get a pot of coffee at this time of the night?"

"That's no problem at all. I'll have one sent up to your room in five minutes."

"I'll wait for it," Susan offered quickly. She didn't want

anyone to see what was on the bed or to wonder why the police were visiting the celebrating couple in the middle of the night.

"Whatever you prefer, but there's no place to sit in here."

Susan got the point. They didn't want outsiders around, either. "I'll be outside, in one of those wing chairs by the fireplace."

"I'll bring you a full pot and two cups in just a few minutes."

Susan didn't have the nerve to ask for another cup—how would she explain?—so she just smiled and left the room.

It wasn't until she was sitting by the still-flickering fire that the enormity of what had happened hit. And the complexity. Where was Doug? Had he left the inn without his wife? Had he killed his wife and then left the inn? Had he killed his wife, put her in the Henshaws' room, and then left the inn? Had . . . ?

"Oh, Mrs. Henshaw, is something wrong?"

Susan looked up into the worried face of Alvena Twigg. "I'm just waiting for a pot of coffee. Jed and I always have coffee before we go to sleep," she lied, realizing she was staring rudely at the elderly woman. Alvena was enveloped in a voluminous nightgown of crisp white cotton, its high neck edged with cotton lace. Matching cotton lace ringed the cotton nightcap perched precariously on her braided red hair. Alvena's gown was freshly pressed; she had not, Susan realized, been to bed yet, either.

"What an excellent idea. I frequently have trouble sleeping. I've never tried coffee." Alvena's light blue eyes twinkled, and Susan wondered if she was being laughed at.

"It often works for us," she insisted, and decided that a change of subject was in order. "The party tonight was wonderful. You and your sister are sensational innkeepers."

"We do pride ourselves on how well we run the inn. Of course, it's Constance's life's work. I had other interests. I'm retired, you know."

"No, I didn't." Susan was relieved the topic had changed, but she wondered when the coffee was going to appear. Jed would be wondering where she had vanished to. "What did you do?"

"Oh, I ran the district's high school," Alvena answered proudly.

"You were the school principal?" Susan had a difficult time imagining this woman controlling that particular age group.

"No. I ran the office. I was school secretary. I worked for six different principals during the fifty years I held the job."

"Fifty years!"

Alvena smiled. It was obvious she had gotten this reaction before. "I started the summer after I graduated from high school. I was eighteen years old. I retired in June exactly fifty years later. I worked two days more than fifty years, in fact."

"Amazing!" Susan said sincerely. "You must have enjoyed your work."

"I was much more important than most people realize. It's the secretary who runs the office, you know."

"Of course. And you must have seen most of the people in this town go through that school."

"Exactly!" The smile on Alvena's face had become distinctly smug. "I could tell you the most amazing things about some of them. Of course, I don't. I consider my position to have been one of trust, and I do not betray that trust."

"That's very good of you," Susan said.

"You'd be amazed how many of my students—I call

them all my students although I never actually taught them, of course—have died recently," Alvena continued without acknowledging her comment.

Luckily a young man bearing a tray with coffee, milk, sugar, and two cups and saucers appeared then, for Susan had absolutely no idea how to respond.

FIVE

SUSAN SAID GOOD NIGHT, PICKED UP THE TRAY, AND HURried toward the stairway. She glanced back over her shoulder. Alvena was staring down into the fire, a smile on her face.

Susan ran into Brett at the top of the stairs.

"Susan, where have you been?" He took the tray from her. "Jed was starting to worry about you."

"Never mind about me. How did you get back so quickly?"

"Nothing like a police cruiser with flashing lights. We're not all that far from Hancock—not if you don't have to stop for traffic lights or obey the speed limit."

"I can't tell you how relieved I am to see you."

"I don't know how much help I can be. This isn't Hancock. In fact, the local police should be arriving any minute now."

"The local police! How do they know about this?"

"I called them. Susan, I had to," he added seeing the dubious expression on her face. "They'll understand why you called me first. After all, I'm a personal friend of yours. But they would not understand if I didn't call them as soon as I knew about the body. According to Jed, it's pretty obvious there's been a murder here."

"I suppose." Something rustled nearby, and Susan realized someone was moving around behind the door they were passing. "Shhh. We . . . we don't want to wake anyone."

"Susan . . ." Brett looked down at her and didn't finish whatever he was planning to say. Instead, he balanced the coffee tray on one shoulder, reached out with his free hand, and opened the door to the room she and Jed were not going to get a chance to sleep in.

Jed was sitting in the wing chair, his head thrown back, eyes closed. He looked pale, exhausted—even old, Susan realized suddenly.

"Jed? Are you all right?" He opened his eyes and looked at her, smiling as he had smiled for over thirty years. "Fine. Just a bit worried about you. Where have you been?"

"I was getting coffee. Downstairs. Then I ran into Alvena Twigg, and we had this weird conversation—"

"Never tell that woman anything. Just about the time everyone else in town has forgotten whatever it is, Alvena Twigg hauls it out and you're embarrassed all over again."

Brett, Susan, and Jed turned and faced the uniformed officer standing in the open doorway.

"Son of a gun! Pete! I heard you'd come back to Connecticut!"

Brett and the officer greeted each other cordially. "Just started here a few weeks ago," the handsome younger officer replied.

"Then this will be your first case?" Brett glanced over at the body on the bed.

"Not counting the kids who broke into the Episcopalian church to throw water balloons from the steeple, and a speeder or two."

"How do you know about Alvena Twigg?" Susan asked.

"I grew up here and, more importantly, went to school

here. Miss Twigg was the high school principal's secretary. Everyone knew her."

"She must have been a memorable person," Susan said absently, looking over at Ashley's body.

"Frankly, I'd forgotten all about her. It's Miss Twigg who remembered me. And who decided to reminisce in front of a room full of men I'm supposed to be leading."

"How embarrassing!" Susan exclaimed.

"That's one word for it. But we're not here to talk about me. Who found the body?"

"Perhaps I should introduce Peter Konowitz, Chief Konowitz of the Oxford Landing Police Department," Brett said. "Peter used to work for us in Hancock, but I don't remember if you've all met. This is Mr. and Mrs. Henshaw. Jed and Susan."

"I thought I knew most of the men and women on the force," Susan commented, squinting at him.

"I was only around for a summer, and I believe my tenure was during the time you were investigating a murder in Maine, Mrs. Henshaw," Peter answered, walking over to the bed and staring down at the body. "You both found her?" He asked the question without turning around.

"I found her," Jed spoke up.

"I was taking a bath at the time," Susan explained.

"Where?"

Susan was surprised by the question. "In the bathroom, of course. Over there." She pointed.

"So she was killed while you were in an adjoining room taking a bath."

"No, of course not!" Susan protested, horrified by the idea. "She was dead before I got into my bath. But I didn't see her," she added quickly. "The bed was covered with gifts."

"Gifts?"

"Presents for Jed and myself. We're celebrating our thirtieth anniversary."

"If the bed was covered with gifts for you and your husband, where was the body?"

"She was under the stuff . . . gifts," Jed answered, sounding tired. "I'd better explain. You see, my wife and I came up here to go to bed after our party ended downstairs and found that the bed was quite literally piled high with presents for us—"

"I offered to help Jed move them—" Susan broke into his explanation.

"Susan also wanted to take a bath and I thought it would be easier—and faster—to move things without her around," Jed interrupted. "Susan loves opening presents, and I was afraid that once she started we'd never get to bed," he added to Brett.

Brett glanced around the crowded room and smiled. "I can see how that would take a while."

Susan decided it was time to tell the story in her own words. "But I fell asleep in the tub, and when I got out Jed had found Ashley."

"And called me," Brett added. "You did call me right away, didn't you?"

"Yes. I had no idea what else to do. She was obviously dead. I knew a doctor couldn't help her. I didn't know what else to do," Jed repeated.

"And when your wife got out of the . . . uh, tub . . . you told her about this?" Peter Konowitz asked.

"No, Susan came into the room and saw the body. I was on my cell phone. There." Jed pointed. "The calls to and from the inn go through an old-fashioned switchboard. I didn't want anyone to overhear my call. I suppose I should have called the local police department, but I just didn't think. I called Brett—at his home."

"We're old friends," Brett explained to his colleague.

"Yes. Well, I called, and then Susan went to the kitchen to get some coffee. I stayed here." He looked over at Ashley. "I didn't know how to cover the body. I didn't want to call anyone, and I couldn't get a sheet without disturbing her. And she really doesn't look all that bad—just . . . well, just dead."

Everyone stared at the body.

"Does anyone know who she is?" Peter Konowitz asked.

"We all know her," Brett answered. "This is Ashley Marks. You may have heard of her."

"The woman on trial for poisoning her husband?"

"She was acquitted yesterday," Brett said.

"Yeah, that's what I heard." Peter walked around the bed, examining the body more carefully. "So how did she turn up here, do you think?"

"She was a guest at our party," Susan explained.

"You invited a woman accused of murdering her husband to a party celebrating your thirtieth wedding anniversary? Good God! No wonder you're always stumbling over dead bodies. . . . I mean . . ." Peter glanced at his former superior, and then looked away quickly.

"Ashley is our next-door neighbor," Jed explained. "We thought it would be rude not to invite her."

"And we didn't know she was going to be acquitted. We sent out the invitations over six weeks ago," Susan added. "I mean, we had to invite her, but we never actually thought she would show up."

"Especially not like this." Peter motioned toward the bed.

"She didn't show up like this!" Susan protested.

"The Markses were at the party earlier in the evening," Brett explained.

Peter looked dubious. "Together?"

"Yes."

"That must have surprised you and your guests," Peter said.

"To be honest, I was more annoyed than surprised. I mean, they were getting an awful lot of attention. On the other hand, now that I think about it, I can see why they came."

Peter looked puzzled. "Why?"

"Well, they had to appear in town sometime. And think how difficult that would be. They would keep running into people one at a time and having to be polite and say everything is okay over and over again. I mean, once or twice would be difficult. Dozens of times could drive anyone nuts! By coming to our party, they got it over with all at once."

"But why together?" Peter asked.

"Why not?" Jed asked, surprised by the question.

"She was arrested for the attempted murder of her husband, right?"

Brett nodded. "True. And she was acquitted, remember."

"But still." Peter apparently couldn't think of anything else to say.

"You probably haven't been following the case, but everyone in Hancock sure has. And we all know that they've been together throughout the entire trial," Susan said. "Doug was in the courtroom each and every day, according to the newspaper articles. He didn't think she was guilty. At least that's what he told the press over and

over again. It was even on network news one night—until
the latest scandal in Washington."

"Odd that a Connecticut story got so much attention
anyway," Peter said. He was still staring at the body. "I
mean, it's not as though the Markses were famous—or
even related to anyone famous."

"It was the fact that Doug maintained Ashley's inno-
cence that interested the press," Brett said. "They repeated
that fact over and over."

"I haven't been paying all that much attention, frankly,"
Peter admitted.

"Well, changing jobs and moving and all . . ." Brett
said.

Susan glanced over at him. It wasn't like Brett to be so
vague. "Doug was not only in court every day of Ashley's trial, he sat right behind her. He got there as soon
as the doors to the courtroom were opened and waited
for her entrance. They hugged and kissed each day when
she arrived and hugged and kissed before she was led
back to jail each night. At least that's what the newspaper reported."

"And they came to your party together?" Peter asked.

"Yes."

"And they left together?"

Susan glanced over at Jed. "Yes, they did, didn't they?"
He shrugged. "I assumed so."

"So where's the faithful husband now?" Peter asked.

"Good question," Jed said.

"Why are you looking for him?" Susan asked.

"For a few reasons," Peter answered. "First, someone
has to inform him of his wife's murder. And, of course,
he'll have to be questioned concerning his movements
since leaving here tonight."

"So you think Doug killed Ashley," Susan said.

"Peter didn't say that he did," Brett reminded her. "But as far as we know they left the inn together. A few hours later Ashley was back here. . . . What are you looking at?" Peter was now kneeling down by the bed, peering at Ashley's face.

"Just wondering how she died." Peter stood up and stretched. "I don't know why we're assuming this was murder. There's no evidence of violence."

Brett frowned at his colleague. "An autopsy will show how it happened. But I think we can assume it was murder. Look how the body was arranged. Whoever killed her also hid her under all those presents. That is what it looked like to you, right?" he asked Jed.

"What do you mean?"

"You said you took the presents off the bed."

"Yes."

"Did you get the impression that they had been carefully piled on her? I guess what I'm asking is whether or not it's possible that the gifts were placed on the body accidentally."

"I don't think that's possible. She's not . . . she wasn't covered with anything. And it's not as though she's flat. . . . I mean, the first layer of gifts were placed very carefully. Bigger boxes on either side of her and . . . sort of a bridge formed across her by the larger gifts so that she wasn't squashed or anything."

Peter stopped staring down at Ashley and looked across the bed, obviously interested in Jed's words. "Almost as though the murderer was taking care of her? Like a husband might do?"

Jed thought before answering. "Not necessarily. Every-thing was placed very carefully, but that may have been because whoever placed the gifts on the body was worried about them falling."

"Afraid something might break?" Peter asked sarcastically.

Susan had turned and was examining the gifts now piled all over the room. At his words, she turned back. "Are you suggesting that a murderer is unlikely to care about something so . . . petty?"

"I can't believe that a person who is so casual about human life would be so careful with a bunch of . . . of stuff. It's not consistent. It doesn't make sense," Peter said, walking out of the room.

"At least he didn't insist that we go back to the police station for questioning," Jed said.

"No, he didn't, did he?" Brett mused.

Susan frowned. A whole lot of things weren't making sense. She just hoped she would be allowed to go to bed before that changed.

SIX

THE SKY IN THE EAST WAS BARELY BEGINNING TO LIGHTEN as Jed drove into his driveway.

Susan pressed the automatic garage door opener and turned to her husband. "Jed—"

"Susan, I figure we don't have all that long before every reporter in this part of Connecticut is trying to get hold of us," he interrupted her. "And I'm just hoping the police give us an hour or two before they think of other things to ask. I don't know about you, but I've got to get some sleep. . . . My God, what is that noise?"

"Just Rock and Roll greeting us. Our canine house guests, remember?"

Jed pressed the accelerator as the garage door swung up. "Rock and Roll, my foot. Dribble and Drool is more like it!" The car moved into the garage, and the barking got louder.

"I just hope Clue's okay," Susan said, referring to the family's golden retriever. Clue had been an active, happy companion—until Rock and Roll, Chrissy and her husband's bull mastiffs, had arrived for a visit. Then Clue spent most of her time moping, feeling underfed and unappreciated. "Rock and Roll keep stealing her food."

"Clue can stand to lose a few pounds," Jed said, sliding

out of the car and stretching. "I hate to admit it, but I'm just too old to pull an all-nighter."

"I'm thirsty. I'm going to make some chamomile tea. Would you like some?"

"No, thanks." Jed opened the door connecting the house with the garage, and a mound of fur propelled itself into his chest. "Oooph! Down, Clue! Down!"

Susan grabbed Clue's collar and yanked her back onto four paws. "Come with me, Clue. I'll get you a cookie after I've had my tea. Jed, you go on upstairs. That racket Rock and Roll are making must have woken up the kids. Tell them to plan on fixing their own breakfast and, for heaven's sake, to let us sleep as long as possible."

Jed padded up the wide carpeted stairs to the second floor of their colonial home, and Susan walked into her country kitchen, filled a teakettle, and put it on the stove. She turned on a burner and sat down at the large pine table in the middle of the room. Clue flopped at her feet, sighing loudly. "I think I know how you feel," Susan said to the dog. She didn't have a whole lot of energy; on the other hand she wasn't particularly sleepy. She sat there until the kettle began to boil, and then she got up and made herself a cup of tea, got a dog biscuit for Clue and . . . and sat back down and stared at the table.

She was nervous, keyed up. Usually she'd just take a nice warm bubble bath, but her last bubble bath hadn't turned out to be terribly soothing. And if she started thinking about that, she'd never get any sleep. She looked down at the dog. "How about an early-morning walk, Clue? Just let me find some flip-flops or some Keds and we'll get going," she added, knowing she could assume an enthusiastic response from the dog.

It was a gorgeous morning. The sun was already warm.

The automatic sprinkler system had drenched the sidewalk, and Susan's rubber soles squished in the puddles. She turned right at the street, noticing that the Markses' new green Jaguar was parked at the top of their drive as though nothing untoward had happened—as though Ashley and Doug had partied until late and were sleeping in. For a moment, Susan wondered if she should walk up to the house and knock on the door. If Doug was home, she could offer her condolences. And then she realized that she was being stupid. The police would have called Doug hours ago. More than likely, he was at the Hancock Municipal Center answering their questions right now. Or making arrangements for his wife's funeral—although that wouldn't happen until the autopsy was completed. She shook her head. She had to stop thinking about Ashley . . . or Ashley's body. She looked down. Clue was enormously interested in something at the curb. "Oh, no! Come on, Clue! Heel! Now!"

After years of reluctant attendance at obedience classes, Clue understood the words and knew what to do—even though it was obvious that she found the squashed squirrel immensely more compelling. The dog sighed, got into position, and accompanied Susan down the road.

Anyone walking by would assume this was usual for the pair—anyone who didn't know them. But Kathleen Gordon wasn't fooled. She jogged around the corner, long hair flying out behind her.

"Hey, isn't it a bit early to be working on dog training? Besides, I thought you and Jed were spending the night at the inn. What are you doing here?" Her words came out between deep gasps for air.

"We were, but something happened," Susan explained as Kathleen reached her.

"Susan, you can tell me all about it. But first, do you have any juice in your refrigerator? I'm ready to pass out."

"Of course. Let's go back to the house. Did you run all the way here from your home?" Susan asked as they turned around.

"Yes. I ate so much at your party last night that I thought I'd at least get a start on burning some of it off." Kathleen was breathing much easier now. "So what are you doing home so early? Is Jed with you?"

"He's asleep."

"You left him sleeping at the inn and came home to walk Clue? Oh, Susan, you should have given me a call. I'd have been happy to take Clue out for you."

"Kathleen, Jed's not at the inn. We both came home. We had to. Ashley was in our bed."

Kathleen started to laugh. "You're kidding me! Was Doug there, too?"

"No, of course not."

"Why of course not?"

"Because she was . . . She is . . . Kathleen, Ashley's dead!"

Kathleen grabbed Susan's arm. "What did you say?"

"Ashley's dead. Someone murdered her. She was in our bed. At the inn. Underneath our gifts. Listen, come into the house and I'll tell you all about it."

"Good idea."

Neither woman spoke until they were in Susan's kitchen. Clue ran upstairs to join Rock and Roll. Kathleen helped herself to juice from the refrigerator, and Susan sat down at the table, her untouched cup of tea waiting for her.

"Now start at the beginning. You did say Ashley was under your gifts on your bed at the Landing Inn, didn't you?"

"It sounds a little weird when you put it like that," Susan said, getting up and putting the kettle on.

"That's how you put it."

Susan looked down at her teapot. "I know. And it's true. Jed and I went up to our room together and discovered the bed piled high with presents. Jed said he would clear the bed while I got a bath. He found Ashley underneath."

"What was she wearing?"

Susan was surprised by the question. "A gorgeous peachy silk dress. It had those little cap sleeves. I can't wear them—my shoulders are too broad—but on Ashley, they looked stunning."

"What she wore to the party."

"Yes, of course. Oh, you're wondering if she had gone home and changed."

"Exactly."

"No, she looked the same way she had looked at the party—only dead, of course."

Kathleen poured herself another glass of juice and sat down at the table. "How did she die?"

"We think she was poisoned."

"Who's we?"

"Jed and I. Peter doesn't agree."

"Who's—"

But Susan knew what was coming. "Peter Konowitz. I should say Chief Konowitz. He's the police chief in Oxford Landing."

Kathleen frowned. "Is that name familiar for some reason?"

"It wasn't to me, but he did work in Hancock for a while. In fact, he was here the summer you and I spent Fourth of July week up in Maine. He must have worked here longer, of course. But I don't remember meeting him. And apparently he didn't remember meeting me."

"I suppose I heard about him from someone. I assume he's in charge of the investigation. And you said Brett was there?"

"Yes. Jed called Brett when he found Ashley. And Brett called Peter."

"Of course."

"Brett said something about contacting Doug, but I don't know if he did or not."

"Oh, I'm sure he did. Doug is probably somewhere being questioned right now." She took another sip of her juice. "Why did you think she was poisoned?"

"Well, she was dead. She obviously had been killed. I mean, if she had died of natural causes she wouldn't have had gifts piled on her, right?"

"You think that the person who killed her put her on your bed and then covered her with gifts, right?"

"Exactly!"

"Why?"

"Why what?"

"Why was she in your room? Why was she on the bed? Why did someone think covering her up was a smart thing to do?"

Susan looked at Kathleen. "Good questions. Very good questions. I don't have any idea."

"Well, it's early days yet," Kathleen said. "You know what I'd really like to know?"

"What?"

"Who knew that was your room. There are nine rooms in the inn, right?"

"In the main building. Eight more in the annex across the street."

"And I assume your room is the biggest?"

"Nope. There's one suite that's much bigger. Ours isn't particularly special—but it's nice and private on that side of the building."

"Was it locked?"

"Yes, but the inn isn't exactly up-to-date in that respect."

"No little cards with magnetic strips to let you into the room?"

Susan laughed for the first time since seeing Ashley in her bed. "Nothing like that. The doors have these big metal keys. I suspect I could break into a room there without any trouble at all."

"But how would anyone just looking in the door know that you and Jed were staying in that particular room?"

"No one else would have a room full of gifts."

"The gifts weren't always there," Kathleen pointed out. "At the beginning of the party, they were piled on a long trestle table in the room where the television is located."

"Constance and Alvena call that the Southern Parlor," Susan commented.

"Is there a Northern Parlor?"

"I have no idea." Susan paused. "You know, I didn't see any gifts."

"That's because one of the Twigg sisters stood at the door, greeting your guests and directing people toward you and Jed. Guests who brought gifts were also told where they should be left before you saw them."

"Oh . . . I guess that was a good idea."

"I gather you didn't know about it."

"No, I thought we'd discussed everything when we went over party plans, but gifts never came up."

"Well, the Twiggs—it seems strange to call them that, doesn't it—were prepared for them. But the question is, when were they moved into your room?"

"Why?"

"Well, I think we can assume that if Ashley was on your bed, whoever moved the gifts in there would have mentioned it."

"Good point. Of course, we don't know if Ashley was killed in the room or killed somewhere else and moved there."

"Susan, we're not investigating this murder, are we?"

"No, I guess not. I mean, I haven't thought about it in those terms. I just have lots of questions. After all, she did end up in my bed."

"True."

"Under my presents—which are now being held by the local police. Peter said something about dusting them for fingerprints."

"You're kidding."

"No. Don't you think they'll find any?"

"They're bound to find some—and I suppose the murderer's could be among those of the gift givers, the Twigg sisters, members of their staff, the salespeople who wrapped them, and anyone else who came in contact with them since they were wrapped up. On the other hand, once those people are eliminated, if someone's prints turn up over and over again, it's possible that that someone is the murderer."

"Do you think it's Doug?" Susan asked.

"That's what everyone's going to be asking when they hear about this." Kathleen put her arms on the table and looked at Susan. "What do you think?"

"I don't see him as a murderer. I mean, I wasn't really surprised when Ashley was arrested for poisoning Doug. Well, I was surprised that anyone was poisoning Doug, but it made sense that if anyone was, Ashley was. Does that make sense?"

"You don't like Ashley."

"Can't stand her. And you know what's worse? I feel guilty about the way I feel. I've never not gotten along with a neighbor before. We've lived in this house for almost twenty-five years. We've had lots of new neighbors. And I've never felt this way about anyone else."

"Susan, it's not you. It's Ashley. She just wasn't the type to be a good neighbor. Let's face it, she was bossy and self-centered. Not a good combination."

"That's true. But, you know, I've been thinking about it, and I think I've come to agree with Doug."

"About what?"

"I don't think she was the person who was trying to poison him."

"Really? Most of the people I know wouldn't agree with that. Everyone's been talking about the trial for months. And everyone seems to think that Ashley was guilty as hell."

Susan shook her head. "No. If Ashley had decided to poison someone, that someone would be dead. Ashley is competent as well as determined."

Kathleen seemed to muse on Susan's words. "You're right about that, but it just leaves us with one question: Who is competent and determined and wanted Ashley dead? Because that person seems to have succeeded in killing her."

SEVEN

KATHLEEN AND SUSAN WERE SITTING QUIETLY AT THE kitchen table when Chrissy and Stephen, dressed in running clothes and followed by their dogs, burst into the room.

"Mom! What are you doing here?" Chrissy cried out before remembering her manners and greeting Kathleen.

"Didn't your father tell you we'd come back early?" Susan asked.

"He was in the hallway upstairs just a while ago, wasn't he?" Stephen turned to his wife. "I told you I heard someone!"

"Drib . . . Rock and Roll made all that noise and you didn't get up to see who—or what—it was?" Susan asked.

"Mother, if we got up every time Rock or Roll barked, we'd never get any sleep," Chrissy protested. "They're very sensitive, you know."

Everyone looked down at the sensitive pair now collapsed on the floor. They were licking each other's hind parts. Clue watched jealously.

"Why are you here, anyway? I thought you and Dad were spending the night at the inn."

Susan paused. "Well, I suppose you'll hear on the evening news. Ashley Marks was killed."

"So?"

"She . . . Her body was found in our room at the inn."

"Mother! You're kidding! Why does this type of thing always happen to you?"

Susan opened her mouth to protest any part in this event, but Stephen got there first. "It isn't your mother's fault if this Ashley Marks was killed in her room. After all, she didn't do it. . . . You didn't, did you, Mother?" he ruined his defense of her by asking.

"Of course not!" And she had always thought her daughter had married an incredibly sensible young man.

"And there isn't anything to connect you to this Ashley Marks, is there?"

"Well, she was our next-door neighbor. . . ."

"See," Chrissy cried. "There's something about her. She attracts dead bodies!"

Susan couldn't let this go by without protesting. "I certainly do not! Dan and Martha lived in that house for over thirty years and nothing happened to either of them. It's not my fault that the people who moved in would turn out to be the type of people who seemed to get poisoned for some reason or another."

"Who else was killed?" Stephen always got to the point.

"No one. But as you've probably heard, Doug Marks was poisoned. He didn't die, but Ashley was arrested for attempted murder, and then acquitted yesterday."

"And now someone has murdered Mrs. Marks," Stephen said, nodding his head. "That's very interesting."

Chrissy looked at her husband, a shocked expression on her face. "Stephen, just for a minute there, you sounded like my mother when she begins to investigate a crime."

"You have to admit, it's a fascinating puzzle."

"I don't have to admit anything. In fact, I don't find it interesting at all!" Chrissy had had her blond hair cut short since she got married, and she ran her hands through it, causing it to stand up in the air. "Besides, I thought we were getting up early because we wanted to go over to the park and let the dogs run."

Stephen's reaction to this was all a mother-in-law could desire. He leapt to his feet and ordered the dogs to do the same. In a few minutes—in the time it took to convince Clue that she really didn't want to go on another walk— Susan and Kathleen were alone again.

"So, where were we?" Kathleen asked.

"They make a nice couple, don't they?" Susan said, staring at the door swinging closed behind her daughter and son-in-law.

"Very. Chrissy is looking happy and healthy."

Susan leaned across the table and grabbed Kathleen's wrist. "You noticed too, didn't you?"

"What?"

"Chrissy's gained weight."

"Well, maybe a little, but it doesn't seem to have hurt her looks. She's positively glowing." Kathleen's eyebrows leapt up. "Susan, I know what you're thinking! You think she's pregnant!"

"I think it's a possibility. She and Stephen are on this new health kick, and I overheard them talking about her 'taking extra vitamins during this time.' "

"During this time! That does sound like she could be pregnant!" Kathleen looked as happy as Susan. "You'll be a grandmother. We'll have a baby around again. Won't Emily and Alex be thrilled?" she asked, referring to her own children.

"Well, maybe Emily." Susan doubted if many ten-year-old boys were enthralled by infants.

"Does Jed know?"

"No, I decided not to say anything to him. Chrissy and Stephen will be here until the end of the week. So there will be lots of opportunities for them to announce their big news. And I think we should let them do it in their own time and their own way."

"Of course. Oh, Susan, a baby! You know, I think I'll get out that afghan I was knitting for Alex and didn't finish in time for Emily's birth and work on it again. I'd just love it if Chrissy's baby would use it."

"But you won't say anything to anyone."

"Of course not! And you'll let me know the second you're sure."

"Of course!"

They were still beaming at each other when Brett appeared at the back door. "I don't suppose those happy expressions mean you've figured out who killed Ashley Marks."

Susan and Kathleen exchanged glances. "No," Susan answered. "We were just laughing at Chrissy and Stephen and . . . um . . . their dogs." She got up from the table and headed to a counter covered with imported small appliances. "Coffee?"

"Sounds great." He pulled out a seat from the table, spun it around, sat down, and draped his arms over its back.

"You look exhausted."

"I am. Mentally and physically. It was hard work telling Doug that his wife had been poisoned."

"And was it news to him?" Susan asked quickly.

"Yup. According to Doug, he and Ashley had an argument at the inn—probably about that stupid joke he made—and she told him to go home alone and took off down some sort of path by the river."

Kathleen leaned forward. "Do you think he did it?"

"You know how some cops are always telling you that

they can tell when a guy is lying? Well, I'm not one of those guys. Doug seemed sincerely surprised—shocked, really—and distraught at the news. But for all I know, he has a graduate degree in theater from Yale and it was all an act." Brett shrugged. "I've been wrong so many times, I don't even bother trying to guess." He looked over his shoulder at Susan, busy at the counter grinding beans. "But you have excellent instincts, and they are your neighbors. What do you think, Susan? Could he have killed his wife?"

Susan poured the ground beans into a paper cone, dropped the filter in its holder, pressed a few buttons, and turned around slowly. "I suppose so. If he believed she was trying to kill him, he might have decided the only answer was to do her in first. Of course, that wouldn't explain why he was such a staunch supporter of her during her trial."

Kathleen laughed. "Maybe he knew she would be found not guilty and he was afraid of what she would do to him when she was released if he wasn't publicly supportive."

"That might not be as far-fetched as it sounds," Brett said. "There were a lot of people who thought the DA didn't have much of a case, and it's entirely possible that Doug was well aware of that fact. Heaven knows, he was interviewed more times than anyone else during the investigation. If he thought she was going to be found innocent, he might have decided supporting her was safer than not supporting her."

"That doesn't make any sense," Susan protested. "Why wouldn't he just leave her? Get a divorce? Just get in the car and drive away, for heaven's sake?"

"Maybe it wasn't that easy for him to do," Brett suggested quietly, picking up his coffee mug.

Susan had heard that tone of voice before. "You know something!"

"I don't know anything about the case. But I do know that a marriage can be complex and demanding in ways that outsiders cannot begin to imagine."

"Milk?" Susan looked over his head at Kathleen.

"No thanks. This is excellent. Almost as good as the coffee back at the inn."

"Sounds like you haven't been to bed yet, either," Susan commented.

"Nope. And there's no reason to think today is going to be different."

"Susan says the chief of police over there used to work for you in Hancock," Kathleen said, pouring sugar into her coffee.

"Yeah. Peter Konowitz. Did you meet him when he was here?"

"I don't think so."

"We were in Maine while he was here," Susan explained. "Remember? Over the Fourth."

Kathleen raised her eyebrows. "We were in Maine a few weeks. How short a time was he here?"

"Only a few months. Peter Konowitz was a very ambitious young man. He saw that there wasn't going to be a lot of movement in the hierarchy here, and he moved on. I think he may have gone to New York City. I don't remember exactly. I do remember suggesting a larger department where he would get more experience doing different kinds of things, where there'd be more room for advancement."

Kathleen's eyebrows continued their upward climb, but she didn't say anything more.

Susan yawned. "Wow, I wasn't tired until I sat down, but now . . ."

Brett was on his feet immediately. "I should be on my way."

"You never told us why you were here," Kathleen pointed out.

"I dropped Doug off at home, and frankly, I stopped over to suggest that you might look in on him."

"You want me to tell you what sort of mood he's in? If I think Doug killed Ashley? I'd be happy to help," Susan offered quickly.

"Susan, I wasn't thinking investigator. I was thinking neighbor. Doug's in a bad way. When I left him, he was going to call their daughter and tell her about Ashley's death. I just thought it might help if he had someone around for a bit—until Signe arrives."

Susan stood up, any idea of going to bed evaporating. "Of course. I wasn't even thinking about Signe. I'll leave a note for Jed—in case he wakes up—and go right over."

"Thanks. I know Doug's had enough of police in the past few months, so I didn't want to barge in, but I hate the thought of him being alone."

"I've got to get back to my family. The kids will be late for Sunday school if I don't hurry, but I'll be free in a few hours. Shall I come back over?" Kathleen asked.

"Sounds good to me," Susan answered.

"Fine. And I'll look around in my closet and see if I can find that knitting." Kathleen winked at her friend as the three of them left the kitchen.

"You knit?" Brett asked, obviously surprised.

Susan was a loyal friend. "Kathleen is a wonderful knitter," she lied.

"Well, what do you know. You women have hidden talents."

The three friends split up in the driveway, Brett offering Kathleen a ride home in his police car, and Susan heading straight across the lawn to the Markses' house.

The first thing Ashley Marks had done after she and Doug moved into the house had been to hire an expensive designer from New York City. The decorator had examined every inch of the large 1930s colonial and decided on what he called the European touch. Apparently when he thought of Europe he thought of crumbling castles rather than Scandinavian modern. After refinishing the golden oak floors and staining them black, he'd had the walls painted ochre and had hung heavy layers of ugly purple velvet at the windows. All the furniture—and there was a lot of it—was ornate and artificially aged. Susan thought the place looked awful. But when Ashley was arrested, the decorating scheme had proven its worth. Once the curtains were closed, no one, from nosy neighbors to the dozens of press people, had been able to peer into the house.

She wasn't surprised to find the curtains drawn again this morning. She picked up the heavy brass door knocker, which was shaped like an urn, and let it drop. The hollow clunk that action produced seemed unlikely to attract the attention of anyone inside.

But Doug Marks wasn't inside. He was walking around the corner of his home. Apparently he had been gardening. His hands and the knees of his chinos were covered with soil, and he carried a basket overflowing with weeds. He smiled when he saw her. "Hi, Susan. I was wondering if I should call you today. Your party was wonderful. I just hope Ashley and I didn't disrupt it too much."

Susan, who had spent the last few minutes trying to think of something consoling and original to say to this man, was completely nonplussed. Fortunately, Doug appeared to be in a talkative, cheerful mood, and didn't notice.

"I'm thinking of replacing the swimming pool with a Japanese garden and small koi pond. What do you think?"

"I . . . Sounds lovely."

"It's something I've wanted to do since we moved in here. But Ashley wasn't fond of the idea. She always said fish made her nervous," he explained cheerfully.

"I . . . How unusual. I mean, they're supposed to be relaxing, aren't they?"

"Ashley was a very unusual woman."

"Yes, of course she was," Susan said. This was something she could hang a sympathetic statement onto. "I'm so sorry about . . . about what happened last night. We'll miss her. She was a wonderful neighbor. . . ." She stopped speaking, realizing how unlikely it was that Doug would believe that lie.

But Doug didn't even seem to be listening. He was sorting through the wilting plants in his basket, apparently searching for something. "Look at this," he said, finally finding what he wanted. "This is the most invasive weed I've ever seen. The backyard is overrun. I'm tempted to have the entire place dug up and reseeded. Do you and Jed have a landscaping contractor you're happy with?"

"We've used the same person for years and years. I can give you his name, but this late in the season . . ." She allowed the sentence to go unfinished.

"I'd appreciate that. He may have an opening you don't know about. And I would love to get going on this project." Suddenly his voice dropped, and the expression on his face changed. Susan thought he looked like a bereaved husband for the first time. "It will take my mind off things, you know."

"It's an excellent idea," she enthused. "Your yard takes too much work to maintain the way it is. Martha Hallard loved her rose gardens, but I've never thought they were worth the effort it takes to keep them looking good—all that pruning and fertilizing in the spring and fall—and all the poisonous sprays it takes to keep them looking good in the summer. It's amazing no one was ever made ill by them all." She suddenly realized what she was saying, shut up, and glanced over at Doug. But he hadn't seemed to notice; he was still sorting through the dying plants in his basket.

EIGHT

"AND THEN—THANK HEAVENS—SIGNE SHOWED UP, AND I left the two of them together."

"Odd." Jed was making his way through a huge sandwich stuffed with the cold cuts Susan had bought to make sure Chrissy and Stephen didn't starve while they were visiting, and he didn't, apparently, want to take the time to reply.

Susan, resisting the obvious comments about cholesterol, continued. "It is, isn't it? I mean, if I'd been murdered yesterday, I doubt if you'd be out gardening today."

"Probably not. Is there any more iced tea?"

As Susan told Kathleen later, the surprising thing wasn't that she and Jed had been married for thirty years. The surprising thing was that, at that very moment, she hadn't picked up a heavy pot and beaned him with it right there at their kitchen table despite those thirty years together. As it was, she went over to the refrigerator, pulled out the pitcher of tea, and refilled his glass. Then she left him to enjoy his lunch and went down into the basement to see if they had another bag of dog food. The last had vanished apparently overnight.

While she was there, she decided to look in the freezer. Doug and Signe wouldn't feel like cooking, and Susan was too tired to spend a lot of time at the stove. But she thought she had a large Tupperware of coq au vin. It would thaw as she napped, and she'd take it next door around dinnertime. After a few minutes of moving around a dozen pints of Ben and Jerry's ice cream—there had been an excellent sale at the grocery—she found everything she was looking for. When she climbed back up the stairs, she had a bag of Science Diet hanging from one hand and a large plastic container of chicken in the other. Jed was no longer at the table, although he had left behind his dirty plate for her to remember him by. Susan looked around. The counters needed wiping. The dishwasher needed running. The tile floor was covered with dog and people prints.

Susan was exhausted. Cleaning could wait. She dumped the dog food and the Tupperware on the kitchen table, called to Clue, and headed upstairs for a much-needed nap.

Her last thought, as she drifted off to sleep, was that she should set an alarm: She didn't want to sleep away the afternoon.

Her first thought, when the phone woke her less than an hour later, was that she should have turned on the answering machine. She really needed more sleep. Since no one else seemed inclined to answer, she reached out and picked up the receiver. "Hello?"

"Mrs. Henshaw? It's Signe. Signe Marks. Could I come over and talk to you?"

"I . . . When?" Susan asked, struggling to wake up.

"Now. Please, it's important."

"I . . . Of course."

Signe hung up before Susan could say more. She stretched and put her head back down on the pillow. Where was Signe calling from? How long would it take her to get here? She was just beginning to drift back to sleep when the doorbell rang.

Clue jumped off the bed and flew into action. By the time Susan made it downstairs, the dog had worked herself into a tizzy. Susan grabbed Clue's collar and opened the door.

A beautiful blond young woman stood on the welcome mat. She wore a white linen tunic over a short, straight, black linen skirt. Italian sandals displayed red-painted toenails—evidence of a recent pedicure. Her long hair was swept off her high forehead with a black-and-white polka-dot silk scarf. Twin gold-cuff bracelets were pushed up on her tanned arms, and black Gucci sunglasses covered her eyes. Her nose matched her toenails—probably because she was sobbing loudly.

"Signe! Oh, my goodness, come in. What's wrong?" The words escaped Susan's mouth before she realized how stupid they were.

"Oh, Mrs. Henshaw. You wouldn't believe what's happened." Signe allowed Susan to lead her into the house. Over her shoulder, Susan saw a large truck with Fox News Television painted on its side pull up to the curb before the house next door.

"Come on into the living room. I'll get you some . . . some tea or something." Susan led Signe to the couch and retrieved a box of Kleenex from a drawer in a nearby coffee table. "Here."

"Thanks. I'm sorry to be so . . . so soggy. It's just that I'm so upset."

"Of course you are."

"I don't know what to do," Signe said.

Susan thought for a moment. "Perhaps your minister . . . or priest . . . should be called to help out now."

"What could our minister do?" Signe sniffed.

"Make arrangements for the funeral. Or do you think it's too early to think about that?"

"I . . ." Signe removed her sunglasses and stared at Susan. "Funeral? Oh, you're talking about Mother. It's not my mother I'm worried about now. It's my father."

"Of course. He must be devastated," Susan murmured, thinking that perhaps Doug had waited until his daughter's arrival to break down.

"He's not devastated! He's crazy! He's on the way to the police station right now. I'm afraid that he's going to do something terrible!"

"What?" The doorbell prevented Susan from asking any more questions. "I'll get that. You stay here. It could be those awful reporters."

But it wasn't a reporter, awful or otherwise. It was Erika Fortesque—Brett's bride, Susan's friend, and, Susan suddenly remembered, Signe Marks's employer. So when Erika asked, "Is she here?" Susan knew exactly who Erika was asking about.

"In the living room. But, Erika . . ." Susan reached out and grabbed her friend's arm as she rushed by. "Signe says her father went down to the police station. She seems to be worried about what he's going to do there."

"That's why I'm here." Erika looked down the hall. "Can she hear us?"

"I don't think so." Susan lowered her voice. "What's going on?"

"Brett called me. And you have to promise you'll never tell anyone that he did—don't even mention it to Brett. He'd kill me if he knew I was talking to you."

"I won't tell anyone anything. But what's going on?"

"About ten minutes ago Doug Marks walked into the police station and demanded to speak to Brett. When Brett appeared in the foyer, Doug announced that he had killed his wife."

"Who else was in the foyer?"

"That's just the problem. You know how the press have been swarming around looking for a story. Well, there were a half dozen reporters hanging around for a scoop—and they got one. There's no way to keep this quiet now. That's why Brett called me."

"I'm glad he called, but I don't understand," Susan admitted.

"Brett says he doesn't believe Doug killed Ashley. He didn't go into the details."

"So?"

"It's Signe. Doug is afraid Signe is going to be arrested. That's why he confessed!"

"Why would he do that?"

"He's protecting me. My father thinks I killed my mother."

Susan and Erika spun around. Signe was leaning against the wall, sniffling.

Erika rushed to her side. "Signe . . ." She wrapped her arms around the young woman, and her embrace inspired a fresh bout of tears.

"Maybe you could get some us some tea or something?" Erika suggested, leading Signe back to the living room.

"Of course." Susan hurried toward the kitchen. She could use a shot of caffeine, too. And some food.

Fifteen minutes later, when Susan returned to the living room, she was carrying a full tray and Signe seemed to have regained her composure. "I thought you might like something to eat," she explained, pushing aside a pile of magazines with her foot and placing the tray on the large coffee table in front of the couch.

Signe looked up at her and almost smiled. "That's sweet of you."

Susan started to fuss with cups and saucers, cream, sugar, and artificial sweeteners. Once everyone had tea, she put out a wedge of Brie, a straw basket of water crackers, and a plate of Mint Milanos. Then she sat down and waited. Erika looked at Signe and raised her eyebrows. Signe took a deep breath. "Okay. If you think she can help."

"Signe has a big problem," Erika began.

Susan picked up her cup and sipped.

"You see, my father has—or thinks he has—a good reason to believe I killed my mother," Signe explained.

"What?"

"It's sort of a long story. And there are some things I don't want people to know about me . . . about my life." Signe looked over at Erika.

"Things have happened in Signe's life that are a little . . . well, a little odd," Erika said.

"And you're afraid not everyone will understand," Susan suggested quietly.

"Exactly." Signe looked down into her cup as though expecting to find something fascinating there.

"I think you're going to have to tell Susan if you want her to help you," Erika said gently.

"I know. It's so hard to talk about." She looked up at Erika. "I don't understand myself."

Erika just nodded.

Susan waited, wondering what was coming. Drugs or some other sort of illegal behavior? Could this lovely young woman have been involved in a cult at one time? It was most likely an unwanted pregnancy, although that wasn't usually as shaming as Signe's hesitancy seemed to imply.

"I was almost arrested once for attempted murder." The words were said so quietly that Susan wasn't absolutely sure she had heard them.

"Attempted murder?" Susan repeated when Signe didn't elaborate. "But that's what your mother was arrested for."

"You have to explain a bit better," Erika insisted.

"You see . . . Well . . . there seems to be a theme of poisoning in my family. It started years and years ago. Back when I was a teenager. Back then, my mother came down with the same symptoms my father was suffering from. She . . . she kept going to the emergency room with stomach problems. Finally a doctor there realized she was being poisoned. There was an investigation, of course. The evidence pointed to me. But I . . . I wasn't arrested," Signe said, the words coming out so quickly that Susan had trouble understanding what she was saying.

"You said you were a teenager at the time."

"Yes. I was sixteen. Barely."

"Signe, I know you don't want to talk about all this, but you really do have to explain more." Erika's voice was gentle, but firm.

Signe took a deep breath. "I didn't get along very well with my mother."

That didn't surprise Susan. She had found it difficult to get along with Ashley, and she didn't live in the same house as her. "Sixteen is a difficult age," she said.

Signe brushed her hair off her face and began, haltingly, to tell the story. "It wasn't because I was sixteen. It was because of the way I was raised.

"When I was a kid, I didn't know my mother all that well. I grew up on my grandfather's farm—he raised tobacco and dairy cows. The closest town was tiny—and a fifteen-mile drive away. I went to school by bus and was driven to church on Sunday. It sounds isolated, but it wasn't. My grandparents were from Norway, and they kept in touch with their roots. I learned to dance at the Sons of Norway Viking Hall. My Girl Scout troop's leaders were from Norway, and we learned to cook Norwegian dishes for our cooking badge. My 4-H project was raising goats. You get the idea." She smiled for the first time since entering the house. "It was a wonderful way to grow up. I was surrounded by people who nurtured and cared for me."

"What about your parents? Did they live on the farm, too?" Susan asked.

"No. My father's job kept him overseas, and my mother went along with him. Most summers, they had a one-month leave, but my mother always insisted that being home wasn't what my father needed to relax from his stressful occupation, and anyway, she preferred Paris or London to a farm in upstate Connecticut. As a result I didn't see much of them—at least not when I was young. But when I was fourteen years old, my grandfather died and my parents came home. My father left whatever project he was working on, moved into my grandmother's house, and planned to run the farm. It was a bad idea. My mother hated the farm and didn't like caring for my grandmother, whose health was failing. It turned out that my father wasn't very good at ·farming, so when my grandmother died, he sold the place and they went back overseas. By then I wasn't living at home, of course. I'd gone to college—NYU—and I was living in the city. I've never been one of those kids who return to the nest. Of course, in my case, there wasn't any nest."

"But back at the farm—when you were all living together. You said your mother was poisoned."

"Yes. It was creepily like what happened last summer," Signe continued. "That's why Erika knows about it all. I went a little—a lot—nuts when my mother was arrested."

"I followed the case in the papers," Susan said slowly. "You father was poisoned with insecticides, right?"

"Yes. He still has traces of it in his blood."

"And your mother?"

Signe nodded. "It was exactly the same. My mother became ill and went to the hospital. She was diagnosed as having food poisoning. It happened three times in two weeks, and finally a doctor insisted on some tests. Those tests revealed that she was ingesting poison.

"At first, everyone assumed she had picked up something on the farm. My father was worried and hired a company to come out and do tests in and around the house to discover exactly where my mother was coming in contact with the poison." Signe paused for a few minutes and then, looking straight at Susan, finished the story. "There was poison in the house. It was in my bedroom closet—a bag of it as well as a cup and a whisk, which had obviously been used to mix the insecticide with other ingredients. I was taken into custody that evening."

"I don't understand. You didn't poison your mother, did you?" Susan asked.

"No."

"But . . ."

"But what was that stuff doing in my closet, right?"

"Yes."

"I can only tell you what I told everyone at the time: I have no idea. My room had two closets. I used one for clothing and one for stuff. You know, sports equipment, school things, teenage junk. The poison was found in the back of that closet. It could have been there for months and I wouldn't have noticed. Or it might have been placed there the day of the search."

"They found the poison in your closet, and you were taken into police custody?"

"Yes, and released almost immediately."

"Why?"

"Because my mother claimed to have put that poison there. I really had no idea where it had come from. And my mother stuck to her story. She said she used it on houseplants. Since she wasn't suicidal, the police really had no choice but to let me go."

"What about your father? Your grandmother? What did they think?" Susan asked.

"My grandmother was wonderful. She believed me absolutely. She made an unusually critical comment about my mother, and that was it. My father—back then I didn't know what he thought. But he suggested I go into therapy. I did. To tell the truth, I seriously needed someone to talk to. My therapist was wonderful and a graduate of Columbia. She's the reason I went to college in the city.

"Of course today my father seems to have decided that I'm a murderer," Signe said sadly.

"Do you think your mother put that poison in your closet? Do you think she knew who did?"

Signe's smile disappeared. "Now you know just a few of the questions I've been asking myself for the past ten years."

"Any answers?" Susan asked.

"There are a few things I do know and a few things I've guessed," Signe answered.

Susan leaned back and waited, expecting the story to

continue. She was wrong, There was a knock at the front door, and when she answered it, Susan discovered three policemen and a woman in uniform. They had come to ask Signe to accompany them to the police station. They had, they said, a few questions to ask her.

NINE

Susan and Erika had no idea what to do.

"Do you think we should follow her to the police station?" Susan asked, watching the two marked police cruisers pull out of the driveway.

"I think she already has an entourage," Erika replied. "Look." She pointed to the Markses' house, where a phalanx of TV microwave vans was lining up behind the police vehicles. "If we follow along, they'll just turn to us for information when the official sources don't provide what they're looking for."

"We could call a lawyer," Susan suggested, feeling they should do something.

"Do you know the name of a good criminal defense lawyer?" Erika asked.

"What about the woman who defended Ashley? She won."

"She won because the investigation was messed up by the prosecutor. Signe may not be so lucky." Susan and Erika turned around to see who was speaking.

"I came in the back door," Kathleen explained. A large straw tote, yellow yarn trailing from the opening across its top, dangled from one hand.

"Signe is not guilty," Erika insisted.

"We believe that, but this is a terrible mess, isn't it?" Susan asked a rhetorical question.

It was one of the many things the three women standing at the window watching the parade of cars could agree upon.

"I suppose Brett already knows about Signe's arrest," Erika said quietly.

"Probably," Kathleen agreed.

Susan turned away from the window. "How well do you know Signe?" she asked Erika. "I know she works for you, but . . ."

"I know her better than I do most of my employees," Erika answered. "She's a remarkable young woman. She applied for a job in the city while she was still in college. I needed good salespeople in my SoHo shop, but I needed them on Friday and Saturday nights. Customers flock into my store while they're out gallery hopping, so it's open until eleven. Then the final tally on the computer as well as all the cleanup has to be completed before everyone leaves for the night. Not many college students are interested in working that schedule. Signe swore it was just what she was looking for, and she was telling the truth. She's smart, well educated, and has sensational taste. She started that year, graduated the next, and she's now managing both that store and the one on Madison Avenue."

"What sort of background does she have?" Kathleen asked. "What was her college major?"

"She was a fine arts major—she makes sensational jewelry and has produced some nice tapestries—and she had a minor in marketing. She had planned on working in an art gallery rather than someplace as commercial as Twigs and Stems, but we handle more and more craft items—high-end stuff. Signe went with me on my last buying trip to Brussels, and she was a huge help. She has quite an eye as well as a head for business. In a few weeks she'll be taking her first solo buying trip to Milan."

"If she isn't arrested," Susan said.

Erika frowned. "Yes, of course. If she isn't arrested," she agreed sadly. "Susan, you have to do something. I can't believe Signe murdered her mother, but who knows what that chief of police might do."

"What do you mean?" Kathleen jumped in to ask.

"Look, I know neither of you would repeat this, but Brett has a very low opinion of Peter Konowitz."

"Does he think he's incompetent?" Susan asked.

"Did Brett fire this guy?" Kathleen asked.

"No, but I don't think he encouraged him to hang around Hancock, if you know what I mean."

"I don't," Susan said quickly. "Are you saying that Brett tried to get rid of him, or was glad when he left, or what?"

"I can't tell you. I didn't know Brett when Peter Konowitz worked in Hancock, so I don't know the entire story. But Brett didn't get home until the sun was coming up this morning, and he got a call from this Konowitz guy almost as soon as he walked in the door. After he hung up the phone he said something about PK screwing it all up again and suggested I head over this way in case Signe needed my help. I'll find out more tonight—or whenever Brett has a free minute to talk."

Susan looked at Kathleen. "I don't suppose you know anything about this guy?"

"I may. I think he came to Hancock around the time I left to marry Jerry. I may have met him. I know I heard a lot about him. He was the talk of the department for much of the time he was here."

"Why? Was he incompetent?"

"Nope. Just a bit overly enthusiastic for a department

like ours. That and a vivid imagination made him a lot more trouble than he was worth in some people's opinion."

"What do you mean?" Erika wanted to know.

"It's not easy to explain. Say there was a burglary. No weapons involved. No assault or anything of that nature. The house is empty one evening. No one bothers to turn on the alarm system and some jewelry and a computer are snatched. Happens all the time in Hancock."

"A routine case," Erika said, nodding.

"Exactly. Only Peter didn't—or couldn't—act as though it was routine. He jumped in as though it was a major case, wanting to investigate everyone who had access to the home in the past year, checking out the company that provided security, talking about setting up a sting operation to catch the burglars. It was a pointless waste of time and upsetting for everyone involved."

"Sounds like Brett must have been glad when he moved on."

"Thrilled is what I heard," Kathleen said. "Peter Konowitz isn't a team player. And that's hard on everyone on the force—especially the person who's in charge."

"Brett said that he was ambitious—that a police department the size of the one we have here in Hancock didn't provide enough room for him to advance. So why is he working in an even smaller town now?" Susan asked.

"That's not unusual. Peter Konowitz moved to a bigger department to get experience and then moved to a smaller one to become chief of police." Kathleen shrugged. "That's the way promotions work for people willing and able to move around."

"I suppose it's not important here anyway," Susan said.

"Oh, it's important," Erika said. "After all, if Peter and

Brett didn't have some sort of relationship, we would never have known that Signe might be in trouble."

"Do you think Brett will have advance notice of whatever else happens?" Susan asked Erika.

"I have no idea. And I hope Signe is only being questioned—that she isn't being considered the primary suspect in the case, frankly."

"But what if she is?" Susan asked. "What are we going to do then?"

"Then you're going to have to find out what's been going on in that house next door," Kathleen said.

"We're not just talking about the present," Susan said. "Signe admits this all started years ago—on her grandparents' farm."

"Which is near where it all ended," Erika added.

"What do you mean?"

"Signe grew up about fifteen miles from Oxford Landing. Didn't you realize that when she was telling us about her past?"

"I had no idea! How do you know?"

"Brett and I got lost on the way to your party. We became intimately acquainted with that part of Connecticut," Erika explained. "Signe's mentioned her grandparents' farm to me over the years, and I recognized the name of the town when we drove through it—for the second or third time—on the way to your party."

"You really were lost," Susan said, momentarily diverted.

"You know the little towns up that way—many of them were built around a colonial green, and so the roads going in and out of town don't make a whole lot of sense. We circled many statues noting an obscure historic event more than once. Anyway, that's how I know how close the two places are."

"What an odd coincidence," Kathleen said.

"*Odd* is just the word for it," Susan agreed. The three were silent for a moment before she continued. "What do you think we should do now? It really isn't our place to call a lawyer for Signe."

"I'd hate for Signe to think we've abandoned her—or for her to think we don't care," Susan said slowly. "After all, whether we want to be or not, we're involved here. Whoever killed Ashley left her body in my bed."

"So what do you want to do?" Erika asked.

"I think I'll call and leave a message on Doug's machine. I can tell him that we're thinking of him and, of course, the usual anything-we-can-do statement. If he wants to take us up on it, fine. If not, we've offered."

"Okay. And I think we should go to the inn for an early lunch," Kathleen suggested.

"Revisiting the scene of the crime?" Erika asked.

"Exactly."

"I think it's a great idea," Susan said enthusiastically. "Let's take the Jeep. It's just possible that the police will have released my presents."

"Your presents? Why did they impound your presents?" Erika asked.

"They were in our bedroom—where Ashley was found. In fact, she was found underneath some of them." Susan paused. "It's a little creepy to think that I may end up using something that lay on top of a dead woman."

"Didn't you say Jed found her body?" Kathleen asked.

"Yes. I was in the bathtub, and he was clearing the bed."

"So you don't actually know which gifts were . . . in contact with Ashley."

"Not actually." Susan grimaced. "No, I don't."

"But you know your friends really wanted you and Jed to have those gifts," Kathleen continued.

"I do know that. So you think I should just ignore where they were and . . . and enjoy them?" Susan asked.

"Yes."

"Definitely!" Erika agreed.

"Then let's go!"

"I need to call Jerry to make sure he takes care of the kids for the rest of the day."

"And I should leave a message on our answering machine for Brett and let him know I'll be out until dinner."

"And I'd better leave a note telling the first person home to walk Clue. Who knows how long we'll be gone."

"Let's go over in one car so we can chat on the way," Erika suggested. "Of course, there won't be as much room for presents on the way home."

"So it will give us an excuse to go back again tomorrow if we have to," Kathleen said. "After all, it's not like this all happened in Hancock. It won't hurt if anyone else involved thinks that we're just minding our own business instead of investigating a murder."

"I gather you don't think Chief Konowitz is likely to be too enthusiastic about amateurs getting involved in his investigation," Erika said.

"I think he'd hate it if he knew."

"So we won't tell him," Susan said, standing up. "We'll just be two suburban housewives and one very successful entrepreneur going about our own business. No one can stop us from doing that, can they?"

"Well . . ." Kathleen started.

"We have a reason to return to the inn. Who we talk to and what we talk about is really no one's business," Erika stated flatly.

"So let's make those calls and get going," Susan said.

TEN

THE TWIGG SISTERS WERE SITTING IN MATCHING ROCKING chairs on the wide front porch of their inn, entertaining the local press corps with coffee, doughnuts, local legend, and a sprinkling of fact. They seemed to be enjoying all the attention. And Susan, Kathleen, and Erika appreciated the distraction they provided, allowing the three women to park in a far corner of the not-too-big lot across the street from the inn and then dash around to the back of the main building unnoticed.

Here, away from the eyes of inn guests, the business of giving a party was displayed. Slick, black plastic bags stuffed with garbage were piled high against centuries-old stone walls. Disused plastic crates, names of local dairies embossed on their sides, had been flung upon the remains of a kitchen herb garden, squashing large basil plants while barely making an impression on a thriving bed of mint. Three garbage cans overflowed with empty bottles, causing Susan to wonder if perhaps her headache wasn't the result of something other than Ashley's murder and Signe's arrest.

"I wonder where they are," Kathleen said, ignoring the mess and glancing back over her shoulder at three police cars parked illegally in the spaces reserved for delivery trucks.

"Good question," Susan said. "I'd rather avoid running into anyone official as long as possible. It will give us more time to look around." She glanced at her companions. "Do you think anyone on the local police force will recognize either of you?"

"I doubt if anyone knows me," Kathleen answered. "Except for the one case when I came to Hancock, I never worked around here, remember. And while I was in contact with a few cops from other districts when I was running my security company, I didn't have any jobs this far north." She turned to Erika. "What about you?"

"You know, it is possible. Brett and I have attended quite a few official functions—some local, some state—in the past few years. I can't tell you how many cops I've met. I don't remember many of them, but it's possible that some of them remember me."

Susan and Kathleen exchanged looks. Erika's distinctive style would stand out—and be memorable—in almost any group.

Erika saw the look and smiled. "So I don't know the answer to your question. Sorry. But I agree it's a good idea to avoid as much contact with anyone official as possible."

"Then let's not go through the kitchen. My guess is that any cop in his right mind would head straight for the origin of the inn's homemade doughnuts."

"Good idea." Kathleen nodded. "You know, there's a ladies' room behind the bar. And I think there may be a passage from there straight to the bedrooms upstairs."

"Great!" Susan enthused. "Lead the way."

Kathleen did just that, and in a few minutes they were standing on the second-floor landing outside the bedroom Susan and Jed had planned to share last night.

"So now what?" Erika asked in a whisper.

"I don't know," Susan whispered back.

"Why's everybody whispering?" Dan Hallard had never felt a need to modulate his booming voice, and now was no exception. "You lovely ladies chatting about something you don't want us men to know about?" His words echoed up and down the chestnut-paneled hallway.

"Not really," Erika, the most forthright of the trio, started to answer, but Susan interrupted her.

"Actually, I am planning a surprise for Jed. And Erika and Kathleen are helping me," she added quickly.

"You women and your little secrets. Just let me know if I can be of help. You know me—anything I can do to support a nice long marriage—especially if it's between two of my all-time favorite neighbors. I'm off to join my own lovely lady for a very late brunch. Can't believe I'm hungry after all the food you fed us last night, Susan. We both slept like rocks, but our room's over the kitchen, and the smell of bacon woke me up this morning."

"Dan, I didn't know doctors ate cholesterol," Kathleen kidded him.

"They don't if they're at home and their wife's doing the cooking, but here I can order whatever my little heart desires—even if it doesn't know what's good for it."

"Well, enjoy your meal," Susan said, wanting to get on with their task.

"Thank you. And you enjoy your planning."

"Ah . . . Thanks, we will," Susan sputtered before remembering what he was talking about.

"So what do we do now?" Erika asked when they were alone again.

"We go in there." Susan pointed to the door. A swath of

yellow tape printed with the words *Police Line Do Not Cross* had been taped across it.

"But . . ." Erika pointed to the tape.

"That doesn't mean anything," Susan assured her. "If they really didn't want anyone in there, there would be a police officer posted at the door."

"I'm not so sure about that," Erica said, looking skeptical. "What do you think?" she asked Kathleen.

Kathleen shrugged. "Susan's talked me into ignoring that before—and we've never been arrested."

"Not yet," Erika muttered as Susan peeled down one side of the tape and pulled something from her pocket.

"So convenient when you have the key," Kathleen said, examining the old-fashioned skeleton key the inn provided.

"I think someone may be coming up the stairs," Erika whispered.

Susan turned the key, and they all pushed into the room. "Don't move!" Susan whispered. The order was obeyed immediately. They listened intently. The old, worn floorboards creaked with every step, and whoever had come up the stairs continued on down the hall, entering another room and slamming its door behind him.

Susan sighed with relief. "Whew! For a minute there I thought it was a police officer."

"Let's look around and get out of here before one shows up," Kathleen suggested.

"But there's so much to look at," Erika said. "I can't believe all these people ignored the 'no presents please' note on your invitation."

"But you gave us something. At least I thought . . ." Susan was suddenly embarrassed, not wanting Erika to think she had expected a gift from her.

"Of course we did! You and Jed have done so much for Brett and me. Heavens, we probably would never have gotten married if you hadn't kept pushing us together, inviting us to the same parties and all. And you gave us that wonderful engagement party! Heavens, I can't count all the things you've done for us. We wanted to give you something nice."

"Jerry and I felt the same way," Kathleen added. "You introduced us to each other. On the other hand, I can't believe you were involved in this much matchmaking. There must be fifty gifts here."

"Fifty-seven was my count."

The correction came from behind. Spinning around, they discovered Alvena Twigg standing in the doorway. "I'll just close this door so we're not interrupted, shall I?" she twittered, suiting action to words as she spoke. "I'm so glad to see you and your friends, Mrs. Henshaw. My sister and I have been wondering if you were going to show up today. You must have come in the back way?"

"Yes," Susan admitted.

"Excellent idea. So many problems getting through the foyer with all the policemen and the esteemed members of the press corpse. That's what my dear father used to call them: the esteemed members of the press corpse." Smiling, she began to flutter around the room, straightening up a package that had fallen off its pile here and fluffing out a curtain there. Susan, Kathleen, and Erika watched silently.

"Interesting group of people, the esteemed members of the press corpse. Very well dressed as a rule, but such a display of bad manners! Not only are they inclined to shout, but they have no compunction about interrupting each other. And no respect for personal property. We are always having to ask guests to stop sitting on the porch railings—they're over a hundred years old, after all. So I shouldn't, perhaps, be surprised by how many of the esteemed members want to perch there. But no one has ever crushed the flowers and hedges like this group. Disgraceful. And they don't seem to know how to pick up after themselves. They leave coffee cups—half full and likely to be tipped over—in the oddest places; I found two in the pie chest just outside this doorway a few minutes ago! If we give them paper napkins, they toss them on the ground or in the fireplace. Surely anyone can tell we're not going to start a fire in the middle of August. And if we give them cloth napkins, they toss them in wastebaskets as though they're disposable. One wonders where—and by whom, oh yes, by whom—these esteemed members of the press corpse were raised."

Susan blinked and tried to think of something to say.

"Why were you wondering if Susan was going to come here today?" Erika got straight to the point.

"Heavens, because of the murder! Everyone knows that Susan Henshaw investigates murders. Why, when Mrs. Henshaw called to set up an appointment to see the inn, I turned to my sister at that moment—right at that moment—and said, 'Do you think a visit from Susan Henshaw means we're going to have a murder here?' That's just what I said. And look what happened!" She turned from the hideous watercolor she had been ineffectively straightening and stared at the bed. All three women looked, too. "A body! Just what I was waiting for!"

"You were waiting for a murder to happen? Here?" Susan had no idea what else to say.

"Why are you so surprised? They do sort of follow you around, don't they?" Alvena Twigg opened her blue eyes wide and peered at Susan over the top of her metal-rimmed glasses.

"I . . . Not really. I just have happened to . . . you know, just been around when someone was killed." Susan struggled with an explanation that made sense.

Alvena looked startled. "Really? I thought . . . well, I thought it was like being accident prone."

"You thought Susan was murder prone?"

Susan glanced over at Erika, who seemed to be having a difficult time not laughing.

"I've never had anything to do with a murder happening," Susan protested.

Alvena Twigg looked offended. "Of course not. I'd never think such a thing. It would be cheating!"

"Cheating?" Kathleen repeated the word.

"Yes. I mean, where would be the challenge? If Susan— you don't mind if I call you Susan, dear, do you?" Alvena continued without giving Susan time to answer. "If Susan killed someone and then investigated, well, what would be the point?"

"Uh, well, that's true, of course," Kathleen agreed.

Susan felt obliged to protest again. "I wouldn't kill anyone!"

"Of course not, because then you couldn't investigate, could you? At least not legitimately."

Alvena Twigg had such an earnest expression on her face that Susan decided there was no reason to continue along this line. "I . . ." She glanced at her companions and began again. "We are, of course, wondering who killed Ashley."

Alvena Twigg leaned closer and lowered her voice. "So you don't think it was her husband."

"Well, I really don't have any idea. . . ."

"But he would be foolish to kill her so soon after her

release. It makes him such an obvious suspect, don't you think?"

"I suppose, but . . ."

"You want to speak to me, of course," Alvena continued without allowing Susan to finish her thought.

"Yes, we do," Erika said.

"Although many investigators begin by looking into the victim's life," Alvena suggested.

"That's no problem. The Markses are Susan's next-door neighbors," Kathleen explained.

Alvena's eyebrows rose. "Why, how convenient for you," she said.

"They moved in less than a year ago. I don't know them all that well," Susan explained.

"Of course. There's really no reason to investigate until the deed is actually done, is there? I often found that to be true when I was working at the school. There were, of course, students who were known to be troublemakers. Every year our doors would open on another class of freshmen, and every year I would look out into the first rows of the auditorium—the classes were seated together, freshmen in front and then sophomores, then juniors, and on up to the seniors in the back of the room." She stopped speaking and looked at her audience checking to see, apparently, if they were capable of comprehending this complex layout. "And I would look for the troublemakers. You could almost always pick them out. The boys who wore leather—and that was the rule for over four decades. The girls wore too-short skirts, too-tight sweaters, and too much makeup. The actual details changed with the current fashions, but the intent—to attract those bad boys in leather—remained amazingly consistent. Anyway, once I knew who would cause trouble in the coming years I would just sit back and wait for it to happen. Perhaps it's like that for you?"

Before Susan could think of an answer, the door opened. Apparently she wasn't going to be given an opportunity to answer. She and her friends were about to be arrested.

ELEVEN

"IF THIS IS THE WAY THE NEXT THIRTY YEARS OF OUR MAR-
riage is going to continue, perhaps I should put a lawyer on
retainer. Or possibly Chad could be talked into attending
law school after Cornell."

"Jed, don't say anything to either of the children! I don't
want them to know I was almost arrested."

"Hon, it's a little late to try to keep the last few hours a
secret. Chrissy was the first one home today, and she listened to the messages you left on the machine. She tracked
me down and told me what had happened."

"But she wouldn't say anything to anyone."

"She doesn't have to. She was accompanied by a half
dozen old friends from high school. While it's possible our
exuberant daughter has grown more discreet now that she's
a married woman, my bet is that her friends cannot be
depended upon in that regard."

"Oh, no, that's right. They were all going to go to that
awful dive they used to go to after school for dinner
tonight. I'd forgotten. Oh, Jed." She sighed. "The whole
town probably knows by now."

"I think that's a good guess. We'll know more when we
get home. I left the answering machine on." They were
traveling down the Merritt Parkway. The sun was setting;

the forest lining the road was turning black in the dusk; the Mercedes purred. Susan leaned back against the headrest and sighed loudly.

"I cannot believe that idiot hauled us all—except for Alvena Twigg—off to the police station."

"Apparently Alvena was quick enough to slip out into the hallway when the police showed up. You could have done that, too. You did know you were breaking the law when you entered that room."

"Oh, Jed, I've ignored that Police Line Do Not Cross tape before, and I've never been arrested. The problem isn't what I did. The problem is Chief Peter Konowitz. He even made Erika come."

"She did cross the police line with you."

"I know, but she's married to Brett!"

"I don't think—"

But Susan was on a roll. "There must be some sort of professional courtesy, don't you imagine? I mean, threatening to arrest the wife of a fellow chief of police. Well, that's going a bit far, don't you think? It's not as if we'd done something terrible, for heaven's sake! We were just talking!"

"It's not what you were doing, it's where you were doing it," Jed reminded her.

"Yes, but, Jed, I was in our room! We paid for it—in fact, we paid for two nights, remember? We're still paying for that room. Did you tell our lawyer that? Does he know that we have a legal right to be there?"

"Susan, I don't know if that's true. . . . What are you looking for?"

"My notebook. That lawyer should know that I was in our room. That might make a difference to our case."

"What case? I understood that you were released with a warning."

"False arrest. I think we should file a lawsuit. I don't think he should be allowed to get away with it!" She was on a roll.

"Susan . . ."

"I know what you're going to say, Jed, and I agree. We wouldn't want to keep any money we won, of course. I mean, I wouldn't feel comfortable profiting from a police chief's stupidity. On the other hand, perhaps we could donate any winnings to Amnesty International. They're such big supporters of people who are wrongfully imprisoned. That would be appropriate, don't you think?"

"I think—"

"They could even use my case—and the money we win—to raise the level of consciousness about people wrongfully imprisoned in this country and—"

"Susan, I don't think Amnesty International would be interested in the two hours you spent sitting in a comfortable chair in the office of the chief of police waiting for our lawyer to come and straighten everything out. You were treated well. You had a cup of Starbucks coffee in your hand when I arrived, for heaven's sake. And they did release you with a warning."

"I asked for no fat, and I'm sure there was cream in that coffee; so don't imagine they were treating us all that well. And I know I overheard our lawyer say something about me being illegally detained."

"Susan, I think you'd better drop the whole idea of a lawsuit."

"I know I'm being . . . well, I may be being just a bit unreasonable. But, Jed, I'm upset. I have all this energy, and I don't know what to do with it."

He glanced over his shoulder into the backseat. "You could start writing thank-you notes."

Susan looked, too. The police had announced that their anniversary gifts were no longer considered possible evidence and were being released. She had insisted on returning to the inn and picking them up. They had filled their car, Kathleen's SUV, and Brett's police cruiser. There was still a pile left. She smiled, thinking of that. "At least I have an excellent excuse to return to the inn tomorrow."

"Susan, are you asking for trouble?"

"No, I'm asking for my presents. They've been moved from our room to the office, so even that stupid Peter Konowitz can't criticize me for picking them up."

"Susan, you heard what Brett said. . . ."

"Brett said a lot of things—but to the wrong people. I was sure he would give those men hell when he arrived."

"Is that what Erika thought would happen?"

"Well, no. She said he would be angry, but I didn't realize she thought he would be angry with us. After all, we didn't mean to do anything wrong."

"You knew you were breaking the law."

"But only in a minor way." She looked over at her husband. "Oh, Jed, I knew what we were doing was wrong. I just thought I'd be able to get away with it. I did exactly what I was always telling the kids not to do when they were growing up. And I guess I paid for it. Now, after all Chrissy's friends have told their families, I suppose a lot of people are going to know about it."

"Susan, you did see the crowd of press people standing around when we left, didn't you?"

"Yes, but I didn't think they were waiting for us, did you?"

"I certainly did. They were taking lots of photographs of our exit. And I don't think it's because they needed the practice."

"Do you think it was all local press?"

"No, in a case that has become as notorious as this one, I think it's just possible that some of those people may have actually been from as far away as New York City—or even the national press."

Susan flipped down the visor and peered into the make-up mirror that automatically lit up. "Jed, you're kidding. I must have looked a mess!" Actually, she realized, smiling, she didn't look all that bad. Sure she could have used some makeup, but her hairdo had held up and she was wearing a favorite shirt, which looked better now that she'd lost all that weight.

"Susan, Ashley's arrest was big news, but her murder and the arrest of her daughter is humongous. Every sleazy show that pretends to be news while glorifying the misery of others is going to be interested. Remember, the only reason Ashley's trial wasn't picked up by *Court TV* was because that rock singer was on trial for being married to three women at the same time. If he hadn't claimed to be the minister of the universal church of rock and roll and immune to bigamy laws or something equally stupid, this would already be a national story."

Susan leaned forward until the seat belt stopped her descent, then rested her head in her hands. "I never realized . . . Oh, I never even thought about the press. Those poor people."

"You mean Signe and her father?"

"Yes. They've been through so much, especially Signe."

Jed was silent for a moment, needing to concentrate on his driving as two black SUVs, their drivers apparently mistaking the Merritt Parkway for a slalom course, zoomed and swerved in and out through the traffic.

"Idiots," he murmured as they both disappeared over the horizon. "Of course it's different for Signe."

Susan nodded. "Because she's younger."

"No, because you don't choose your parents. Doug could have divorced Ashley, but Signe had no choice— Ashley was her mother no matter what."

"Signe was almost arrested when she was young. For attempted murder."

"Good Lord, where did you hear that?"

"She told me."

"When?"

"A few hours ago. Just before the police came for her."

"Susan, you'd better slow down. This is all news to me."

"The truth of the matter is that I don't know very much. Kathleen and Erika were at the house this morning, and Signe came over. She didn't have time to tell the whole story before the police came and hauled her off. They said it was just to ask her some questions. I do know that she was almost arrested for the attempted murder of her mother—she was sixteen at the time—but she was released because Ashley told the police she'd put the insecticide in Signe's closet . . ."

"Insecticide?"

"She was accused of poisoning her mother. With the insecticide."

"Wasn't insecticide what was used to poison Doug?"

"Yes."

"And how old is Signe now?"

"I guess around twenty-six."

"So this first poisoning event took place ten years ago?"

"Probably a bit more than that."

"Susan . . ."

"I know. It's really weird, isn't it? So you see why we had to go to the inn."

"No, I don't."

"Because the police are making a terrible mistake, and I . . . we . . . Kathleen, and Erika, and I feel that we have to investigate a bit on our own. Erika says that Brett doesn't have a very high opinion of Peter Konowitz, and so we're afraid he—Peter Konowitz—won't see that he's arrested the wrong person and . . ."

Jed glanced over at his wife. "What's wrong?"

"I was so upset that I never thought." She said the words more to herself than to her husband.

"Never thought what?"

"Really, I was so indignant. It never occurred to me."

"Susan! I didn't get much sleep last night and it's been a difficult day, so will you please explain clearly what you're talking about?"

"It never occurred to me that Signe was in the police station," she said slowly. "All the time Erika and Kathleen and I were there, Signe was too."

"You're wrong about that."

"But she was brought in for questioning. Where else would she be?"

"I have no idea, but she wasn't there. That's a tiny little town and a tiny little police station. They have two holding cells. I passed by them both on the way in to pick you up. They were both empty."

"Are you sure?"

"Susan, each one is about six feet square with a pull-down bench in one corner. Believe me, if anyone had been there, I'd have seen them."

"So where was she?"

"They could have taken her to the county jail."

"The county jail? Where is that?"

"I have no idea. I don't actually know which county Oxford Landing is in. Do you?"

Susan shrugged, then realized her husband probably hadn't seen her. "No. But poor Signe. She's such a sweet, young girl, and she shouldn't be in jail. Who knows who else is there with her! She could be hurt. We've got to find out where she is and go right to her." She reached into her Fendi bag for her cell phone.

"Who are you going to call? I don't think Chief Konowitz is going to be happy to hear from you again."

"I'll call Brett."

"He may not be home yet."

"I could call the station and leave a message for him. Or maybe I should call him at home and leave a message there. What do you think?"

"I think we're almost home ourselves. Why don't we go in, get a glass of wine or a cup of tea and maybe something to eat, and we can check our own answering machine at the same time. Maybe Brett has called us."

Susan considered his suggestion. She was surprisingly hungry, and it was just possible that Brett had called and the information she wanted was waiting on their machine. "Okay, but promise me that if Signe is in the county jail— any county jail—you won't object if I go see her this evening."

"Susan, I don't think county jails have evening visiting hours."

"Why not? Hospitals do."

"It's not quite the same thing, you know."

"But if I can see her this evening, you won't object to it."

"Of course not."

Susan was quiet, licking off the last of her lipstick and

worrying about Signe. They were passing the *Welcome to Hancock. Founded in 1772* sign. They had less than five miles to go to get to their house. It didn't take long, but she was relieved when Jed turned the corner onto their street. A lone TV van sat in front of the Markses' house surrounded by the cars of friends and neighbors; Susan turned her head away as they drove up their driveway. The automatic garage door opener allowed them to slip into their garage without confronting anyone. From there it was only a few steps to the kitchen.

Susan had been prepared for the rambunctious greeting of Rock and Roll. And she knew Clue wouldn't be far behind.

But Signe's quiet "Hi" came as a complete surprise.

TWELVE

"SIGNE! WHAT ARE YOU DOING HERE?"

"They asked me a lot of questions and then said I could go home. But I didn't want to . . . to go home. My father's there and I know I should be with him, but all those cars . . . He's not alone. And if I go back to the city, they could just come and haul me off to jail at any time. I . . . I was hoping that if I came here . . . I just don't want them to find me."

"Would anyone else like a drink?" Jed suggested.

Signe looked up. "I'm afraid it would just go to my head. I can't remember the last time I ate anything."

Susan leapt into action. "Jed, I'll have a glass of whatever you're having, but first we need to take care of Signe. There's Brie, Stilton, and some excellent chèvre in the refrigerator. And a baguette in the bread box. If you could quickly make up a cheese platter, I'll run down to the basement and see what's in the freezer that I can defrost for dinner." She was out of the room before she had finished her sentence—and back almost as quickly. "Just don't put any food within reach of the dogs!"

Jed looked down at the three hungry, furry faces that had gathered by his feet before he'd even opened the refrigerator door. "Don't worry."

Signe, Susan noticed, didn't even smile. Susan dashed

down to the large freezer in her basement and rummaged through its well-stocked shelves for the second time that day. Soups, casseroles, chili. She found what she was looking for and smiled. Homemade chicken rice soup—it might not cure a cold or mend a broken heart, but it would be soothing, filling, and nourishing. Tupperware in hand, she climbed the stairs to the kitchen.

Jed was chopping up the baguette with more energy than efficiency, and crumbs were flying everywhere. Signe didn't appear to have moved an inch. Susan rushed to her husband's side. "I'll do that. Why don't you pour us some wine and maybe get a glass of orange juice for Signe."

Jed went to do as she asked, and Susan finished his task. Then she cleaned up, throwing out the chicken that had been getting warm on the counter all day, and placed the frozen soup in the microwave. After pressing a few buttons, she returned to the table, placing the cheese, bread, plates, and napkins before her guest. When Signe didn't respond, Susan spread Brie on a thin slice of bread, put it on a plate, and placed it on the table in front of the young woman.

"You will feel better if you eat something," Susan suggested quietly, pushing the plate closer to her guest.

"I guess." Signe picked up the food and looked at it critically. "I'm allergic to nuts."

"It's cheese."

Signe smiled. "Of course it is. I'm not thinking—or seeing—very well, I guess." She took the smallest bite possible.

"I'm heating up some chicken soup too—homemade. I know it's a little warm for soup, but . . ."

"No, please, it sounds good." Signe put the rest of the cheese in her mouth and almost smiled. "I'm starving."

Now this was a problem Susan could solve. She spread cheese on more bread, got up and punched a couple of buttons on her microwave, and then headed for her refrigerator to collect the ingredients for a salad.

Jed poured glasses of Pinot Noir for Susan and himself, and Susan sipped hers as she put together a salad. "You and I have something in common. I was at the police station over in Oxford Landing today, too."

Signe didn't ask why, perhaps because Susan hadn't told her that she'd been taken there with a police escort. "Actually, I never made it that far," Signe said.

"I thought—"

"I know. I thought they were arresting me too, but it turned out that that weird Chief Konowitz just wanted to ask me a few questions."

"What sort of questions?" Jed asked.

"Why do you call him weird?" Susan wondered.

"It was all so strange," Signe began slowly. "Here I was talking with you and Erika and . . . I'm sorry, I don't remember who the other woman was. . . ."

"Kathleen Gordon," Susan said.

"Well, I was talking to you three and telling you about . . ." She glanced over at Jed. "About my past."

"It's okay. I told him pretty much everything you told me," Susan explained.

"Then you know why I'm the first person the police questioned when my mother was murdered."

"I don't know about that," Jed said. "It seems to me there may be many other suspects. But why don't you go on and tell us what happened after you left here."

"I was taken to the police car."

"Were you handcuffed?" Susan asked quickly.

"No. But there was a rather muscular man on either side

of me and a very large woman walking behind me, so I didn't even consider trying to get away or anything like that."

"If you weren't heading to the police station, where were you going?" Susan asked.

"Oh, we were on our way to the station. At least that's what he told me."

"He being Chief Peter Konowitz?" Jed asked.

"Yes. He told me that he needed to ask me some questions. Well, he said that here, right?" Signe continued after Susan nodded. "I asked him where we were going when I saw the police car, and he said to the station. I don't know why . . . well, I do know. I was in shock. I wasn't thinking. Anyway, we all got into the police car and I assumed we were going to the Hancock Police Station. When the car headed onto the highway I was stunned. I don't remember what I said. . . . Something like where are you taking me. And he said that we were going to Oxford Landing. That's when he offered me his cell phone."

"Good Lord. Why did he do that?" Jed asked, putting down his wineglass with a bang.

"He said I might want to call my lawyer."

"Did you?" Susan asked.

"Did he read you the Miranda warning?" Jed asked simultaneously.

"I don't have a lawyer. And he didn't read me anything at all. It was just a suggestion. It was almost casual, in fact. I turned him down, and he began to ask me some questions."

"What questions?" Susan asked quickly.

"The first was how well I got along with my mother. I told him that I was grown up, had a life of my own, and didn't see either of my parents all that much." Signe paused. "To be honest, I was afraid that maybe I sounded a bit defensive, so I added something about us having never been close. I probably should have kept my mouth shut."

"What did he say to that?" Susan asked.

"Nothing. He asked the same question about my father. And I gave him pretty much the same answer. Then he wanted to know where I was when my mother was killed. I told him home asleep in front of the TV. And then he got a call on his cell phone and almost right away he insisted that the officer who was driving pull into a diner parking lot."

"You're kidding!"

"I know; it was really odd. I got the impression that his phone kept going in and out of service. He kept raising his voice and yelling. I was thrilled that we had stopped, though. I desperately needed to use the bathroom, and they let me."

"They let you go alone?"

"No, the female officer went with me. We weren't gone more than five minutes, but when we got back to the car, Chief Konowitz said that there had been a mistake, that he had more important things to do, and that they were going to drive me back home. Which they did, although I asked to be dropped off a few blocks away. The press trucks that had been tailing us had vanished, and I wasn't anxious to run into any of the reporters who seem to be permanently camped out on my parents' lawn."

"And that's why you came here," Jed suggested.

"Yes. I walked through the backyard. Your daughter and some friends were out there tossing a stick to some huge dogs. They said they were just about to leave and go out to dinner. Anyway, I told them who I was and that I wanted to speak with you about my mother's murder and . . . and your daughter let me in." Signe looked perplexed. "She didn't seem to think it was at all odd."

"Our daughter is accustomed to her mother's rather strange activities," Jed commented, getting up to fetch the wine bottle.

"You came here just to avoid the press?" Susan asked, choosing to ignore Jed's remark.

"Yes . . . No . . . Not really. I came . . . I'm here . . ." Signe paused, took a deep breath, and started again. "To be honest, I was hoping you might be able to explain something. Something my mother said to me."

"What?"

Signe looked from one Henshaw to the other, a sad expression on her face. "Yesterday was awful, and I'm not completely sure I know when everything happened. I wasn't even planning to be in Hancock this weekend. I've been avoiding here because I didn't want to answer questions about why I wasn't in court during my mother's trial."

"Why weren't you?" Susan asked quickly.

"I . . . My parents . . . This is all so difficult." Signe took another deep breath. "You see, my mother's lawyer thought my presence might complicate her case."

"I would have thought it would strengthen it—you know, make it look as though you were being supportive," Jed suggested.

"She—her lawyer—didn't want the press to find out about what happened when I was a teenager."

"I would have thought your mother's lawyer would be thrilled that someone else might be a suspect—no matter who it is," Jed said.

"But think about that time. Signe's mother told the police she had put the poison in Signe's closet," Susan interrupted her husband. "When you think about it, her lawyer was smart. That fact coming out might have done a lot of damage to her case."

Signe nodded. "Exactly."

"It does make sense." Susan looked at Jed.

"So let's get back to the party," he suggested. "You were just saying that you were in Hancock because your mother called you . . ."

"Yes, she wanted to celebrate her 'not guilty' verdict. At least that's what she told me on the phone."

"When was that?" Jed asked.

"Around one o'clock on Friday. I was at the SoHo store. She called me there."

"Right after she arrived home after being freed by the court," Jed said.

"How do you know that?" Susan asked.

"I came home early because Chrissy and Stephen were driving up from Philadelphia. You had an appointment for a manicure—or pedicure or whatever—and you wanted to be sure someone was around to greet them, remember? Anyway, I was feeling sorry for Clue since Slobber and Snot tend to get all the attention when they're here. So I thought I'd take her over to the playing fields by the municipal building and toss around a ball. We'd just gotten started when about twenty press cars and microwave vans pulled into the parking lot. They were all looking for Brett to get his response to the 'not guilty' verdict."

"How did you know that?"

"You know Clue—she considers herself the world's official greeter," he explained to Signe. "Anyway, she took off to see what all the commotion was about, and I dashed right after her. One of the reporters for the Hartford paper grabbed her before she could run in front of a car, and he told me what was going on. He has two goldens of his own," Jed added.

"So your mother called you around this time," Susan said, trying to get back to the story.

"Yes. Mother said she wasn't calling from home, but she didn't explain where she was," Signe said. "Or else I wasn't paying attention. She told me the jury had come back with a 'not guilty' verdict, and she wanted me to know right away. I was so relieved." She pursed her lips and was silent for a moment before continuing. "Anyway, then Mother asked me if I could come to Hancock for the weekend. Of course, I said I would. I explained that I needed some time to get organized, but that I'd be here in the middle of the afternoon. Then Mother said Father was going to take her to dinner, that the food in jail had been repulsive, and we hung up.

"It wasn't until I arrived in Hancock that I discovered that Mother had no interest in celebrating her release with me. I shouldn't have been surprised. I was so happy with the news when she called that I completely ignored the fact that we are not the type of family who gets together to celebrate anything."

"So what happened when you arrived?" Susan asked, thinking how sad that sounded.

"Well, I came straight to the house. Father was home, waiting for me in the living room, but Mother had gone out."

"You're kidding!"

"No, she was getting her hair done and having a manicure and pedicure. At least that's what she told Father when she left home. Apparently she went shopping, too. When she arrived home she was carrying at least a dozen packages from Saks."

"When was that?" Susan asked, wondering if she would have done the same thing after being in jail for over a month.

"She came home around four in the afternoon. Father had made reservations for dinner at a place on the water up near Mystic. He and I had talked it over, and we thought it might be a good idea to go someplace where no one would know them. Of course, it turned out that Mother had other ideas."

THIRTEEN

"WHAT OTHER IDEAS?" JED ASKED.

But Susan knew the answer before the words were out of Signe's mouth. "She had decided to attend your party."

"I gather you and your father were surprised by her decision," Jed said.

"Shocked. We had planned a quiet evening in a restaurant fairly far away and had talked about how to avoid being followed by any press, and all of a sudden Mother is asking my father if his navy Brooks Brothers suit is back from the cleaners and if he thinks it's necessary to buy—" Signe stopped speaking, obviously embarrassed. "Ah, if it was necessary to buy you two an anniversary gift."

"Didn't we have 'No gifts please' printed on the invitations?" Jed asked no one in particular.

"How weird," Susan commented, glaring at her husband. After all, he was the one who was always saying they needed to stick to the subject. "Did your father have any reservations about coming to our party?"

"Yes. He didn't come right out and say so, but I could tell. He told Mother that he was fairly sure he had refused your invitation and that it would be rude to turn up unexpected. But Mother said she had found the invitation on her desk and that, as the RSVP card was still with it, he could not possibly have refused. And she said it was going to be a big party and no one would notice if they hadn't sent in the RSVP. She wouldn't listen to anything else. She was determined to go, and the only decision to be made was what Father was going to wear and when they were going to leave.

"When Mother gets going, Father usually dithers around a bit and then he gives in. He was upstairs looking for his blue suit almost immediately."

"What did you do?" Jed asked.

"This is the odd thing that happened," Signe answered. "My parents were both upstairs getting dressed. I was scrounging around in the kitchen, looking for something to eat, when my mother came downstairs. She was wearing a robe and she looked . . . I don't know. . . . She looked weird."

"What do you mean?" Susan asked.

"She was pale, of course. I mean, it's not as though she'd spent the summer out in the Hamptons. And she'd lost weight in jail, but there was something else. It's going to sound strange, but she looked serious—more serious than I'd ever seen her."

"Did she say anything to you?" Jed asked.

"Yes, she said she had something to tell me. Something important. I had been getting ready to open a can of soup, and I put it away and sat on a stool. I don't know what I was expecting. I was afraid . . . Well, to tell the truth, I thought for a minute that she was going to tell me that she had been poisoning my father, that she was guilty. But she started to talk about you two."

"About Jed and me?"

"Well, mainly you," Signe answered. "She told me that you had been involved in solving murders—not as a police officer, though. That you did it on your own. I didn't know what to say, so I just listened. I think that's when she told me that the reason she and my father had moved to Hancock was to be your neighbors."

"What?" After thirty years of marriage, the Henshaws spoke as one.

"That's what she said. I'm sure of it."

"Did she explain?" Jed asked.

"Did she tell you that she—or your father—had known us before coming here?" Susan asked.

"She didn't explain—" Signe paused. "—exactly."

"What do you mean?" Susan asked.

"Did she say she knew either of us before she came to Hancock?" Jed asked again.

Signe answered Jed's question first. "No, she didn't say anything about that. I've thought this over. I knew you'd ask. All she said was that she and my father moved here— to Hancock—to be your neighbors. But that's not all she said. She also said that if something happened to her, I should remember that it was important that they live near you. That's all there was time for. My father came into the room to ask her to help him pick out a tie, and she didn't say anything else—about you, or moving here, or what she thought might happen to her."

"That's so weird," Susan said.

"What did you do then?" Jed asked.

"Nothing much. I suggested that maybe a present would be a good idea, and I headed downtown to Twigs and Stems. To be honest, I was looking for Erika more than anything. I was glad Mother was found not guilty, of course, but if we weren't going to go out to dinner to celebrate, there really wasn't anything for me to do in Hancock. I . . . You can probably tell that I haven't maintained a close relationship with either of my parents. I thought that checking in with Erika would mean that the trip here wasn't a complete waste of my weekend.

"Of course, Erika wasn't there. The girl minding the store said she had been in earlier in the day, but had gone home to get ready for a party. I had no idea what to do." Signe got up and wandered over to the kitchen window and looked out at the backyard. "There was a present there waiting to be picked up and taken to the Landing Inn. I offered to deliver it, and I did. That only took about an hour. Then I stopped in at the McDonald's out on the highway, ate an incredibly fattening dinner, and drove back to my parents' house. I wasn't surprised to find that they had already left. In fact, I was counting on it."

"What did you do then?"

"Fell asleep in front of the TV. I was exhausted. I didn't even wake up when they first arrived home."

"They arrived home? Both of your parents?" Susan jumped in with a question.

Signe looked surprised. "Yes, of course. . . . Oh, I see what you mean. I . . . I thought my mother and father had come home together. And they weren't all that late, either. When did your party end?"

"Heavens, it was well after one A.M. when we finally went upstairs, wasn't it?" Susan checked with Jed.

"At least. But Ashley and Doug left before it had really gotten started, remember." He looked at Signe. "When did your parents arrive home?"

"The news—the eleven o'clock news—was just ending."

"It's probably a half hour drive to Hancock from Oxford Landing that time of the night," Jed said. "Maybe less."

"But that's an hour round-trip," Susan said slowly.

Signe looked at Susan, a puzzled expression on her face. "When did you find Mother?"

"A little after one, but she must have been murdered and placed on our bed quite a while before that. I mean . . ." Susan looked at Signe. "You look a bit pale. This must be awful to hear. Maybe—"

"No, I'm okay. I need to know about this. Really. Go on."

Susan pursed her lips and thought for a moment. "It's the time frame that puzzles me. I thought . . . I knew your parents left the party early, but I just assumed that they never left the inn."

"Or my father either?" Signe asked.

"I didn't really think about that. I just assumed they were together . . . until your mother was killed that is," she added.

"So you think my father killed her."

"Of course not! I . . ." Susan stopped and tried to think of a nice way to answer the question. "Look," she began slowly, "that is what most people will—or are, I guess—thinking."

"But my father came home early. I spoke with him."

"Signe, I hate to ask you this," Susan said. "And I know the way the question sounds, but were you watching TV in the family room next to the kitchen?"

Signe looked surprised, but answered promptly. "Yes."

"And your parents entered the house through the garage. That is, they came in through the kitchen."

"Yes." Signe paused. "That is, I assume they did. I didn't actually see both of them. That's what you're getting at, right?"

"Yes. Who . . . Which one did you see?"

Signe looked scared. "Father. He . . . he came to the doorway and said that Mother was tired, so they'd left early and were going straight to bed. He . . . he asked if I needed anything. I said no. Father said that we'd all have a big breakfast together in the morning and for me to get a good night's sleep. I . . . I said good night and turned back to the television. I meant to go up to bed, but I just wasn't all that sleepy after my nap. I watched a Cary Grant movie on TV for a while, and then, around the time I started to doze off again, the phone rang with the news about Mother's murder."

"You answered the phone?" Jed asked the question.

"Yes."

"Who called?" Susan asked.

"I think it must have been Chief Konowitz, but I'm not sure. He introduced himself right away, but I wasn't paying much attention. I was half asleep. All I heard was a male voice asking who I was, and when I told him, the caller said that my mother was dead and that he would like to speak to my father right away. I hung up."

"You what?"

"I hung up. I thought it was some sort of joke, frankly. You have to understand how strange things had been in that house for the past few months. My father had stopped answering the phone completely. He said the only people who called were reporters or idiots—people making crank calls, suggesting the names of lawyers for my mother, and other sorts of junk that either upset him or hurt his feelings. He had been using the answering machine to screen phone calls since the day after Mother was arrested. I just assumed that this call was one of the ones he had described to me.

"Anyway, the phone rang again, and I picked it up planning to tell off the idiot on the other end of the line—only it turned out to be Erika. She knew about the murder, had called my apartment in the city, and when she didn't find me in, she thought I might be here. She . . . she told me that my mother was in fact dead." She frowned and looked down at the floor.

"And you went upstairs to tell your father," Jed prompted when Signe had been silent for a moment.

"Yes. That's exactly what I did."

"And what did he say?" Susan asked, hoping she didn't know the answer to her question.

"Nothing. He wasn't there." Signe looked at the Henshaws. "I know what you're thinking, but my father would never ever have killed my mother. I'm sure of it."

"What did you do then?" Susan asked.

"I didn't know what to do. I walked around the house for a bit. I think I turned on the radio. I was thinking that perhaps the news of the murder might be on. I didn't know what to do," she repeated. "And then . . ."

"And then," Susan prompted.

"Then my father walked in the front door."

"Where had he been?"

"He couldn't sleep," Signe insisted. "He told me that he couldn't sleep so he went for a walk. He didn't really go anywhere in particular. He said something about walking around the block a few times."

"Did you tell him about your mother's death?" Susan asked gently.

"Yes. Of course. What else would I have done?"

"He must have been shocked," Susan suggested.

"Did he tell you why your mother had stayed at the inn after he left?" Jed asked.

"Yes. He said that something had happened at the party that upset them and they had planned on leaving together, but while they were walking to the car, they'd had an argument about something he had said to someone, and my mother stalked off. He said he tried to follow her, but she just took off down some path by the river and he got lost. Anyway, he couldn't find her, so he finally came home."

"He left her at the inn?" Susan asked.

"Yes, he said she knew so many people at your party that he was sure she would find a ride home. He didn't say anything to me when he got home because he didn't want me to worry. But it turned out that he was so worried he couldn't sleep." Signe stopped speaking and looked up at the Henshaws. "I know it sounds odd, but it could be true!"

"I suppose . . ." Susan started.

"You have to understand what I'm going to say to you," Signe said urgently. "I know Father. He did not kill my mother."

Susan patted Signe on the shoulder. "It doesn't matter what we believe. What matters right now is what the police think happened."

"They're going to look to the family for suspects first, aren't they?"

"Probably," Jed answered.

"But that doesn't matter in the long run," Susan added quickly. "There must be other people who wanted your mother dead." She realized that what she was saying was not necessarily comforting and stopped.

But Signe didn't seem upset by Susan's words. "I guess. I don't know much about their lives. My father could tell you about that—if you can convince him to."

"Why would he need convincing?" Jed asked. "He certainly would want suspicion to fall away from the family."

"Of course, but he's spent years and years protecting my mother."

"Your mother always struck me as a very strong person," Susan said.

"She was. It's just . . ." Signe took a deep breath and then exhaled. "It's a little difficult to explain."

"Try."

Signe started by asking a question of her own. "Did you get along with Mother?"

"We've always gotten along with our neighbors," Susan said. "We make a point of doing so. Of course, your parents hadn't lived in Hancock all that long, and we were very friendly with the Hallards. They were already living in the house that your parents bought before we moved to Hancock. Martha Hallard was the first person to knock on our door the day after we arrived here. Dan Hallard is a gynecologist. He delivered our son Chad."

"You're saying that my parents couldn't have replaced the Hallards in such a short time, but you're not answering my question. Did you get along with Mother?"

Susan and Jed exchanged glances. "Not really," Jed answered.

"It's just that—" Susan began to excuse Jed's lack of tact.

"It's just that Mother was an almost impossible person to get along with. You don't have to tell me that. You're being nice, and there's no real reason to. I . . . I care a lot about my parents, but Mother and I have always had a difficult relationship. I still have feelings for her, of course, but I know her too well to be blind to her faults. But you don't have to tell me any more. Most people have trouble getting along with Mother. She was demanding, domineering, and difficult." Signe's lips crumpled into a tiny half smile. "The three Ds. That's what my grandmother used to say about her—that she represented the three Ds."

"You could say that about a lot of people, but most of them have not been murdered," Jed reminded her.

"I know. It's just that Father spent an awful lot of time keeping other people from knowing how horrible my mother could actually be. That's what I meant when I said he protected her."

"How did he do that?" Jed asked.

"Well, there were simple things. Like he would send flowers to someone she offended by being what she called honest. I don't know how much time you spent with Mother, but she always claimed to place a high value on her honesty."

"I think I know what you mean," Susan said. "Ashley did tend to tell people what was wrong with them or their family or . . . or even their yard. I remember when she and your father moved in last spring. I have a fabulous bed of peonies lining the driveway. The weather was perfect for them last May, and they were looking their best. I invited your parents over for drinks the day after we met, and I'd picked a large bouquet for the mantel in the living room. Of course peonies do attract ants, and I thought I'd shaken off the blooms enough, but there was one ant crawling on the mantel. Your mother spied it and made a comment about how she would never have such filthy flowers in any house she lived in. I know it sounds innocuous, but there was something about the way she said it that made me feel as though I'd done something much more terrible than bringing a little garden ant or two inside. I . . . I don't know why it upset me, but it did."

"I do. You were trying to be a good hostess. You were offering the best you had to some people you didn't know, and Mother turned it around and made you feel as though you had done something wrong. What did Father do?"

Susan smiled at the memory. "He made a joke at the

time. To be honest, I don't remember exactly what he said, but I do remember appreciating that he was trying to make me feel better. Then, the very next day, he sent over that little watercolor." Susan pointed to a small, framed painting sitting on a stand under a lamp. "He wrote a note telling me how much he and your mother appreciated our hospitality and kindness to them, and he enclosed that. I had it framed," she explained.

Signe got up and looked down at the picture.

"It's a peony," Susan added.

Signe nodded. "I know."

"He didn't actually mention what had happened over the flowers and the ant. I mean, it was such a small thing. . . ."

"But it was a hurtful thing," Signe said. "And my father knew that. So he did what he could to make it up to you. And, being his kind self, he did it in a way that didn't reflect badly on my mother, as well."

"You know, you're right. I hadn't thought of it that way before. You say he's done that type of thing before?"

"All the time. Why?"

"Well, a man who took care of his wife like that surely shouldn't be considered a possible murder suspect, could he?"

"There are just two problems with your idea," Signe said. "First, my mother offended so many people over the years, how will anybody find the time or energy to search out a suspect?"

"And what's the second problem?" Jed asked.

"We have to convince Chief Konowitz to look at all those people instead of Father or me."

FOURTEEN

"SOMEONE NEEDS TO CHECK OUT YOUR PRESENTS. I THINK Wet and Wild have been sampling in there." The front door slammed, and Susan realized their son had just exited the building—again.

Susan and Jed were sitting quietly in the living room. Signe, having seen her father's car drive up to his house, had left half an hour ago, but the Henshaws, both tired, hadn't moved. Now Susan opened her eyes and glanced over at her dozing husband. "Do you think he'll manage to spend the entire summer here without having a single intelligent conversation with us?" she asked.

"Who?"

"Chad!"

"I don't know what you mean. We've had lots of intelligent conversations. He and I had a long discussion about the politics of appointing minorities to the Supreme Court just the other day."

"That's not the type of conversation I'm talking about! I'm interested in personal things. You know, if he's serious about any one particular girl, what he plans to do after he graduates. Things like that."

"You want to sit on the edge of his bed, ruffle his hair, and hear all about his day," Jed suggested quietly.

Susan grimaced. "Okay. Yes, that is exactly what I want."

"And you think that would be appropriate at this time of his life?"

"I know it wouldn't be. But it's what I want. He's nice and polite and everything, but I miss the closeness we had. You know?"

"I know. But he's a great kid, Sue. He . . ." Jed stopped and scratched his head. "What did he say as he went by? Something about the dogs and our presents?"

"Oh, Jed! Our presents!" Susan jumped to her feet and ran out of the room.

They had decided to leave their anniversary gifts in Jed's study, thinking they could use his desk to organize the thank-you note writing process. They hurried there now.

"I guess," Jed said as they stopped in the doorway, "we're going to have to keep this door closed."

A large wicker basket of cheese and crackers that had been on Jed's desk was now scattered about on the Aubusson rug. The mastiffs had managed to remove the cellophane and had consumed most of the cheese, crackers, wrappings and about half of the basket itself.

"Oh, no! Is the card around somewhere?"

Jed walked over to the mess. "A card? You're worried about a card?"

"We need to know who to thank, Jed."

"I guess. Too bad those beasts can't write. They're the ones who should be saying thank you for that gift." He turned around and examined the piles of presents for the first time. "Wow! We're going to have to buy a wine cellar for the basement."

"Hm. There are lots of bottles here. Wine and champagne. I peeked at some labels."

Jed was doing the same, slowly wandering around the

room. "Looks like we're going to be well stocked for the winter. Hon, are you sure you want to get involved in this murder?"

"We're already involved!" Susan picked up a rectangular box and shook it. "What do you think this is? A book?"

"I don't know. Susan, this is an odd family. Signe seems sweet, but she was accused of attempted poisoning when she was young. And you know you never particularly liked Doug or Ashley. Why don't you just let the police do their thing, and we can enjoy the rest of the summer?"

"I don't think Signe killed her mother."

"I don't think we know Signe all that well. And I thought that story she told about Ashley and Doug moving to Hancock because we live here was just plain weird."

"You think she lied?"

"I don't know what to think. It seems to me that someone is lying. Certainly Doug's story about the fight and then coming home alone but not wanting Signe to know he was alone is suspicious."

"It sure was! But that would have been Doug lying, not Signe."

"Why are you so sure that Signe's telling the truth?" Jed asked. "You don't know her at all."

"I know. But you should hear the way Erika talks about her. She really relies on her in her SoHo store, and I think Erika's a wonderful judge of people."

"I agree, but that doesn't mean you have to be involved in the investigation of her mother's murder."

"I don't like Peter Konowitz."

"I can't imagine many people do, but—"

"And he threatened to arrest me for being in my own hotel room."

"He had a perfect right to—"

"He'll arrest the wrong person. I just know it."

"And you're worried that it might be Signe."

"Yes. She's such a sweet girl, and I feel as though she needs my help."

"Is it possible that this has to do with the fact that your own children need less and less of you?" Jed asked gently.

"I suppose. Maybe. But, Jed, if she's innocent—"

"Look, you're going to do what you're going to do. I know that. But, for God's sake, be careful, hon. Poisoning is an easy way to kill someone. And I don't want you to be next."

Susan held a bottle of Tattinger's sporting a silver bow and a tag around its neck up to the light. "What do you mean? Why do you think it's any easier to poison someone than it is to kill them in some other way? Because there's no blood?"

"Because you don't have to be around. You could poison a person's food or drink and then vanish. The death—and all its disgusting side effects—can happen without you."

"That's true. I don't think I've ever thought about it before." She peered at the foil cap around the bottle in her hands. "You don't think . . ."

Jed grinned. "No, I don't think any of our guests was trying to kill us."

"That's not what I was thinking. Suppose Ashley ingested the poison at our party. Maybe it wasn't even meant for her. Maybe the poisoner was trying to kill someone else."

"You know, that's just possible," Jed said. "Ashley could have gotten the poison by mistake and died, then been brought up to our room. Although I don't understand why anyone would put her on our bed and cover her with our presents if she wasn't the intended victim."

"And she probably didn't die that far away from our room. The inn was full that night, and remember, the farther you carry a dead body, the more likely it is that someone will see you doing it."

"That's true," Jed agreed.

"Is it possible to take a poison and not die immediately?" Susan asked.

"I would imagine that it would depend on the type of poison ingested."

"And we won't know that until the autopsy is completed."

"No, you won't know that until the autopsy is completed and you can find someone to share the results of the autopsy with you. Remember, this isn't Brett's case."

Susan ignored him. "Do you think they work on Sunday?"

"It depends on what 'they' you're talking about."

"The county medical examiner. That's who does the autopsy, right?"

"I guess each county has its own medical examiner, but remember not every county is as populated or as wealthy as ours is, Sue. I don't know who would take care of this type of thing in Oxford Landing."

"This is getting more and more confusing. We really don't know anything at all."

"We know Ashley was murdered. We know whoever killed her moved her body into our room, piled all our presents on top of the body, and then left it—her—there for us to find. You know, we might know something else."

"What?"

"That whoever did this—whoever moved the body into our bedroom—wanted you to get involved in the murder investigation."

"Why do you say that?"

"Susan, have you ever found a body and then not investigated?"

"No, but that doesn't mean . . . Well, the truth of the matter is that . . . Jed, what would anyone do when they found a body?"

Her husband laughed. "Susan, most people would run like hell in the opposite direction. Or go home and hide under the bed. Or—most likely—call the police. Most people would never, ever think of trying to find out who the murderer is."

"I guess that's true, but—"

"But you have to do what you think is right. I know." Jed paused and looked around the room. "So what are you going to do now?"

"Why don't we start opening presents? We're going to have to hide in the house until we see what's in all these."

"Why?"

"Jed, I can't risk running into friends all over town who went to the trouble and expense of buying us gifts and not thank them immediately! Some people would be offended!"

Jed pursed his lips. "I suppose you have a point. Listen, this won't take forever if we get organized. Bottles first. I'll sit at the desk and write down what was given as well as the name of the giver. You know, we could do a form thank-you on the computer." He glanced over at his wife and read—accurately—the expression on her face. "No? Well, let's get going anyway."

Susan loved getting presents, and Jed's practical approach to the towering piles of wrapped gifts seemed to be lacking in enthusiasm. On the other hand, as much as she loved getting presents, she hated writing thank-you notes. Maybe getting Jed involved would be a good thing.

If he could write a thank-you note on the computer, he could write a couple of dozen longhand. "There's a copy of the guest list right under your desk light. You can just write on it."

They got to work. Susan pulled bottles of champagne, wine, and liquor from their elegant wrappings. Jed wrote down the salient facts next to the name of the person or couple who had given each gift. They were having a good time, talking about the various vintages, what they would serve them with, who they should invite to share some of the more precious bottles, when Susan found it.

"Jed! Look at this!" She held up a bottle with a fancy label.

"Isn't that the wonderful white wine we had on our last trip to Lucca?"

"It was. Now it's an empty bottle."

"You're kidding! Is it broken?"

"Nope." Susan turned the bottle upside down. "Looks to me like it was emptied the normal way. Someone probably used a corkscrew. I just hope it was someone with enough sophistication to appreciate what he was drinking not one of the kids who were passing appetizers."

Jed had gotten up from the desk and moved to his wife's side. "Susan, don't you think this is a little odd? Don't you think we should report it?"

"But we don't know who did it. What do you expect the Twiggs to do? Question their entire staff about one missing bottle of wine? Not that the bottle's missing—just the contents." She giggled.

Jed reached in his pocket for a handkerchief and, protecting his fingers, removed the bottle from her grasp.

"You can't cut yourself. Nothing's broken," Susan said, seeing what he was doing.

"Susan, this could be evidence."

"Evidence?"

"What if this bottle was filled with poisoned wine? What if that's what killed Ashley?"

"You think someone in Italy . . . Oh, you mean someone opened the bottle at the inn, added the poison, and then served it to Ashley."

"It's possible."

"I guess. Maybe someone invited her to our room, offered her wine that had already been poisoned, and then . . . Oh, Jed, that might be the first concrete evidence we've come across!"

"The bottle has to be tested."

"Of course."

"That's why I'm holding it so carefully. We have to get this bottle to the Oxford Landing Police Station as soon as possible."

"Are you nuts?" Susan jumped to her feet, sending wrapping paper and cards cascading to the floor.

"What exactly were you planning to do with it?" Jed held the bottle away from his grasping wife.

"I thought of maybe mentioning it to Brett."

"Who would then tell you to call the Oxford Landing Police Department. Or, perhaps, offer to have it taken there by someone from the local department."

"You don't know that's what he would do," Susan insisted.

"Yes, I do. And so do you."

Susan frowned. "I suppose. But we don't want one of our good friends to be a suspect in a murder investigation just because he generously gave us this present."

"What are you doing?" Jed asked as Susan sat back

down and began to rummage around in the papers at her feet.

"Looking for the card."

"What card?"

"The one that came with that bottle," Susan answered. "Although I didn't notice . . ." She reached down and scooped up a white silk bag printed with the image of a white dove. "This is it!"

"What?"

"The bag that bottle came in. Oh, but there's no note. There wasn't a card on the outside. I noticed that when I pulled off the ribbon, but some people have put notes inside the bags, and I thought there might be one in here. But there isn't."

"So you don't have to worry about incriminating anyone we invited to the party. Now let's call Oxford Landing."

"I don't know, Jed. This changes things."

"What?"

"Well, now we not only don't know who killed Ashley; we don't know if she was the person who was meant to die."

"What do you mean?"

"Well, we don't know who the bottle is from, but we do know one thing. We know it was in with our gifts. It may have been intended for us."

FIFTEEN

SUSAN AND JED WERE WALKING THE DOGS AROUND THE block.

"Did we have a real meal today? I know we've been eating constantly, but I'm talking about real food. You know, meat and vegetables."

"Please don't mention food. Those beasts will start begging again." Susan reached down and ran her hand over Clue's solid head. She glanced at the bull mastiffs, striding by Jed's side. "I'm glad you're here to walk them. They don't listen to a word I say. And I'm always afraid they'll pull me down."

"They're actually sweet dogs," Jed said, trying to untangle the two leashes he held in one hand. "Just a bit over-enthusiastic perhaps."

"Yeah, just a bit," Susan said as the larger of the mastiffs spied a chipmunk crossing the street and lunged after it.

"You just have to keep control." Jed jerked on the leash, and the mastiff sat down with a bump. "And you didn't seem to be bothered by their enthusiasm an hour ago."

"To be honest, I was thrilled," Susan said, smiling. The call to Chief Konowitz had brought almost immediate results. He had shown up at their front door, a scowl on his face. But it wasn't the scowl that had interested the mastiffs. It was the splash of catsup on his uniform shirt. Acting as though they had been starved for years and catsup was their favorite nourishment, the dogs had thrown themselves on the police chief, licking enthusiastically.

Jed had been horrified, Susan thrilled. Like Queen Victoria, Chief Konowitz had not been amused. But he did have a way with dogs. "Sit," he ordered. The dogs sat, and the Henshaws rushed forward to apologize for the animals. But Peter Konowitz was not interested in hearing their explanations. "I understand you have more evidence in the Marks case," he stated flatly, staring around the room as though he expected to find yet another body.

"You won't believe what we found!" Susan said.

"Perhaps what I won't believe is that you found it," he had replied ominously as Susan handed the bottle to him.

Fortunately, Chief Konowitz had announced his intention of immediately placing the empty wine bottle in the hands of his forensic team and had departed. "Otherwise," Susan said, as she and Jed discussed the day's events, "I might have grabbed that bottle back and used it to hit him over the head."

"Hon, Peter Konowitz is the best reason I know to stay out of this. He doesn't like us, and he'll resent anything you do."

"I know. I'll just have to stay out of his way as much as possible. And I know how to do that," she added earnestly. "Remember, Brett wasn't all that enthusiastic about my involvement in his investigations to begin with. I used to investigate and avoid Brett at the same time. So I can do that with Chief Konowitz now."

Jed smiled, but he didn't say anything.

Susan glanced over at him and laughed. "You're thinking that he still isn't always appreciative of my help, right?"

"Right now I'm thinking that after thirty years of marriage, I've finally learned to keep my mouth shut."

"Oh, Jed."

They continued around the block, but the subject of the murder didn't come up again.

The Hancock police chief's cruiser was parked in their driveway, and they could see Brett leaning against the rail on their porch steps as they got closer.

"I wonder . . ." Jed began.

But Susan was a mother. She didn't wonder anything. She moved straight to panic. "The kids! Do you think there's been an accident? Come on, Clue," she ordered, starting to jog.

The mastiffs picked up the chase, dragging Jed behind. They came together on the steps in one lunging, drooling bunch, and by the time Jed had untangled the leashes, Susan had been assured of her children's safety.

"So what can we do for you?" Jed asked, following the mastiffs into the house.

"I'm actually here to ask Susan for a favor," Brett explained.

"If you don't need me, I'll make sure the dogs have water and then I'll head on up to bed. Frankly, I'm exhausted. And Sprinkle and Spray are sure to wake us up when Chrissy and Stephen get home."

"Good idea." Susan was enthusiastic; she wanted to speak to Brett alone.

"I wanted to speak to you alone," Brett said, echoing her thoughts as she led him into her living room.

"What's up?"

But Brett asked a question instead of answering hers. "You're investigating Ashley's murder, aren't you?"

"Well, it did happen in my hotel room, and I know the wrong person is the major suspect, and . . ."

"Susan, I'm not going to suggest you stop. In fact, I'm here to encourage your investigation."

"You're kidding." Well, it was true. There was a first time for everything, she thought.

"No, I'm completely serious."

"Why?"

"I need your help."

"I didn't think Hancock had anything to do with this investigation."

"That's not true for a couple of reasons. Sit down and I'll explain."

Susan sat and waited.

"In the first place, we rarely reopen a murder investigation without new evidence in the case. But the case of Doug being poisoned was never completely closed. And something else has happened, of course: Ashley was poisoned. Just because her murder didn't happen in Hancock, there are too many connections to Doug for the cases not to be connected. I think we have a poisoner loose, possibly in Hancock. And I can't ignore that fact. I can't directly investigate the Oxford Landing murder, but I can look into the original case again."

"So you have officially reopened the case."

"Yes."

"Who . . . ?"

"Susan, we're looking everywhere. Into Doug's present-day relationships and into his past. We haven't come up with a single thing. Doesn't surprise me, frankly. We didn't find any suspects except for Ashley the first time around."

"So why do you need my help? Do you want me to ask Doug some questions—you know, without him knowing that the answers he's giving me are going straight to you— or what?"

"What. Remember, I said that I need your help for a couple of reasons." Brett stopped talking and took a deep breath. "Susan, this is very sensitive. And I can't tell you how much I hate talking about it. The papers are always full of stories about the Blue Wall—how policemen protect their peers. You know the type of thing."

"Sure." She leaned forward, more curious than ever. Did Hancock have a crooked cop?

"I don't think cops who do bad things should be protected, but you've got to understand that being a police officer isn't like other jobs. And even in a quiet suburb like Hancock, every officer knows that his or her life may depend on a fellow officer. So a reluctance to criticize peers is really self-preservation as well as loyalty."

Susan understood what he was saying, and the expression on his face showed how difficult it was for him to say it. She only nodded.

"So you must understand that what I'm telling you is completely confidential—and must remain so. I think Kathleen may know something about him, but no one else. I don't believe I've even mentioned this to Erika."

"I won't tell anyone."

"It's about Peter Konowitz."

"Really! I knew there was something odd about him. What did he do? Something illegal, right?"

"No, in fact, Peter did the right thing. It didn't make him popular. It's actually made him incredibly unpopular, but he did it anyway. You gotta give him credit."

"What did he do?"

"Peter's a stickler for rules. He doesn't like to see them broken. He doesn't even like to see them bent."

"I know that from personal experience," Susan said.

Brett's face lost its solemn look for a moment. "That's right, you do. You and Kathleen and Erika. Well, then you understand a bit. We're not talking Serpico here. Peter hasn't been, as far as I know, involved in uncovering anything like police brutality, illegal acts, or racial profiling—all things any good cop hates. Rather, Peter has a habit of noting any little infringement of the rules and then reporting it to his superiors."

"Sounds like he wouldn't be a very popular officer."

"Damn right. He wasn't liked when he was here in Hancock. I actually suggested that he would be happier moving to a larger, urban department. I thought that if he was around more and more serious corruption, he would focus on that and be . . . well, less of a pest."

"And more of a conscience to his department," Susan suggested.

Brett seemed relieved by her words. "Yes, exactly."

"And did it work?"

"Apparently not. I've been asking around. He left Hancock over seven years ago, and I understand he's worked with five different departments since that time."

"Is that unusual?"

"Very. Not many cops jump about from place to place. And, while you could look at Peter's moves as attempts to improve his career, I think there may have been something else involved. I suspect he simply couldn't get along with his coworkers and was encouraged to leave all his various positions."

"I gather you've contacted people in the other places he worked?"

"No, but over the years, they've been in contact with me. You see, I'm on Peter's resume as a reference. Unfortunately."

"He couldn't have used your name without permission."

"No, I gave it. Years ago when he wanted to leave Hancock, he asked me if I minded being listed as a reference. Since I had suggested that he would be happier someplace else, I didn't feel I could refuse. Especially as I had never expressed to him my concerns about his ability to get along with his fellow officers."

"Oh . . ."

"It's a mistake I've never made again. I should have told him outright that he was alienating himself from his coworkers and that it was dangerous, stupid, and arrogant of him. Instead I foisted him off on a precinct in New York City and assumed he would learn his lesson there."

"I gather he didn't."

"Nope. Well, not at least that I know about. And it's not as though I've been following his career step-by-step. But from what I do know, he's moved to smaller and smaller departments, and I do believe there always have been some questions about his ability to work with his fellow officers. At least that's the impression I get from the questions that I'm asked by whoever is hiring him."

"So how did he get to be police chief in Oxford Landing?"

"Who knows? It may be that no one wanted the job. It's a small town—probably doesn't pay all that much. And he does have some connections there. He grew up in the area. At least that's what he told me."

"Were you contacted as a reference?"

"Nope. But he worked in Hancock four or five jobs ago. So why contact me now? And, as I said, he knew people there. They may not have felt it was necessary to do a thorough check on him. Small towns can be like that. Hell, Hancock is like that."

"I guess. But what does this have to do with me?"

Brett sighed and ran his hands through his hair. "Susan, I hate to ask you this. I . . . I was hoping you would snoop around a little and find out some things."

"Brett, I'm always glad . . ." She looked at him suspiciously. "This has something to do with Chief Peter Konowitz, doesn't it?"

"I need some information about him."

"Brett, I just told Jed that I was going to stay away from him."

"Why?"

"Because he hates me. At least he acts like he does. This afternoon I called him. . . . Well, I called the police station in Oxford Landing and spoke with the officer who answered the phone. And I told him that Jed and I had found an empty wine bottle in our presents. I mean, it was in with our presents. It may even have been one of them. But now it was empty, and we thought that maybe Ashley had drunk from it. That maybe it had contained the poison that killed her."

"It's possible, I suppose. So you called the Oxford Landing police," Brett prompted.

"Yes. We thought we had to, of course. And the first thing we know Chief Konowitz is at our door to collect the bottle."

"That's part of his job."

"It's not part of his job to be so nasty. I mean, I understand what you mean when you say he doesn't get along with people. He's awful! He made me feel guilty, and all I was doing was trying to help out the police."

"Does that mean you won't help me out?"

Now it was Susan's turn to sigh. "Exactly what do you want me to do?" she asked.

"Keep your eyes open and please, Susan, stay out of Chief Konowitz's way."

SIXTEEN

Early the next morning, the Twigg sisters were enjoying a second cup of breakfast coffee on the wide front porch of the Landing Inn when Susan drove up. She forced a smile on her face, waved, and steered her Cherokee into the parking lot across the street. In the time it took Susan to join them, Constance had disappeared.

"My sister has a busy day planned. In a few minutes, she's meeting with a prospective customer looking for a location for a Christmas wedding reception. Then she has a brunch meeting with a woman who is sampling our cuisine for a party she's giving in a few months. And, this afternoon, three of our suppliers are going to be here promoting new products. Of course, I feel that our dear inn isn't quite the sort of place to try out new products, but Constance felt she had to meet with them. My sister is more modern than I am."

"You think the inn is perfect just the way it is," Susan suggested, sitting down in the rocking chair Constance had just vacated.

"Exactly!" Alvena turned pink with pleasure. "You do understand. So many people don't. Including my dear sister sometimes, I'm afraid. She can be so very modern."

"Perhaps that's what makes the Landing Inn work—your

reverence for the past and your sister's . . . ah, modern flair." The words sounded superficial to Susan. Did Alvena share her opinion? But apparently they were just what the other woman wanted to hear.

"You are so perceptive! That's exactly what makes our inn unique. Of course, it's not always easy to arrive at a consensus. Sometimes my sister and I have the most dreadful arguments. But my father provided for that in his will. We simply take turns being right. My father was such a wise man. Isn't that a brilliant solution?"

"It sounds like it," Susan said, realizing she sounded doubtful. "But how does it work?"

Alvena leaned forward to peer at Susan. "I just told you. We take turns being right."

"You mean you alternate making all the decisions?"

"No, because, of course, sometimes we agree. And that's that. We alternate making the decisions concerning those things we disagree on." She sighed loudly, giving Susan the impression that Alvena had explained this many times before. "It's simple. Suppose I say—as I did say recently— that I believe it would add to the inn's ambiance if we had new table linens woven by one of the local weavers. I was thinking of heavy napkins made from natural linen, actually. There is a weaver a few towns away who is doing the most beautiful work. Her fabrics are gorgeous, heavy but with a silky hand. Of course, I was the first to admit that replacing the regular linens we get from restaurant supply outlets would be expensive, but I, for one, thought the outlay was justified. It's the small details that mean so much. Don't you agree?"

"Well, yes. I guess so."

"But you see, my dear Constance didn't. She thought what we were using was adequate. That's her exact word:

adequate. I want more than adequate for the inn. Much, much more. I want everything to be perfect. And the linen napkins and cloths I found were perfect. Unfortunately, it was Constance's turn to make the decision, so I had to accept less than perfect. Once again."

"It's the inn's loss." Susan hoped that it was the right thing to say.

Apparently it was. Alvena reached out and patted Susan's arm. "Exactly! You put that so well. 'It's the inn's loss.' I shall remember that phrase. It's the inn's loss," she repeated.

"And the next time it will be your turn to decide what to do, right?"

"Oh, I've already had my turn. You won't believe what that silly Constance wanted."

Susan had yet to see anything silly about Constance at all. She leaned forward. "What?"

"She thought we should install central air-conditioning in the entire inn. It's so foolish of her. She drew up plans and ordered information from a few suppliers over the Internet, but of course I said no."

"There are individual air conditioners in each room, and they do seem to keep everything nice and cool," Susan said, nodding.

"Yes, and it would be horribly expensive and destructive to install central air-conditioning! Constance should have known that. She suggested the same thing last year, and I said no then. Silly Constance!"

Susan would have called Constance wily rather than silly, but she decided it was time to change the subject. "I hate to bother you, but I'm here to collect the last of our anniversary gifts," she explained.

"Of course." Alvena stood up immediately. "So many lovely things. You have very generous friends."

"We did ask that they not bring gifts. It was printed right on the invitation."

"Then they are especially generous, aren't they?"

"Yes, I guess that's true. And you and your sister have been very kind to store these things for us."

"Well, I feel it was the least we could do. After all, it must have been such a shock to find that woman in your bed. I can't tell you how badly I felt about that. A murder on your second honeymoon. Of course, you're used to this type of thing, aren't you?"

"But Ashley's murder had nothing to do with me!" Susan protested.

"Now, now, that's not what Peter says, and he would know, don't you think?"

"Peter who?"

"Why, Peter Konowitz, Chief Peter Konowitz. He's running the investigation of Mrs. Marks's death. I would have thought you would have remembered him."

"Yes, of course. I just wasn't thinking of him as Peter."

"He'll always be Peter to me. I knew him when he was young, you see."

"That's right. I'd heard he grew up around here."

"In the next town over, but he attended Central High— all the children whose parents didn't send them to private school go there—and I got to know him very well during his tenure there."

This was exactly the type of information Susan had come here for. "Really? I remember you saying you were the school secretary."

"Yes, for over fifty years."

"Does that mean Peter Konowitz was one of those boys who spent a lot of time in the principal's office?"

"Why yes, he . . ." Alvena stopped and wagged her finger at Susan. "Oh, you naughty woman you. I know what you're thinking, and you're completely wrong."

Susan was so taken aback by being referred to as a naughty woman that she was speechless. Fortunately, Alvena wasn't.

"Peter wasn't in trouble. He was one of the nicest boys in the school. He got good grades, dressed well, was one of the stars of the baseball team. He was always well groomed—he never wore his hair long and stringy as so many high school boys do. He belonged to many of the school's clubs. He even received an award for his part on the debating team from the state when he was a junior."

"He must have been very popular," Susan muttered.

"Well, that's just the problem, see. For some reason he wasn't. I mean, I loved him, and I know most of his teachers must have liked him; but the students . . . Well, what can I say? High school students have never been especially good judges of character. Poor Peter ran for office four years in a row, and each time he lost. It was heartbreaking. Of course, it was because he ran for office that I got to know him so well."

"Why?"

"Well, the student elections were monitored by the vice principal. Everything went through his office—you would not believe what some of the students thought was appropriate for campaign posters and slogans."

Susan, thinking back to her children's school years, knew that nothing would surprise her, but she didn't argue. "So he was in the office a lot?" she prompted.

"Yes. And he was such a polite young man. He'd come in and just stay around to chat. Not many young men did that, I can tell you."

"No, most young men don't appreciate women of our

age," Susan said tactfully, although, of course, Alvena was probably twenty years older than she.

"Exactly. And we have so much to teach them,"Alvena added, then giggled and blushed. "Oh, I don't mean that! But you do understand what I mean."

"Yes, of course. So you got to know Chief Konowitz well?"

"I like to think so."

"That must be very comforting for you. In case you have any problems here that require police involvement."

"Until yesterday we never had reason to call the police to the inn."

Susan had not realized Constance had joined them.

"Oh, Constance, that's not true. We have had to call them before," Alvena protested. "Why just last week—"

"I was referring to a serious problem, and I'm sure Mrs. Henshaw does not want to sit here and discuss our unruly guests, Alvena," Constance said. Her tone, Susan thought, would wilt most anyone's enthusiasm.

But apparently Alvena was more accustomed to her sister. "But remember that guest who tried to steal the trundle bed in room seven and the one who decided to repaint all Mother's dear, dear watercolors hanging in room three?"

"Alvena, those were minor problems, and I'm sure Mrs. Henshaw is not interested."

Actually, Susan wouldn't have minded meeting the person who shared her opinion of the inn's artwork, but she decided that the conversation would go nowhere with Constance around. "I suppose I'd better get on with what I came here to do. It's almost time for brunch," she added, glancing at her watch.

"That's why I'm here," Constance explained. "Those damn suppliers have screwed up and they're arriving two hours early. I was hoping you would entertain a Ms. Jinx Jensen for brunch, Alvena. I've already ordered—"

"You mean Jinx is here?"

"Yes, I believe that is her first name. She was at your party the other evening, wasn't she?"

"She was, and I didn't get a chance to speak with her. I took some classes at the local college a few years ago, and Jinx was there working on her degree. We got to know each other when we joined a support group for returning students." Susan didn't add that they had investigated a murder together. She thought for a moment. She had things to do, but nothing that couldn't be put off for a few hours. "Would it be possible for me to have brunch with her? You said you'd ordered, but—"

"That would solve our little problem, wouldn't it, Constance?" Alvena enthusiastically responded to Susan's question.

Her sister was less enthusiastic. "You would have to choose from the regular menu," she warned. "I only ordered one sample meal."

"That's no problem at all. I . . . Jinx!"

Jinx popped her head in the doorway. "Well, here you are. The perky young woman at the desk said I would find you all out here, and she was right. But I must tell you, she seems to need some help. The phone was ringing, guests were checking in and checking out, and I noticed two men with large briefcases coming up the sidewalk."

The sisters got moving with surprisingly little stiffness for women so old. "I'll go bring the reps around to the office. You better spend some time at the desk. I don't know why we can't find more competent help," Constance complained, striding away without waiting to see if Alvena followed her orders.

"There's a table reserved for you out back," Alvena told Jinx, fluttering around. "I do need to help out at the front desk. First impressions are always so important, don't you think?"

"Yes, but . . ."

"Perhaps I can help if Jinx has any questions. Remember, I just planned my own party," Susan offered.

"And if I have any questions that Susan can't answer, I'll ask you or your sister later," Jinx said.

"If you're sure . . ."

"We're positive. And we'll feel dreadful if we keep you any longer," Susan assured Alvena.

"Well, then I'll go help out. Do have a lovely brunch. And, if you have some time, fill out one of our guest satisfaction forms. There's one on each of the tables. We do depend on our guests to make sure our dear inn is up to snuff." Alvena started from the room and then turned around. "Be sure to try the creme Courvoisier for dessert. It's my favorite. A wicked number of calories, but worth it, I think."

"We will," Susan assured her.

"Yes, we will."

Apparently unable to think of anything else to suggest, Alvena fluttered off. Waiting a few minutes to be sure they were alone, Jinx shook her head. "I love this place. I loved your party. But those two women are going to drive me nuts. How about a drink?"

"An excellent idea. I was so thrilled to see you the other night, but we didn't have a chance to really talk. And I have so much to ask you—starting with who was that hunky guy you were with?"

Jinx threw back her head and roared, "My nephew! Oh, Susan, it is good to see you! Everyone else I know thinks

I'm pining away in my own little world, depressed and alone."

"That doesn't sound like you," Susan said as they headed toward the dining room.

"It isn't. But I can understand why they think that. I have spent much of the past year and a half alone in my condo."

"Why? What happened?" Susan cried.

"I was busy. Writing my book. That's why I'm here. My first novel is going to be published in two months, and I've decided to give myself a book party."

Susan threw her arms around her friend's neck and hugged her. "Jinx, that's fantastic news. What is it called? What's the book's title?"

"*Men I've Killed and How I Did It.*"

SEVENTEEN

"IT'S AUTOBIOGRAPHICAL. I HAVEN'T ACTUALLY KILLED anyone, of course. But I do spend a fair amount of time discussing the changes in my attitude toward the opposite sex over the years. My publisher suggested the title. He thought it would sell."

Susan laughed. "Probably will. I'll buy a few copies. I want to read it, and it sounds like it would be a great present for some of my friends. Which reminds me: I told the Twigg sisters that I was here to pick up Jed's and my anniversary gifts. Don't let me forget to do it."

Jinx's eyes twinkled. "Susan, if that's why you're here, why are you worried about forgetting?"

"Well, you could say I have ulterior motives. I'll tell you about it when we're alone. Here comes a waiter."

Susan and Jinx were given the best table on the deck, and chilled Sauvignon Blanc was poured for them without either woman asking. "Can't complain about the service," Jinx commented, picking up her glass and squinting at the golden liquid.

"The food is great, too."

"Is that why you chose to have your party here?"

"No, we gave the party here because this is where we spent our honeymoon. I hadn't even thought about this

place in years and years—and then we were having cocktails with some neighbors and started talking about the
party. Someone . . ." She paused. "I think . . . Well, that
doesn't matter now. Anyway, it was suggested that we think
about coming back here to give the party. I thought it was
a great idea—and it was, although not for the reasons we
thought it would be."

"What do you mean?"

"Well, in lots of ways the inn is nicer now than it was
then. The food is sure better. And the public rooms have
been updated. They've taken away the 1950s fake pine
colonial and put out some wonderful antiques. And it's not
that the bedrooms aren't nice—they are. They're . . . well,
they're just not what we're used to anymore."

"You're saying that your life has changed more than the
Landing Inn has."

"Exactly. And, frankly, I hadn't been confronted with it
before. We've become more Four Seasons than Oxford
Landing Inn. We're used to lush marble bathrooms, king-
size beds with masses of pillows, discreet artwork hung
above fashionable furniture. Our bathroom here didn't
even have a shower, the tub was stained with decades of
lime and rust, and while the room was comfortable that's
about all I could say for it. And the pictures on the wall are
a horror—watercolors done by the mother of the current
inn's owners. I'm afraid she had neither talent nor training—and was possibly color-blind as well."

Jinx laughed. "You don't make it sound very appealing."

"You know, that's wrong. It is appealing—except for the
artwork—but this was the first time I've wondered if we've
become snobs and . . . I don't know." Susan frowned and
played with her wineglass. "Maybe we've become too

dependent on things we swore wouldn't matter when we got married."

"So you've changed. Everyone changes. At least you and Jed changed together and managed to stay married. That's a real accomplishment."

"I know. I've thought that, too. But I keep thinking that when we got married we dreamed of going around the world on steamers, camping or staying in hostels."

"You could still do that."

"I guess. But do we want to do it anymore? Oh, this looks lovely." Susan changed the topic and looked down at her plate. Roasted corn, tomatoes, avocados, and strings of red onions had been laid over arugula.

"Dill corn muffins, Cheddar shortbread rounds, walnut whole wheat rolls, garlic salt sticks." Their waiter pointed out the selection of breads in the basket he placed on the table between the women.

"Thank you," Jinx said, reaching for the little china crock of butter. "Has Jed talked about retiring anytime soon?"

"He talks about it, but we haven't made any plans. I think once Chad is settled . . . We've always talked about leaving Connecticut, keeping the house in Maine, and buying another—or a condo—somewhere warm."

"By the time Chad is out of college, you'll have grandchildren and you won't want to leave them. What's that expression on your face?"

"Chrissy's pregnant! I've been thinking about other things so much that I almost forgot."

Jinx jumped out of her seat and reached across the table to hug Susan. "What fantastic news! You're going to be a grandmother! When is the baby due?"

"She hasn't told me. In fact, she hasn't told me she's pregnant. I just found out."

"Still the detective?"

"I guess. In fact, I'm—"

"—looking into the murder of Ashley Marks," Jinx finished Susan's sentence.

"How do you know?"

"Susan, everyone knows. Has there ever been a murder in your vicinity that you ignored?"

"Well, no, but . . . well, I've been asked to help with this one. Officially."

"Really?"

"You don't have to sound so surprised!"

"I remember that the local police, when we were taking college classes, were anything but thrilled by your involvement."

"Well, the local police here don't really know about it," Susan admitted. "Do you remember Brett Fortesque?"

"The incredibly good-looking man who runs the police department in Hancock? Of course. How many women would forget meeting him?"

"He's asked for my help. He . . . You won't say anything about this to anyone else?"

"Who shouldn't know? The sisters Twigg? The local officials?"

"The local officials." Susan paused. "The local police chief once worked in Hancock—for Brett."

"And Brett Fortesque thinks he's a corrupt cop!" Jinx suggested.

"No, nothing like that," Susan insisted. "Brett just thinks it would be better if Peter Konowitz doesn't know that I'm looking into Ashley's murder."

"Who is Peter Konowitz?"

"The chief of police here in Oxford Landing." Susan hesitated. She trusted Jinx, but she knew Brett wouldn't want her to repeat too much of what he had told her. "It's not that Brett doesn't trust Peter, but I know he thought that Peter would be better off in a large police department. He worked in New York City after Hancock."

"Oxford Landing isn't exactly an urban area. Wonder how he ended up here?"

"That's simple. He grew up here. He probably has friends here." She remembered what Alvena Twigg had said about this and rushed on. "And professional contacts, of course. Peter Konowitz is still pretty young to be a police chief. Actually, I don't know a whole lot about all this—yet. I suppose I'll find out more as I investigate the Markses."

"How are you going to do that here?"

"I'm not sure. I was talking with Alvena Twigg. She seems to know a lot about everyone who grew up in the area. But, you know, I just had a great idea. I should check with the local paper. There may have been stories about the Markses."

"This area is pretty rural. Are you sure there is a local newspaper?"

"I think I saw what looked like one on the coffee table in the front parlor. Wait, our waiter will know." She waved to the young man who was standing nearby ready to do their bidding.

"Ma'am?"

The question was addressed to Jinx, so she answered. "Could you possibly find a copy of the local newspaper for us?"

"Of course. They're in the foyer. I'll pick up copies for both of you and be back immediately."

"Is the service always this good, or is this just a sales pitch?" Jinx asked.

"It's pretty good," Susan said. "Back in the winter, things were different. They were slightly understaffed when we were doing some of the party planning, but once summer arrived, the place was swarming with willing and helpful college kids."

Their willing and helpful waiter must have also been on the track team; he reappeared promptly, papers in hand. "There's a weekly newspaper and a shopper that comes out weekly, too. I picked up both. Many of our guests seem to enjoy going through the real estate ads, looking for vacation homes, you know."

"Please, I'm a writer. One small apartment is more than I can afford," Jinx said.

Susan looked up and grinned. It was obvious that Jinx had enjoyed announcing her newfound career. And, gratifyingly, their waiter was impressed.

"Really? A writer? What's your name? Would I know it? Have I read anything you've written?"

"No, my first book is due to be published in October."

"Really? I'm majoring in English lit, and I want to write. What's the name of your book?"

"*Men I've Killed and How I Did It.*"

"Oh, a mystery novel. I'm afraid I'm studying more literary work." It was obvious to both women that his interest had all but vanished. "Well, I'd better bring you your soup."

"I guess the title doesn't appeal to everybody."

"Well, he is male. Perhaps he considers you a threat."

Jinx whooped her enthusiasm at this suggestion and reached for her wineglass. "I think that deserves a toast. I've waited almost sixty years for men to think of me as a threat!" Then raising her glass, Jinx said, "To me! And all the other threatening old bags!"

"You are not an old bag!" Susan protested, picking up her glass.

"Well, maybe not old."

They both laughed and tapped their glasses.

"I'll skim through the shopper while you look at the—" Jinx glanced down at the table. "—at the *Oxford Democrat*," she finished, reading the header aloud. "But I don't see why these papers would have anything about the Markses in them. They don't even live here anymore."

"These issues won't. I thought I'd find out where their offices are located and go over this afternoon and see if I can go through their archives."

"That's a great idea! No wonder you solve so many murders!" Jinx cried.

Unfortunately, their waiter appeared with two cups of gazpacho at just that moment. "The chef also makes a wonderful chive vichyssoise," he said, putting the cups down hurriedly, grabbing their empty salad plates, and moving immediately to the other side of the room.

"I think we scared the poor guy," Jinx said.

"I suppose more of his customers discuss real estate than murder," Susan said. "So, do you want to come along with me?"

"To the office of the *Oxford Democrat*?"

"Yup!"

"If you hadn't asked, I'd have invited myself. But there is just one thing."

"What?"

"Constance Twigg promised to send out a dessert plate with samples of all their goodies."

"And I told Alvena that I would be sure to try something called creme Courvoisier," Susan said.

"So, dessert first, investigate later."

"Sounds like a great plan," Susan agreed, laughing.

EIGHTEEN

"I THINK WE MISSED IT!" JINX PEERED THROUGH THE WIND-
shield of Susan's Cherokee.

"Not again! We've circled this block at least three times.
How could we possibly have missed it? Maybe we don't
have the correct address," Susan suggested.

"It's printed right here." Jinx looked down at the newspaper grasped tightly in her hands and then back out the
window. "This is a short block. There's a luncheonette, an
auto supply store, a five-and-dime—closed—a newsstand,
a pharmacy, a store that sells work boots and hunting and
fishing supplies, and a diner. Oh, wait! Slow down! Look
at what it says on that sign!"

"Which one?"

"Sam's Sporting Supplies. Up there."

Susan put her foot on the brake and looked in the direc-
tion Jinx had indicated. "Sam's Sporting Supplies. Work
Boots our Specialty. Ammunition. Fly Rods. Bait. We have
Blood Worms. Expert Taxidermy. Office of the *Oxford
Democrat*. Sam Redman, Editor in Chief."

"There's an empty parking spot at the end of the block."

Susan pulled in, switched off the engine, and turned to
look at her friend. "Amazing. A newspaper office above a
bait shop."

"Look again," Jinx suggested.

The second floor of the building was fronted by double plate-glass windows displaying all manner of dead animals frozen into what were, to Susan and Jinx, rather odd poses. "The taxidermist seems to be upstairs," Susan said. "So where are the newspaper offices located?"

"Why don't we go in and ask?" Jinx suggested. They got out of the car, and Susan pressed the key to lock it.

"Sounds good to me."

The building was old—perhaps as old as the Landing Inn. The door creaked as they pushed it open, and the floors echoed the sound as they walked down the aisles between displays of fishing creels, camouflage clothing, camping equipment, and hand-tied flies. "Who would have thought that there were so many different kinds of dried bait," Susan said, peering down at what appeared to be a large, dehydrated worm.

"Ugh. On the other hand, look at him!"

Susan looked away from the displays to see what had softened her friend's voice. "Oh . . . hi," she said. A tall man, possibly in his mid-fifties, was walking down the open knotty pine staircase at the back of the store. He was wearing hiking boots, worn jeans, and a red T-shirt. His clothes hid few, if any, of his muscles.

"Good morning, ladies. What can I do for you?" His voice was deep, and he brushed graying hair off his forehead as he spoke.

"We're looking for the newspaper office."

"Well, then you're in luck. You've found it. I'm Sam Redman, editor in chief. What can I do for you? Announcements of upcoming events have to be submitted at least a week early. All press releases should be submitted in writing. Advertising rates are reasonable and posted on the door of my office upstairs." Sam was tanned, and when he smiled, the deep wrinkles that formed around his light blue eyes only added to his considerable charm.

Susan introduced herself and Jinx before continuing. "I'm afraid what we want is a bit more complicated than any of those things."

"Well, I can deal with that. Since I don't seem to have a steady supply of customers down here, why don't we all go up to my office where we can sit down, be comfortable, and you can just tell me what you want."

"Great!" Jinx said, just a bit too enthusiastically. "You lead the way," she continued, grabbing Susan by the sleeve.

"Wha—" Susan looked at Jinx as Sam Redman started up the stairs.

"He isn't wearing a wedding ring. See if you can move the conversation around to whether or not he's married," Jinx whispered.

"Why me?"

"It will be less suspicious coming from you!"

"What happened to that liberated woman you've become?"

"She tends to vanish in moments of stress."

"I'm sorry? I didn't hear what you were saying."

"I was just telling Susan what an interesting store this is," Jinx lied. "Not that I know anything at all about stuff like camping and so on. I'm more of a city girl myself."

Sam Redman turned and smiled at Jinx. "If there's anything I love, it's trying to teach a city girl to appreciate the great outdoors. Right this way, ladies."

Susan and Jinx glanced at each other and hurried after him.

The office of the *Oxford Democrat* was the entire top floor of the sporting goods shop. There were three worn, golden oak desks and two large printing presses. "We're modern. We don't lay out the paper in hot type anymore," Sam explained. "My grandfather used to run the paper, and I grew up in this office. I can't bring myself to get rid of the presses."

"Have you ever thought of doing small press runs of handmade books?" Jinx asked, walking over to the closest of the huge machines. "There's not much money in that type of business, but—"

"Sounds like just the thing for me, then. I specialize in doing things that aren't profitable—which is why I run a sporting goods shop and newspaper without a whole lot of help. I can't tell you how many times a day I run up and down that stairway."

"What about the taxidermy part of the business?" Jinx asked, glancing at the animals in front of the windows.

"Friend of mine does that. Can't get too excited about stuffed dead animals myself," Sam Redman answered.

"Then we won't take up too much of your time," Susan said. "We'd like to go through your files. We're doing research on some . . . uh, events and people in Oxford Landing."

"You're welcome to see what you can find. You are here because that Ashley Marks was killed at your anniversary party, aren't you?"

"Well, sort of," Susan admitted, hoping she wouldn't be forced to explain further.

"Tell you what. You can scrounge through my files as much as you want to—with two conditions."

"What?"

"Everything has to be put back where you found it— exactly. Every time I let someone look around in here, I end up regretting it. I'd like this time to be different."

"It will be!" Jinx assured him. "What else?"

"I'd like an interview with Mrs. Henshaw for the next issue of the paper. A lot of the social life of Oxford Landing takes place at the Landing Inn, and the murder of a guest there is big news."

Susan frowned. "Okay. I guess . . ."

"You talk with Susan, and I'll take a look at your files," Jinx suggested, heading toward the largest desk. An IBM computer sat on top, its screen saver displaying species of freshwater fish.

Sam Redman spoke up. "Not there. Over there." He nodded toward the back wall of the room. Neither Susan nor Jinx had noticed before that it was lined with floor-to-ceiling file cabinets. "Unless you're looking for the second week of May 1971, every issue of the *Democrat* ever printed is in those cabinets."

"Where's the missing issue?" Susan asked, staring at the file drawers.

"Up on the wall." Sam nodded to four large framed sheets on the wall over the desks. "That's the week my grandfather died. The issue was devoted to him and his life. No ads. I keep it up there to remind me and any stringers I happen to hire what sort of traditions the paper has to keep."

Jinx had been staring silently at the files. When she spoke it was in a quiet voice. "I don't suppose there's an index?"

"Can't say that there is."

Susan looked around. The drawers were dated in a precise hand, but looking for anything related to Ashley and Doug didn't seem possible. "Maybe we shouldn't bother," she began.

"I'll go through everything," Jinx interrupted in a firm voice. "I have the time, and I love old magazines and newspapers. It will be fun." She stood up and strode purposefully to the back of the room.

Sam Redman's eyes followed her. "A woman who thinks going through old newspapers is fun and and needs to learn about the outdoors. Who would have thought she would walk right in my front door today?"

Jinx must have heard him, for she spun around, a smile on her face. "Are you married?"

"Nope. What about you?"

Jinx's smile turned into a grin. "Nope," she said before opening the first drawer and sticking her head inside.

Susan tried to look serious. Jinx really had come a long way from the slightly insecure, recently divorced middle-aged woman she had been when they met. She couldn't wait to read her book. "So what do you want to ask me?" She turned her attention to Sam Redman.

He waved to a chair near the largest desk. "Have a seat."

"I don't know much about the murder," Susan warned him. "I don't even know Ashley all that well. She and her husband just moved into our neighborhood about a year ago."

"That's what I understand. Of course, I have a fair amount of background on her. She's a local, you know."

"I . . . that's right. I'd forgotten they lived around here for a while."

"The Markses lived all over the world: Hong Kong, Switzerland, New York City. But Doug grew up here and his parents lived here. We've seen a lot of the Markses over the years."

"Then you probably know a lot more about them than I do."

"Don't know squat about the murder, though."

"Well, we found her—"

"Mrs. Henshaw, my readers don't fall into any one category. Some grew up around here and have been farmers—mostly tobacco or dairy—all their lives. And some were big deals in New York or D.C. and moved here to get away from it all. We even have the remnants of a hippie commune up north. They've sold out and become one of the largest and most prosperous providers of organic produce on the East Coast. What I'm saying is, there are lots of different levels of education in our readership. But there are some things I suspect all of them will want to know."

"What?"

"Just how did Ashley turn up in your bed, what was she wearing, and what did you and your husband do when you found her?"

"What was she wearing?"

"Rumor around here is that she was naked."

"Good heavens! No, she was dressed the same way she had been at the party, in a silk dress. It was peachy colored. She had had shoes dyed to match. She was wearing them, too! She most certainly was not naked."

"Too bad. That would have made the story a whole lot more interesting. And it might have encouraged some of the young men in the area to get interested. Keeping our youth reading the news was one of my grandfather's favorite causes."

"Fully dressed," Susan repeated firmly.

"Alas. Perhaps we can run a dirty limerick contest. Just kidding.

"So, Ashley was lying on your bed, fully dressed, when you and your husband returned to your room after the party was over."

"Underneath our presents."

"I heard there were presents involved somehow. Surely, she wasn't completely covered with these presents."

"Yes. Completely. We had no idea she was there when we entered the room."

"You have very generous friends," Sam said.

"We requested no gifts. It was on the invitation." Susan was beginning to wonder just how many times she had repeated this.

Sam chuckled. "I wasn't suggesting that you were greedy or anything. Just commenting."

"Of course. They were generous. Unexpectedly so. If we had known we were going to be given so many gifts, we would have prepared a place for them to be stored. As it was, sometime during the party, Alvena Twigg spoke to me and my husband about the number of gifts we'd received and I suggested that they be placed in our bedroom. Jed agreed and . . . well, when we went upstairs and unlocked the door . . ." She stopped speaking.

"Mrs. Henshaw, you were saying that when you and your husband went up to your room . . ."

"We found all the surfaces covered with gifts—not only the bed. We were quite surprised."

"So you took all the gifts off and found Ashley."

"Sort of. I mean, that's not the way it really happened. I was tired, and Jed, my husband, suggested I take a bath and, while I was doing that, he'd clear the bed. I guess I was in the tub when Jed found her."

"You guess?"

"Well, I know I was. It's just that he didn't say anything right away. I got out of the tub and came back into our bedroom and Jed was standing next to the bed, talking on his cell phone."

"And Ashley was lying in your bed?"

"Yes. We were both shocked, of course. Jed was on the phone with the police. They arrived, asked a few questions, and we went home. It's not much of a story, I'm afraid."

"And it's not the whole story either, is it?"

"What do you mean?"

"Well you and your charming friend are here looking into the murder, aren't you? Isn't she going through my files checking to see what stories we've run on the Marks family?"

"Well . . ."

"Gotta tell you that I hope that's what she's doing. It would sure make my job easier if someone else did a little background research for me."

"Jinx . . ."

Jinx joined in the conversation. "I've already found one or two references to the Markses. But this is going to take days." She smiled at Sam Redman, and Susan noticed she had reapplied lipstick while they were talking. "I hope you don't mind if I hang around for a while."

"Why, I always enjoy the company of a smart, good-looking lady. And you're welcome to any information that helps you find the murderer. Just want to ask one thing."

"What?"

"When you know who did it, you tell me first. It's been a long, long time since the *Oxford Democrat* broke a big story."

"We'd be happy to do that, wouldn't we, Susan?"

"Sure."

"And I'll do you a favor in return. I'll help Jinx go through those files."

"Oh, great," Susan said, hoping courting and research were compatible occupations.

NINETEEN

Susan had left Jinx and Sam Redman poring over newspapers from the last millennium and gone home, Sam having offered to take Jinx to dinner at the Landing Inn; she would be able to retrieve her car when they had tired of their task.

Her house was unexpectedly, and uncharacteristically, quiet. Clue was asleep on her cedar bed in the kitchen, apparently having abandoned her career as family greeter. A glance out the window explained the unusual calm: The mastiffs were dozing in the shade in the dog run that had been built for, and rejected by, Clue. There was a note on the kitchen table.

> Sue,
> Chad and I took the dogs for a run at the nature center and have now headed out for dinner and a movie. Chrissy and Stephen are shopping for a baby present for a friend, then going to dinner at the Hancock Inn. Don't wait up.
> Love, Jed

Susan began to smile. A free evening. Just what she needed. She poured herself a glass of V-8 and plopped a bag of low-fat popcorn in the microwave. Once the popping sound had ceased, she grabbed her main course and made for Jed's study. She loved opening presents!

. . . Almost as much as she hated writing thank-you notes, she realized two hours later, staring down at the creamy Crane's note card in front of her. Susan's sixth-grade teacher, Mrs. Sweeney, had insisted that starting a thank-you note with the words "Thank you for the . . ." was unacceptable. Susan was on her seventh note before she decided to abandon that advice. By the time Chad and Jed came into the house, still discussing the special effects of the action feature they'd attended, she had a respectable pile of envelopes ready for stamps.

"Hi, sweetie," she said to her son as he swept by the door.

"Hi ya, Ma! Did anyone call?"

"A young woman named Kelly called around nine."

"Way cool . . ." If Chad finished that sentence the words were lost in the sound of his feet hitting the stairs as he bounded up to his room.

"So how was the movie?" she asked as Jed bent down to kiss her fevered brow.

"Fun, loud, and without a plot. You would have hated it."

"What did you have for dinner?"

"Pizza."

"Sounds like an ideal male bonding evening."

"How was your day?"

"Not bad. I ran into Jinx at the inn, and we went on to the office of the local newspaper. As a matter of fact, I left Jinx there. She and the paper's editor seem to have hit it off."

Jed yawned. "Sounds interesting, but I think I'd better go upstairs. I'm exhausted, and I have to get to work early tomorrow." He started to leave the room and then turned back. "Where do we keep the Pepto-Bismol these days?"

Susan refrained from commenting about trying to eat like a twenty-year-old at age fifty-five and directed him to the correct corner of their medicine cabinet. "I'm ready to turn in, too," she added. "It's been a long day."

The next morning, Jinx was on the phone before Susan had finished her first cup of coffee.

"Sam and I are going to be busy all day," Jinx announced after a quick greeting. "I'm off to the newspaper office now, but I wanted to tell you that I'll give you a call as soon as we find anything more."

"Great. What did you come up with yesterday?"

"Just the ordinary press-release stuff, but Sam's really a good investigative reporter, so . . . Oh, Lord, he's knocking on the door and I haven't even got my mascara on. Gotta run."

A loud click told Susan that she had been abandoned. Oh well, she had things to do too.

Susan's mother and Mrs. Sweeney would have been proud of how promptly she was getting to work on her thank-you notes, she decided about an hour later, backing out of the driveway. Her husband had taken the early train to the city. Chad and Clue had gone for a long run—apparently this Kelly lived on the other side of town. Stephen had driven the mastiffs to Long Island Sound, hoping, he said, a swim would be as good as a bath. Chrissy was sleeping in. Susan smiled. Pregnant women needed extra sleep. Her daughter hadn't said anything yet, but Susan had begun counting the months. An April baby would be nice, she thought, parking in the lot behind the Hancock Post Office. As usual, there was a line inside; she walked to the end of it, hitched the heavy box of envelopes up in her arms, and leaned against a wall, prepared to wait.

"Susan! I was just thinking about you!" The professionally streaked hairdo Susan had been admiring turned around; it belonged to Martha Hallard.

"Martha! I was just admiring your new hair color!"

The women hugged as much as they were able, each holding a large box at the same time.

"What's that?"

"Thank-you notes. What are you mailing?"

"You know those wonderful spice blends for seafood that they sell at the market here? I can't get them in Arizona. I'm stocking up! Next I'm heading to that tea shop on Main Street. Their chamomile mint tea is one of the things I miss most about Hancock—that and our wonderful old neighbors like you and Jed."

"Believe me, you can't possibly miss us as much as we miss you!"

"Oh, Susan, I told Dan we should have held out for a different buyer! But the Markses paid cash, and Dan was anxious to move before winter set in and he couldn't get his damned daily golf game!"

"Didn't Dan tell me that you were going to take up the game once you got to Arizona?"

"He may have told you that. He may even have believed it. But I had no intention of following a little ball around a golf course in a tiny cart. You know that's not my idea of fun."

"So what are you doing in your retirement?" Martha had been one of Hancock's most successful realtors.

"Having a ball. I'm docent at the local botanical garden two days a week. I'm taking weaving classes from a woman who was taught to weave by her Navaho grandmother. I belong to two reading groups at the library. I teach Sunday school at our church. And I'm collecting antiques to furnish our home. I want everything to be southwestern, but special."

"Sounds like a wonderful life."

"It is. And it's been a lot of work, but I've taken the time to keep up with the trial and all."

"That's right. Dan said you get the local paper sent to you there. Martha, what do you think of it all?"

"You're asking me? I thought you'd have the scoop on the Markses. After all, you live right next door."

"They never really mixed with the rest of the neighborhood," Susan started to explain. "Ow!" She spun around to see what—or who—had run into her spine. A tall young man dressed all in black and sporting tattoos where his clothing failed to cover him looked embarrassed.

"Sorry, lady. Didn't mean to hurt you. But I'm in a bit of a hurry. The line's moving, and you two aren't."

"Oh, I'm sorry. We haven't seen each other in so long. We were catching up."

"Why don't you come to the tea shop with me? We can walk. It's only a few blocks away. We can have a snack and talk," Martha suggested, hurrying toward a suddenly free postal clerk.

"Great." Susan moved up to the counter as the next clerk became free. "One hundred first-class stamps."

"We only have the pasted variety," the young woman behind the counter stated flatly.

"Fine with me. I'll just wash down the taste of the paste with iced tea."

"This place is sensational!" Susan said, looking around. The tearoom was lined with dark linenfold walnut paneling, but every flat surface—counters as well as tables—was covered with polished copper. Copper urns boiled water, and copper knobs made it possible to get into the many drawers of tea. The effect was rich and comforting.

"You've never been here before?" Martha sounded amazed.

"You know me. I'm a coffee drinker. Although this iced herb tea just might change my mind. What's in it again?"

"Ginger, hibiscus, and orange peel, but we're not here to talk about the tea. I'm dying to know more about the Markses."

"I was hoping you could tell me about them. Like where did they get all the money they needed to pay cash for your house? Eight-fifty was the asking price, right?"

"Yes. And they paid it. Said the house was exactly what they were looking for and they had the money and wanted a quick closing. Suited Dan just fine. I wasn't quite so happy. I'd have liked to spend more time sorting and packing. I can't tell you how many boxes of junk went to Arizona from Hancock and then just had to be thrown away there."

"Do you know where it came from?"

"What? The junk? I suppose years and years of living—"

"Not the things you took to Arizona. The Markses' money! Where did they get all that cash?"

"I understand they owned a farm somewhere upstate which they had sold to a developer. It must have been a large farm. I got the impression that money wasn't going to be a problem for the rest of their lives—or the lives of their children, for that matter."

"Well, that's not good news," Susan said, thinking of Signe.

"I don't agree. Now that that awful woman is dead,

Doug has the time and money to find someone else and live a nice life."

"Wow! You really didn't like her."

"Couldn't stand her. I remember the first time we met. She and Doug came to an open house that we gave the weekend the house was put on the market. There were lots of people milling around, but she made a definite impression on me. She hardly looked at the house. Actually, I was a bit surprised when they made an appointment to come back. They struck me as the type of people who would look at a lot of houses, wasting a realtor's valuable time, and then vanish into the world of 'we're not ready to buy just yet.' "

"How can you tell?"

"In the first place, most of those people are incredibly critical, stupidly so. They make appointments to see a perfectly restored Victorian and then they wander from room to room comparing it—unfavorably—to a custom-built contemporary. Most serious buyers only look at homes they would consider buying. Of course, there are buyers who don't know what they want—modern, colonial, whatever—but those types tend to be exceptionally uncritical. They love the old-fashioned fireplaces in the colonial homes and the open plans of the contemporary. They talk about what they would do if they lived in a Queen Anne Victorian with lots of stairs or how they can understand the reason most fifties ranches have almost nonexistent dining rooms upstairs and huge rec rooms in the basement. They're my favorite kinds of shoppers. The ones who are smart know what they can afford and how many beds and baths they need. And many times they stumble right into the perfect fit without worrying about the style of architecture."

"But the Markses weren't like that."

"No. I don't have any idea how they ended up in Hancock, but—"

Susan leaned forward. "Really?"

"Really what?"

"What you just said. Why did they come to Hancock anyway?" Susan asked, wondering if Martha knew about Signe's earlier explanation. "We have great schools, but the Markses were well past worrying about that. I love Hancock, but our taxes are high and the homes expensive. And I don't believe they had any friends in the area. At least they never mentioned any to me, and I don't remember meeting anyone who knew them before they arrived."

"They didn't know a soul. I'm sure of that. I remember Doug said that it was a fresh start for them. I hadn't spent a lot of time with Ashley at that point, but I could already believe they needed one."

Susan nodded. "She really had the most amazing ability to alienate people."

"Amazing is the right word. The first time I met her I wanted to kill her."

"What happened?"

"I was sitting at my kitchen table during the open house. It's strange selling your own home after decades of giving sellers advice on how to move theirs. I really felt I had to do it right. Of course the place was clean and had fresh flowers and green plants everywhere. And I turned on every light in the place. Then I did what I tell clients to do: I stayed out of the way but was available to answer questions. So I sat in the kitchen with tea, fresh home-baked cookies, and the information sheets on the house on the table."

"You baked?"

"Yes. I convinced the owners of the specialty shop that

used to be out on the highway to sell me the dough. I sliced it, put the cookies on the baking sheets, and had warm—if rather lopsided—gingerbread ready before the first looker entered the house. I always tell owners that the smell of home cooking can sell a home."

Susan, whose favorite gingerbread recipe contained fresh, candied, and ground ginger, reminded herself that she wasn't here to argue with anyone else's idea of home cooking. "And that's where you were when you met Ashley?"

"Yes. She came into the room, followed by her husband as always, looked around, and did a pretty good imitation of Bette Davis. You know, her 'what a dump' scene in *All about Eve*?"

"She called your kitchen a dump?" Susan was indignant. "I always loved your kitchen. That wonderful seating area in the bay window. That old Wedgewood stove . . . Oh, she probably didn't appreciate the stove."

"Or the old pine cabinets or the hand-painted mural on the walls around the soapstone sink, et cetera, et cetera, et cetera. By the time she got through looking around and making loud comments about everything she despised, I was ready to kill her. She was quite literally driving away potential buyers."

"Do you think it was deliberate on her part? That she had decided she wanted the house and was hoping no one else would bid for it?"

Martha frowned. "I don't think so. Although I did consider that possibility at the time. But then her husband came by with an offer for the asking price . . ."

"What's wrong?" Susan asked when her friend didn't finish her sentence.

"You know, that may have been exactly what she was doing."

"But you just said—"

"I just said that Doug made the official bid on the house. But her name wasn't on the bid. It's just possible that Doug was making the first independent move of his life when he bought our house."

"Why do you say that?"

"Look, Susan, I didn't say anything to anyone at the time. I mean, I mentioned it to Dan when we saw the first stories about Ashley's arrest in the *Herald*, but he said— and I agreed with him—that Doug was just making one of those comments that husbands make all the time, and that it didn't mean anything significant."

"What did he say?"

"He said his wife was going to kill him for buying a house in the suburbs."

TWENTY

"AND THEN, OF COURSE, SOMEONE TRIED TO DO JUST THAT."

Martha nodded. "I assumed she was guilty, and I assumed she would be found guilty. Reading the stories in the *Herald* . . . Well, I never thought she'd go free."

"Which is why you didn't tell anyone about what Doug had said to you."

"Exactly. It seemed unnecessary. And Dan's right. Husbands say that very thing about their wives all the time."

"True, but . . ."

"But most husbands don't have to worry about their wives actually doing it, and it's just possible Doug did. I've thought about that."

"Did he sound . . . I don't know . . . more serious than Jed might sound making the same comment?"

"I have no idea. I didn't think there was anything unusual about it at the time—except that it seemed to be so unlike Ashley to allow Doug the freedom to make such a decision on his own. Heavens, I sold homes for almost thirty years. There was only one other time that I know of that a married man bought a house without his wife's approval. And that marriage lasted only a few years. Buying a home is something a couple does together. Period."

"If Doug bought the house and Ashley hated it, it would explain a lot of things," Susan mused.

"Like what?"

"Well, for starters, like the fact that Ashley changed everything she possibly could." She looked up and watched the expression on her friend's face change—for the worse. "Oh, Martha . . ."

"Susan, Dan and I had a good life in that house. We raised three great kids there, and we made the right decision when we decided to move to Tucson last year. I'm being foolish and sentimental when I start thinking that it should have been left the way it was. Hell, over the years we obliterated every trace of the Coles as well."

"Who were the Coles?"

"The people we bought the house from. They built that house."

"I hate to make you feel worse, but Ashley not only remodeled and redecorated but she made everything ugly and depressing."

"What did she do? Paint all the walls black?"

"No, but everything she did was overdone—you know the type of thing—each window was draped in at least two layers of fabric; the walls were papered, stenciled, gilded, with borders and fancy doodads. Her color scheme was black, ochre, purple, and gilt."

"Sounds hideous."

"It is. And expensive. She had people in doing faux finishes for months. And you know how, when you go to a lighting supply store, you wonder who buys all those ugly fixtures?"

"Ashley Marks?"

"Yup."

"Damn. I knew we should have taken the carriage lamp in the foyer to Arizona with us."

"You can. The Markses left it out for the garbagemen. But I picked it up and put it down in the basement. I thought maybe Chrissy and Stephen might like it someday. But it should stay with you."

"Susan, how sweet."

But Susan was interested in getting back to their subject. "You know, now that I understand that Doug picked out the house, what Ashley did makes sense. She just didn't love old colonials the way you and I do. And she spent a huge amount of money trying to turn one into a modern trophy house— like the ones in that new development outside of town."

"But just because she had no taste doesn't mean she was poisoning Doug because he picked out their home without consulting her."

"True. Although it's an excuse many women could understand—if she had gotten a completely female jury . . ."

Both women laughed.

"Of course, she got off anyway. Apparently because the investigation was inadequate or something," Susan said more seriously. "Brett said he wasn't surprised that Ashley wasn't convicted."

"From reading the paper, I didn't get the impression that there were any other suspects."

Susan thought of Signe and decided not to bring her into the conversation. "No, the paper didn't mention anyone."

"What did they do once they moved in besides redecorate?"

Susan dropped the packet of Equal she had been playing with onto the tabletop. "What do you mean?"

"What church did they join? Did Doug play golf at the Field Club? Did Ashley join an aerobics class? What sort of connections did they make in the community?"

"Besides being the sole supporter of decorating firms without taste? To tell you the truth, I'm not sure."

"Susan, that doesn't sound like you. You lived next door to these people for almost a year."

"I know. And we did our best to be neighborly. I was on their doorstep with freshly baked cinnamon rolls the morning they moved in—and Ashley explained that she and her husband had given up sweets years and years ago. I mean, she took them and said thank you and then made me feel as though I had shown up with a bag of heroin as a welcome-to-the-neighborhood gift. But we invited them over for a barbeque in the backyard the next weekend. You know, to meet the neighbors and all."

"And?"

"Actually, that went pretty well. Ashley ate salads and ignored the meat. But Doug ate everything in sight and thanked me more than once for the delicious cinnamon rolls."

"Who else did you invite?"

"Let me think. Kathleen and Jerry, of course. And our immediate neighbors. And Dick and Barbara from the Field Club. I thought the Markses might be interested in joining, and Dick is head of the membership committee now. Oh, and Brett and Erika. More because of Erika than Brett, though."

"What do you mean?"

"Well, Signe, the Markses' daughter, works for Erika in the city. You know, they did have a connection to Hancock before they arrived here: Erika!"

"Which also means they had a connection to the police

department. Erika and Brett have been together for years, right?"

"Yes. And Erika really seems to depend on Signe. I can't imagine that Brett and Signe wouldn't have met over the years—probably many times."

"Which also means that her parents probably had met—"

"Not necessarily. Signe and her parents weren't close, but I can't imagine that the Markses didn't know about Brett and Hancock. It's certainly possible that Signe's connection to the town is one of the reasons they looked for their new home here." She didn't think it was necessary to mention Signe's tale of her mother's reason.

"Do you think it means anything?"

"I don't know. It is odd, though, isn't it? I mean you look for good medical care, schools, public facilities, whatever when you decide to move. But there aren't a whole lot of people who would look for a friendly police department, unless . . ."

"Unless you were planning on committing a crime . . . like a murder," Martha finished Susan's thought out loud.

"I guess." Susan was having trouble imagining what—if anything—this might mean when Martha surprised her again.

"Of course, I'd be more inclined to accuse Doug of his wife's murder if Ashley had been shot."

"Why?"

"Well, he loves guns, right? At least that's what he told me."

"I never heard anything about that."

"Then I guess the soundproofing does work."

"Martha, what are you talking about? What soundproofing? And how do you know Doug loves guns? Did he just walk up to you and say, 'I love guns'?"

"Of course not! But when he was looking at the house that very first day, he said he needed to have a practice range built in the basement. In fact, he was very enthusiastic about the basement. You know we never finished it the way so many in the neighborhood did and it is—or was— just an open space with a small laundry area at one end and pool table and Ping-Pong table at the other. Doug told me he was going to have the entire room soundproofed and a shooting range installed."

Susan was stunned. "Next door? There is a shooting range in the house next door and I didn't know a thing about it? Is that legal?"

"I assume he has a permit to own the guns, and we're talking about the inside of his home. It's perfectly legal."

"I can't believe it."

"Susan, you'd be amazed what people have in their homes."

"Like what?" Susan asked, momentarily distracted.

"Well, like bomb shelters full of survival gear, or walk-in safes full of original artwork."

"But a shooting range?"

"That's what he was planning on. Have you ever been in the Markses' basement?"

"No."

"Then I'd bet it's there. He was really enthusiastic about the possibility."

"He never mentioned guns to me. I wonder if Jed knows."

"Did they become close?"

"No. Jed invited him to play some golf at the club, but I don't think they ever actually arranged a game. Apparently for men, saying let's have a game of golf is like when we say let's get together for lunch sometime—just politeness unless someone actually works to make it happen. Anyway, a shooting gallery in the basement next door is definitely something Jed would have mentioned if he'd known about it."

"Probably."

Susan thought for a moment. "You said the money for the house came from the sale of their farm."

"Uh-huh."

"So you don't know what Doug did."

"You mean professionally?"

"Yes."

"Not really. For some reason I got the impression that he was a lawyer. Maybe he mentioned going to law school or something. Because, come to think of it, I don't know. They lived abroad a lot, though. I do know that."

"Me, too. Martha, you don't think he could have been CIA, do you?"

"Something like a secret agent?"

"Maybe. What do you think?"

"It's possible."

"It would explain everything: The travel. Us not knowing what he did professionally. I know the CIA hires lawyers."

"I think you're thinking of the FBI. Why would the CIA need lawyers? They don't worry about whether or not what they do is legal, do they?"

Susan dismissed this with a wave of her hand. "The guns in the basement! A CIA operative would have guns in his basement!"

"I suppose. But if Doug was a secret agent, he wouldn't tell people about the guns, would he?"

"I don't know. I don't know anything about that world. I don't even read spy novels. But it all fits together, doesn't it?"

"It might," Martha said slowly. "But . . ."

"Oh, damn!"

"What's wrong?"

"Peter Konowitz just walked in the door."

Martha turned and peered over her shoulder. "Who is Peter Konowitz? Do you mean that nice-looking man in the chinos?"

"He's the chief of police in Oxford Landing and a major pain in the butt. Every time I run into him he seems to feel obliged to detain me on some silly charge. Let's get going before he sees us."

The women paid their bill and hurried from the room, moving too quickly to see the slow smile cross Chief Konowitz's face as he spied their departure.

TWENTY-ONE

"So, WHAT'S FOR LUNCH?"

Susan took a deep breath and decided not to kill her only son. But for the life of her, she couldn't understand how Chad could live on his own for ten or eleven months of the year, go to school, get decent summer jobs, have an active social life, and apparently take care of himself. Then, when he bothered to reappear at his family home for short periods of time, he forgot everything he knew about self-sufficiency and needed to be cooked for, cleaned for, and have every single piece of his laundry washed, folded, and put away by his mother. She mentioned none of this. "What would you like?"

"I don't know. What about those sandwiches you make, the ones with cheese and tomatoes and that green sauce? They're pretty good."

Susan rightly interpreted this to mean Brie and tomato topped with homemade pesto broiled on a sliced baguette. It was one of her summer favorites, so even though she wasn't particularly hungry, she agreed to make one for him. At least he had become sophisticated enough to request something other than hot dogs, she reminded herself before noticing that he had just pulled a can of Mountain Dew from the back of the refrigerator. So much for sophistication.

"Mrs. Gordon called about half an hour ago," Chad announced, plopping down at the kitchen table without bothering to get a glass.

"Oh, thanks. I'll give her a yell when I'm done here." Susan took a deep breath. "You know, Chad, your father and I were wondering . . ."

Half an hour later, Susan was explaining to Kathleen how a poorly timed phone call had saved Chad from what might have turned out to be an intimate conversation with his mother. "He was out the door and on his way to the pizza parlor in less than five minutes. From the speed of his departure, you would have thought he was fleeing an interrogation by a member of the gestapo rather than a chat with his mother."

"Kids," was Kathleen's only comment.

Susan smiled. Kathleen's children were six and ten years old—ages when their demands for attention were more annoying than their avoidance of them. "At least Chad gave me the message you had called. For years I didn't think that was possible."

"I've been talking to Erika, and she said something I thought might interest you."

"About Signe?"

"Nope. About Doug."

"That he was a spy for the CIA?"

Kathleen's eyebrows shot up. "He was? I didn't know that! He told me he was a clean-water expert. Was his job a front for something more interesting?"

"He told you he was an expert in clean water? When?"

"I don't know. Probably when we first met. At that party you gave. I'm sure that's true, because we were looking at your pool and there was some algae growing along the edge. I said something about clean water and . . . and, well, he told me water was his field. It's funny; I got the impression that he loved his job. He talked on and on about the challenges of producing water fit to drink in underdeveloped countries and how an adequate water supply was the key to surviving global warming. It sure was a good act. It never occurred to me that he wasn't telling the truth."

"He probably was. The CIA idea was mine," Susan admitted. "He didn't say anything about guns to you, did he?"

"You know, he did. I don't remember how the subject came up, but he told me he collected guns. He'd actually been given his first one when he was just a kid. He grew up on a farm upstate, and he'd always hunted. He said he was planning on building a shooting range in the basement of his new home. I don't know if he actually did it, though."

"I think he did," Susan told her, slightly chagrined. Kathleen had found out more about Doug the first time they met than Susan had known until just a few days ago. Any more revelations like this and she was going to be forced to stop thinking of herself as a good neighbor. "So what did Erika say?"

"She says that Brett told her that he believed the reason Doug supported Ashley—you know, insisted that she was innocent in the press and turned up in court every day— was because he knew who was poisoning him."

"You're kidding! Then why didn't he just tell the police, and then they could have arrested the correct person?"

"I don't know. Erika says that Brett didn't understand, either, but of course, you know what this could mean, Susan."

Susan took a deep breath before saying what she didn't want to say. "That Doug was protecting Signe."

"Exactly."

Susan was silent for a moment.

"Erika is really worried," Kathleen said.

"Can't say I blame her." Susan thought for a moment before asking a question. "What about her mother? Is it possible that Signe poisoned her?"

"Apparently Signe has no alibi. And she was in Hancock that day. Her mother called asking her to join the family for dinner—but then decided to go to your party apparently."

"It looks worse and worse for her, doesn't it?" Susan said.

"Yes."

Kathleen and Susan exchanged a few more words, but neither of them was in the mood for casual conversation. Kathleen was dropping stitches instead of making progress with her knitting, so they hung up.

"How are we going to help Signe?" Susan asked, looking down at her dog, who was lying on the floor by her feet.

Clue thumped her tail, then got up and ran from the room. Susan followed. She didn't have any ideas; maybe the dog did. But Clue was in greeting mode, she realized, hearing the doorbell ring. From Clue's enthusiastic tail wagging, Susan could assume there was a friend on the other side of the door. She opened it to discover Erika there, the worried expression on her face changing into a smile as Clue leapt up onto her.

"Clue! Down!" Erika was a good friend. Susan wasn't even going to try to pretend that this was unusual behavior for the dog. On the other hand, Erika was wearing a hand-woven turquoise tunic over black raw silk slacks, and Susan knew a liberal coat of dog fur wouldn't enhance her outfit.

"That's okay, Susan!" Erika bent down to greet the retriever. "I'm just glad to see a happy face. Brett's walking around looking as though he expects the sky to fall."

"What do you mean?"

"I'm almost afraid to ask. But I think he's afraid Signe's going to be arrested."

"How . . . ?"

"I overheard him talking on the phone. I don't know who he was talking to, but I'm almost sure he was saying something about what idiots the Oxford Landing police were, and that you could depend on them to get things wrong, and that someone was getting an arrest warrant issued. I know he mentioned Signe."

"Why don't you just ask him?"

"Because I'm not sure he would tell me. No, that's not true. I'm sure he wouldn't tell me."

"But . . ." Susan stopped speaking. Erika looked miserable. Susan didn't want to say anything that might add to her problems.

"I knew he took his job seriously," Erika said slowly. "I knew he cared. I knew he had strong ethics. I knew all of that before we got married. It just never occurred to me that he wouldn't trust me."

"I'm sure Brett trusts you," Susan said.

"Then why doesn't he answer my questions about Signe? He knows I care about what happens to her."

"What did you ask him?" Susan asked.

"If Signe had been arrested."

"Already?"

"I don't know! That's what I'm telling you! I asked Brett, and he simply refused to talk about it! I was stunned! I never expected him to do that to me. I didn't know how to respond. I didn't know what to do. I just turned around, walked out of the room, got into my car, and drove straight over here."

"But Signe—"

"I don't know about Signe. I called her on my cell phone while I was driving. No answer. I left a message on her answering machine and in her cell phone's mailbox. She hasn't gotten back to me. Probably because she's sitting in a cell down at the police department."

"Then let's go there," Susan said, jumping up.

"Go to the police station? I . . . I don't know. What if Brett finds out? I don't want him to think I'm interfering in police business."

"Then you just drive, and I'll go in and see if Signe's there. Brett's used to me interfering in police business!"

That put a smile on Erika's face, but it disappeared almost immediately. "It doesn't solve my problem, though. I thought Brett and I had gotten married because we wanted to share our lives. Here something has happened that involves both his professional life and mine, and he's keeping me in the dark. Susan, I just never thought he would act like this."

"Well . . ."

"Of course, I knew that his work involved confidentiality and that sometimes I wouldn't know what was going on. But I never thought I'd want to know, to be honest!" Erika looked at Susan and then down at Clue. "What do you think? Am I being stupid?"

"Erika, you don't believe Signe killed anyone, do you?"

"No."

"And what about Brett?"

"That's just it! It makes no sense! He agreed with me.

We've been talking about almost nothing else since the night of your party. That's one of the things that has me so upset! I can't believe Brett was lying to me about what he thought."

"Maybe he wasn't," Susan suggested quietly. "Maybe something else is going on here."

Erika looked slightly less distraught. "What?"

"Maybe Brett didn't arrest Signe. And maybe he isn't planning to."

"I . . . I don't understand."

"What exactly did Brett say on the phone?"

"Something about a warrant was being issued and Signe being arrested."

"For murdering her mother?"

Erika looked at Susan as though she thought she was mad. "For what else? A traffic ticket?"

"No, but . . ."

"I'm sorry, Susan. I shouldn't snap at you. I just feel as though my world is beginning to fall apart. I know Signe did not kill anyone. I know Brett . . . Well, that's just it, I guess. I thought I knew Brett. I can't believe this is happening. To me . . . to us . . . to our marriage."

Susan wasn't sure what to say. "Nothing is happening to your marriage. You and Brett were meant to be together. This is just one of those difficult times. Every marriage has them."

"Less than a month into the marriage?" Erika looked as though she didn't believe Susan.

"Well . . ."

"And, frankly, I didn't think we'd have most of the problems that other couples have. Neither Brett nor I is young and naive, for heaven's sake. We've known each other for a long time. We're mature people. And we put a lot of thought into this relationship."

Susan took a moment to consider how to respond. Marriage, she would have liked to say, changed a relationship—any relationship. But Erika was a smart, sophisticated woman as well as her friend. She didn't want to risk insulting her or sounding patronizing. Fortunately, Erika's cell phone rang and made a response unnecessary.

Erika answered, and Susan moved away to give her some privacy. But she was barely out of the room before Erika snapped the phone shut and looked up. She was smiling. "That was Brett. He said everything is going well and that there's no reason to worry. And, for a change, he'll be home in time for dinner tonight."

Susan was perplexed. "What about Signe?"

"I asked if he knew how she was—just casually—and he says she's fine. I guess I've been stupid. Brett is a wonderful man and an excellent policeman. And we all know Signe didn't kill anyone. So whatever is going on now will be worked out in the long run. I've been an idiot. I'm forgetting what Brett's really like. Susan, it's wonderful to talk to you. You really help me to see things clearly. I think I'd better get home. Brett may need to talk to me, and I wouldn't want to disappoint him. I'll stop at the liquor store and see if they have some of that Irish ale he likes so much." And, as fast as her Italian sandals could carry her, Erika left Susan's house and hurried, presumably, home to her husband.

Susan grinned briefly, but it didn't take long for a frown to return to her face. Erika may have been satisfied with Brett's reassurances, but Susan wasn't. Something was going on. And she wasn't going to be content until she found out what. She looked down at Clue, lying on the floor, staring at the door with a rejected expression on her face.

"I think it would be a good idea to go down to the police station and check out what's happening in person, Clue. And we'd better go for a walk before I leave. This may turn out to be a long visit."

TWENTY-TWO

THERE WAS NO WAY BRETT WAS GOING TO TELL HER SOME-
thing he refused to tell his wife—at least not outright.
Susan spent the drive to the police station trying to come
up with a reason for him to talk to her about Signe. But
she arrived at her destination without an answer to her
quandary.

There was nothing at the Hancock Municipal Center to
indicate any unusual activity. The library was holding its
regular story time for preschoolers under a large chestnut
tree on the patio surrounding the flagpole. A group of pre-
teens from the youth center were playing soccer on a field
nearby. A meeting seemed to be going on in the mayor's
office. At the police department, it seemed to be work as
usual. There weren't even any reporters around making
pests of themselves by demanding interviews and answers
to their questions. Susan easily found a place to park and
walked up the brick path and through the double doors into
the police station. The young man sitting behind the
counter looked up from his magazine as she entered.

"May I help you?" he asked politely.

"I . . . Aren't you Sean Hoag?" Susan asked.

"Yes, Mrs. Henshaw." He answered without smiling.

"Sean, I haven't seen you since . . . since . . ."

"Since the party you gave to celebrate Chad's high school graduation. It was a pool party. I threw up in the pool."

"That's right. So you're a police officer now?" she asked a bit too brightly.

"Yes, and a dedicated member of AA, in case you're wondering about my drinking."

"I'm sure Brett . . . I'm sure Chief Fortesque only hires the best men," Susan stated flatly.

"Ah . . . well . . ."

Susan smiled as a pink blush spread over Sean's face. "Does Chad know you're still in town? You know he's home this summer."

The blush deepened. "Yes, ma'am. We . . . uh, ran into each other the other night."

"Really? Where?"

"Uh . . ."

"I'll take over here. Take a fifteen-minute break, Officer Hoag." Brett Fortesque stood in the open doorway leading to the offices behind the public foyer. "Hi, Susan. Am I being self-centered to assume that you're here to see me?"

Susan, distracted by Sean's obvious reluctance to talk about his meeting with Chad, didn't answer immediately.

"He's going to be a good cop," Brett said.

"You never would have thought that when he was in high school. When he was growing up, he was one of those kids you don't notice much. He was in Scouts and on one or two teams with Chad, I'm sure, but I don't remember anything much about him until he hit his teens. Then things changed."

"That's right. I remember those days. He was a terror. We probably hauled him down here to the station more than anyone else his age. I think we saw him virtually every weekend. And there were some serious charges. But

I suppose hanging around the police station turned out to be a pretty good thing for Sean."

"You mentored him?"

"I think the term is modeling. He saw the ways cops help people and decided he wanted a life like that for himself. Of course, he had to spend a year or two cleaning up his act before we'd even talk to him about a possible job. But he did that, made it through the police academy with excellent grades, and I was pleased we could find a place for him on the force."

"Where do you think he saw Chad?" Susan asked, a frown on her face. "I got the impression he didn't want to tell me anything about it."

"Who knows? Could have been the drive-through window at the local McDonald's. That's not what you came here to talk about, is it?" Brett leaned across the desk and pressed a button on the console. "I need an officer to man the entry desk for a few moments," he said into the microphone there. "Come on into my office. We can be comfortable and talk." He led the way, apparently confident that his order would be followed and that the next person to enter the double doors would be appropriately greeted.

"Well, okay. You'd let me know if Chad was in any trouble, though, wouldn't you?"

"Susan, Chad is a great kid. Hell, he's become a great young man. You don't have to worry about him."

Susan laughed, relieved. "I'll try not to. But, you know, Brett, I'm here because of Signe."

"Your own kids are fine, so now you're worrying about other people's? Sit down, Susan." He pointed to a chair. "Let's talk."

Susan was thrilled. "This is about Ashley's murder, isn't it?"

"I didn't say that. But I'd be interested in hearing what you think. You were, after all, the first person on the scene as well as being a neighbor of the victim and most of the major suspects."

"Well . . ." Susan leaned back and made herself comfortable in the hard chair. "I've been thinking about all this." She did some quick thinking. She had an opportunity to offer alternatives to Signe as the major suspect. If only she could think of someone. "Have you checked out the staff at the inn?"

Brett leaned his elbows on his desk and rested his chin in his hands. "In what sense?"

"Do any of them have any connection to Ashley? Maybe a relative who might benefit from her death?" Suddenly realizing that she had skirted too close to Signe as a possibility, Susan changed her approach. "Maybe she'd had an affair with one of the men on the staff?"

"Ashley had affairs?"

"Well, I couldn't be sure of that, of course. But it's possible. She and Doug never seemed particularly close."

"But there were rumors?"

"Not really." She looked up at him sharply. "Why? What did you hear?"

"Susan, cops hear a lot of things. Most of them don't relate to any particular crime. And all of them shouldn't be talked about."

"But . . ."

"But we've always had evidence that Ashley was involved with men other than her husband. Yes. In fact, we investigated several possible affairs when we were looking for a motive for someone to be poisoning Doug."

"Really? Anyone I know?"

"Actually, Ashley was involved with a man connected to

Hancock at one time, but their relationship was over before she and Doug moved to town."

"So maybe that's how she knew about Hancock."

It was Brett's turn to look interested in their conversation. "Why were you wondering about that?"

"Well, it seems like an odd place for someone to retire to. Our taxes are high, and the Markses don't have children who would benefit from our schools. Hancock is a great community, don't get me wrong. But we, Kathleen and I, wondered how the Markses happened to end up here. Signe has a connection with Hancock because she works for Erika, but we didn't know if Ashley and Doug had friends in the area."

Brett shook his head. "Not that we could find. And you can be sure we looked."

"But Ashley's affair . . ."

"Over years ago. We could find no connection to the case. And I'm *not* going to tell you the man's name. Period."

Susan frowned. So much for sharing information. "Could you tell me if that man was a guest at our party?"

"He wasn't. And that's the last question I answer about him."

"What about Doug?"

"What about him?"

"Was he involved with other women?"

"No one we could find. And there weren't any hints of any sort of . . . ah, more unusual relationships in his life."

"Oh." Susan hadn't even considered that possibility. Then she had another thought. "Did you know that Doug had a shooting gallery built in the basement of their house?"

"Of course. We got a warrant and searched the place before we arrested Ashley."

"Is it legal?"

"Completely. As long as the neighbors don't complain about noise, there's no ordinance against a private shooting range in Hancock. And that place was soundproof. And, before you ask, Doug has a permit for each and every one of his guns. There's nothing illegal there. Besides, no one has been shot. Unless you know something I don't?"

"No. I was just surprised to find out what was going on next door, to be honest."

"I don't think you have to worry about Doug coming over and murdering you all in your sleep. The man doesn't seem to have had a single aggressive thought in his whole life—against people that is. If you're an animal and in season, watch out! Doug is a serious hunter—deer around here as well as whatever else is in season. And he's hunted all over the world."

"Don't you think most people who kill animals are just a bit more likely to kill people?"

"No, I don't think there's any relationship at all. Period."

Susan opened her mouth to protest.

"I grew up hunting," Brett said, defeating any comment she might have been ready to make.

"Well, then . . ." Susan paused and looked around for another topic, one that involved neither guns nor Signe. Money, she thought. No, that might lead to Signe. "Did Ashley have any enemies?"

Brett shook his head. "You know as well as I do that that woman could irritate almost anyone in less time than it took to say hello."

"She was a little bossy."

"Susan, she was more than a little bossy. She was judgmental, overly critical, completely unable to see anyone else's point of view, and she could be downright nasty to boot. I just thank God that finding Ashley's enemies isn't a problem that fell into the lap of the Hancock Police Department."

"But . . . then what are we talking about?"

"I thought we were talking about the investigation into Doug's poisoning. At least that's what I've had on my mind. I gather you were thinking of other things."

"I . . . I came here because I'm worried about Signe!"

"There's no reason to worry about Signe. She's fine."

"Brett, she's not fine as long as someone else hasn't been arrested for her mother's murder!"

"Susan, I keep telling you that the Hancock Police Department is not investigating Ashley's death."

"I know that Signe may be in trouble." She snapped her mouth shut. She didn't want to mention Erika's name. "I understand that there's been a warrant issued for Signe's arrest."

Brett looked up from the pile of papers he'd been shuffling through on his desk. "Really? Where did you hear that?"

"I . . . I just know it! I don't have to tell you everything I know or why I know it."

"No, you certainly do not; but whatever you think you know, I can assure you that you are wrong. Signe is just fine. Susan, you really don't have to worry."

"How do you know that? You just told me that you have nothing to do with Signe and the investigation of her mother's murder."

"I didn't actually say that."

"Then what?"

"Susan, I can't talk about this."

"But it's not Ashley's murder that I'm interested in!"

"Then—"

"I'm worried about Signe!"

"And I just told you that you don't have to be worried about her."

"But Erika said—" Susan realized what she had been about to say and snapped her mouth shut. She valued Brett and Erika as some of her best friends. And she believed in their marriage. If anything she did or said damaged either of them or their marriage, she'd never forgive herself.

Just as she was about to panic, a slow smile moved across Brett's face. "Susan, I don't know what Erika told you. And I don't want to. I do know that whatever it is Erika did or said, it came out of her concern about Signe; and I can only tell you what I will tell her when I get home this evening." He glanced down at his watch. "Which will be soon, I hope. Signe is fine. You don't have to worry about her. Erika doesn't have to worry about her. And that is really all I can tell either of you right now."

"But . . ."

"Susan, I have legal obligations and personal obligations. I plan to honor both of them. That's it."

Susan stood up. "Then I guess I'd better leave so you can get home to your wife."

"That would be nice." He stood up, too.

"But, Brett, I do have one question."

"Which is?"

"If someone were going to be arrested for Ashley's murder, who would do the arresting?"

Brett didn't have to think to answer that one. "The most likely person to do the arresting would be Peter—Chief Konowitz of the Oxford Landing Police Department."

Susan was out of the door before he had a chance to say good-bye.

TWENTY-THREE

OXFORD LANDING HAD APPARENTLY CHOSEN FUNCTION-
ality over charm when they looked for a place to house
their police department. The one-story cinder block building was separated from the highway by a macadam parking area. Space had been left for a narrow garden between
the building and the parking lot; weeds and cigarette butts
grew there. Susan walked around the mess and into the
building.

Two uniformed officers were chatting, leaning against
the wall right inside the door. A young woman was sitting
at the radio console, chatting on the phone. Susan hesitated, not sure who to approach. Fortunately, one of the
officers noticed her presence.

"Can I help you, ma'am?"

"I'm looking for Chief Konowitz."

"Are you a member of the press?"

"No, I'm—"

"Well, he's busy giving an interview to someone from
the press. He can't be interrupted." The men exchanged
amused looks. "You'll have to wait, no matter what your
business is. There's a chair over there."

Susan took the seat offered and looked around for something to read. A coffee table nearby offered a choice

between outdated issues of *Connecticut* magazine and pamphlets concerning such less-than-fascinating topics as Lyme disease, rabies, and West Nile virus. Susan frowned. She should have stuck a paperback in her purse before leaving the house. She pawed through the magazines. Maybe there was an issue here that she hadn't read cover to cover. Her hands paused over one touting "Inns in Connecticut" on its cover. Hm.

When Peter Konowitz had finally finished his interview and left his office, she was still staring at the magazine article in her lap.

"Mrs. Henshaw? Are you waiting to see me?" he asked after escorting the reporter to the door.

Susan almost dropped the magazine. "I . . . yes, of course, I was," she answered. Then, hoping no one noticed the theft, she dropped the magazine into her purse.

Peter Konowitz either wasn't paying attention or could have cared less about petty theft in the station house. He turned to the woman seated at the console. "Any messages?"

She handed him a pile of papers, and he glanced through them before returning his attention to Susan. "I have to return a few of these calls, but you may as well come in now."

". . . Okay, thank you." She leapt to her feet, pulled her purse up on her shoulder, and followed him into his office, pleased that he wasn't going to force her to wait outside. Maybe she'd learn something from his calls.

Chief Konowitz's office was . . . well, Susan tried to think of the appropriate word. It was startling—amazing— an astonishing display of ego. Undeterred by the cinder block construction, dozens of photographs had been affixed to the walls. Susan leaned forward. There were three presidents: both Bushes and Clinton. Susan recognized a governor of Connecticut, a mayor of New York City, and—maybe—three or four senators or representatives from neighboring states. There were a few females too—one nun and three queens from assorted beauty pageants. Some photos were in black and white, some in color. Some had obviously been taken by professional photographers. Some were blurred enough to assume that an amateur had stood behind the lens. All of them featured a grinning Peter Konowitz. Over the years the uniform had changed, but the expression on his face was the same. Look at me, he seemed to be saying. Look who I'm with!

Susan crossed and uncrossed her legs. She didn't know what to do, and she was having a difficult time appearing as though she wasn't interested in what was being said on the phone. The messages that Chief Konowitz was answering seemed to be from reporters interested in learning the latest in the investigation of Ashley Marks's murder. Since that was Susan's main interest also, she finally just sat back and listened.

And learned nothing. Like the photographs on his office walls, everything centered around Peter Konowitz. Susan, imagining Signe wasting away in a cell somewhere in the back of this bleak building, became more impatient the longer she listened.

Chief Konowitz assured each caller that he was not only in charge of the investigation, but "on top of it." Apparently Susan wasn't the only one who wondered exactly what that meant, because the next answer—she could only guess at the questions—was always something about sorting through evidence, interviewing people who were related to the victim or the place where she was killed, and finally a vague mention of forensics, which could have meant absolutely anything. Susan got the impression that Chief Konowitz was having as difficult a time as she was getting a handle on this investigation.

Caller after caller may not have asked the same questions, but caller after caller got damn near the same answers. Susan was wondering if perhaps Peter Konowitz wasn't wasting his talent as police chief in a small town in Connecticut. She had no trouble envisioning a fine future for him in national politics—perhaps as a spokesman for one of those people in the photographs on the wall. She was just going over the possibilities when Signe's name came up.

". . . Not to worry. Being in custody is as good a place as any for the moment. . . . No, it certainly is not my place to comment on that, but I will say that a professional police department is unlikely to make that sort of mistake. . . . Well, yes, but that was an exception. . . . Listen, I'm doing you a favor by even talking to you. It certainly wouldn't be to my benefit to answer that. . . . If you feel that way, perhaps I shouldn't waste my time speaking with you. . . . No, thank you." Putting down the receiver with a bang, Chief Konowitz tossed the rest of his messages in the overflowing wastebasket by his desk, then looked up at Susan and smiled graciously. "And what can I do for you, Mrs. Henshaw? I assume you've gotten over the shock of finding a body in your bedroom at the Landing Inn?"

Susan was surprised by the question. "Ah . . . yes."

"But I'm forgetting. That was not the first time you've discovered a body, was it?"

What was he getting at? Susan wondered. "It's not something you get used to," she said.

"No, I guess not. So . . ."

"So what?"

"So why are you here?"

"I . . . um . . . I was over at the Hancock Police Station and . . . well, I'm looking for Signe. Signe Marks," she added when he didn't respond.

"And?"

"And . . . well, I do want to see her." Susan wondered if she sounded as foolish as she felt. Why didn't he just come right out and tell her whether or not it would be possible to see Signe?

"Of course." There was a smile spreading across Chief Konowitz's face.

Susan wanted to smack him. "Yes. Well, I was . . . you know, wondering if I could."

"You're asking me if you can see Signe Marks?"

"Yes. I'm her friend. She's my friend. I mean . . ."

"You're friends, I get the idea."

"Yes. So I should be able to see her."

"Do you know anything about the law, Mrs. Henshaw?"

"Yes, of course." Well, not much, if she was being honest. She knew she shouldn't drive through red lights or rob houses—the general concepts, you might call them.

"Then you know that a person who has been arrested for a serious crime—and matricide is a serious crime, I think you would agree—cannot be prevented from seeing her lawyer. But I don't believe the right for friends to pop in for tea, as it were, has been upheld by the Supreme Court."

"I didn't say anything about tea."

"Signe is a prisoner." He paused and grinned before continuing. "And that's all there is to it, Mrs. Henshaw."

"I . . ." Susan had no idea what to say. Then . . . "Why didn't you question me about the murder?"

The expression on Chief Konowitz's face changed. "What do you mean?"

"Well, if you're in charge of investigating Ashley Marks's murder . . ."

"As chief of police in the town where the murder took place, I don't believe I have any other choice," he said.

"Well, then why didn't you or one of your men question me about what happened?"

"Happened? I wasn't under the impression that anything happened. My understanding is that you and your husband discovered Mrs. Marks's body when you went up to bed. Period."

"Yes, well, of course, that's right."

"And what do you have to add to that?"

Although she was ordinarily a nonviolent person, there was something about this man that made Susan want to jump up and punch him in the nose. Reminding herself that slugging a policeman was stupid, immoral, and definitely illegal, she answered his question. "I also live next door to the Markses."

"And?"

"And what?"

"And does that mean you know who killed her?"

"No, but I do know the family."

"Yes, you already mentioned your close friendship with Signe Marks."

"Not close. That doesn't matter! What I'm trying to say is that I would have thought you would have been interested in interviewing me about her and her family and other people, like her husband. You know," she ended weakly.

"I do know." Chief Konowitz had been sitting on the edge of his desk. Now he stood up and towered over Susan. "I know that you are implying a complete lack of professional competence on my part. And I know that I do not like it. I have looked into the murder of Ashley Marks. I have looked into it thoroughly. And I do not like your implication that by ignoring you and your husband, I have not done my job properly. You, Mrs. Henshaw, might consider whether or not you're being just slightly egocentric. I can assure you that hundreds, maybe thousands of proper murder investigations can and do take place without your intimate involvement."

Susan, insulted, stood too. "I . . ." She glanced back at the wall of photographs. "You're calling me egocentric? I . . ." She took a deep breath. "I am not egocentric, and I do not think I must be involved in all murder investigations. But if you think that Signe murdered her mother, you are completely wrong." She turned toward the door and then looked back at him. "And if Signe is mistreated here, if there is even any hint that she is being mistreated, I will find the best lawyer in the state and sue you, this department, and this entire town!" She spun around and grabbed the doorknob.

"So you think your money can ruin me? That's typical of a rich—" He paused. "A rich woman like you."

Susan, who heard the word he didn't say, jerked open the door and stamped out of the office. She couldn't remember ever being so angry. She didn't even acknowledge the officers still sitting around the reception area, but stormed out of the building, got into her Cherokee, and roared out of the parking lot, driving in a manner that would have gotten her a ticket if anyone had been paying attention.

Ten minutes later, calming down a bit, she drove off the road into the lot beside an attractive farm stand. Baskets of squash, tomatoes, corn on the cob, and beans gleamed next to large bouquets of zinnias and mums. Susan realized she was breathing heavily and grinding her teeth. She turned off the engine and got out of the car. Maybe a bit of shopping would help, she decided, spying bunches of gorgeous basil beside little yellow pattypan squash.

Fifteen minutes later she had filled the back area of her car with vegetables, herbs, and even a few jars of locally made blackberry jam. Then she checked the stored messages on her cell phone. There were three, all of them from Jinx.

Susan smiled. Jinx must have found something. Then her smile vanished. She just hoped it was something that would help rather than incriminate Signe. She dialed the number Jinx had left.

A few minutes later, she was off the phone and on her way to meet her friend at the Landing Inn.

TWENTY-FOUR

"MRS. HENSHAW? IT'S NICE TO SEE YOU, DEAR. BUT I don't believe there are any *more* presents for you," was Constance Twigg's greeting.

"I'm here for lunch. I'm meeting someone," Susan added lest the inn's owners believe she just couldn't stay away.

"Oh, well, I can recommend the green gazpacho and the avocado salad with grilled shrimp. Both are delicious."

"Sounds good." Susan started to go back to the restaurant, and then she stopped and turned around. "I was wondering . . ."

"Yes?"

"About the murder."

"Perhaps this is not the place to speak of death. Would you like to come into my office?" Without waiting for a reply, Constance Twigg glided off. Susan felt she had no choice other than to follow. She hurried through the foyer, past the small room where guests were checked in and out, through a door marked Private, and into a lovely sun-filled parlor. She looked around eagerly. All the planning for her party had been done in the bar—not because she was interested in drinking, but because that's where samples of food and decorations had been most readily available. The bar was small and dark and had been cozy in the winter months when she had done the planning.

Constance's office, however, was made for summer. The wallpaper depicted white trellises covered with lush morning glories. Dense green carpet lay on the wide chestnut planks of the floor. Three complementary chintzes covered the upholstered couches and chairs, accented with elegant petit point pillows. A large fireplace surrounded by blue-and-white delft tiles dominated one wall, while bookshelves ran floor to ceiling directly across the room. Antique English brasses hung on the walls, gleaming with decades of hand polishing. Ruffles of white-dotted Swiss fabric framed the many-paned windows. The only discordant note was the state-of-the-art CD player atop a cherry desk. Constance pressed a button as she passed it by, and Bach filled the air.

"Please sit down."

"I'd love to. What a wonderful room!"

"Thank you. Except for our bedrooms, this is the only part of the house that is truly private—and the only part I feel I can really call my own."

"It's gorgeous," Susan said, noticing the singular pronoun. "Is it part of the original inn?"

Constance smiled. "No. I never admit this publicly, but the oldest parts of the inn are the most uncomfortable. This room was added right after World War Two. I'm told the tiles around the fireplace were brought back illegally from occupied Germany."

"Really?" Susan moved to get a closer look. "They look as though they've been here forever."

"That's part of the art of owning an inn like this one. We—and some excellent local craftsmen—have worked very hard to make everything look as though it's been around since 1779, when the original inn was built here."

"How much is original?"

"About half of the main building and most of the foundation. Of course, much of the rest has been restored to resemble how the building looked immediately after the Revolutionary War."

"You've done a wonderful job."

Constance shrugged. "We usually tell guests that it's a labor of love, but to be honest, it can be something of a bore. Around ten years ago I spent a week at an inn in Carmel, California. It was a brand-new building sitting right by the water. It had every bit as much charm as our place—more, in fact—but every time there's a minor plumbing problem at that inn, the owners won't be forced to spend a fortune cutting through lathe, plaster, and worm eaten wood. I think of that inn every time a guest here blows a fuse or a pipe in the attic freezes."

"Then you don't get away much?"

"It's difficult, but that isn't what you wanted to speak with me about. I believe you said something about the murder."

"Yes, of course. You see, I wasn't questioned by the police."

"I should consider that a sign of good luck on your part. Surely you don't want to be questioned by the police? Or . . . ?" She stopped speaking and pursed her lips.

"Or what?"

Constance smiled slowly. "You must know what everyone says about you and murder."

"I know that your sister believes murders happen when I'm around. She apparently thinks I cause them to happen."

Constance waved a manicured hand in the air, apparently dismissing this thought. "My sister has these romantic fantasies. Perhaps I don't listen to her as carefully as I ought. But I can assure you that I don't believe Mrs. Marks was killed here because you were giving a party. I assume that a clever person saw an opportunity to kill Mrs. Marks while everyone was busy elsewhere and took advantage of it. The party could have been given by anyone, it seems to me."

Susan smiled. "Yes, that's what I think. But, to be honest, this is not what interests me right now. You see, the police—the local police—never interviewed me," she explained again.

"And you think they should have done so?"

"Well, I found the body. That is, my husband and I did. And she was my next-door neighbor."

"Of course. I had heard there was a close personal connection between the two families."

"Well, there really isn't. I mean, they moved in less than a year ago, and I'm afraid we . . . well, we weren't close." Why, she wondered, did she keep feeling as though she had done something wrong by admitting this?

"Oh, that's too bad. I thought perhaps you might know something. There is something I've been wondering about."

"Maybe I can help," Susan offered eagerly.

"Why did he stay with her?"

"You want to know why Doug stayed with Ashley?"

"Yes. I mean, she was poisoning him."

"That was never proven," Susan pointed out, sitting back in the comfortable chair and getting ready for a nice long chat on the subject.

"Apparently the police botched the investigation."

Susan was quick to defend Brett and his men. "I don't think you can know that. According to my . . . my sources, the prosecutor went to court without preparing the case properly."

"Court . . . I . . ." Susan was surprised by Constance's laugh. "Oh, you're talking about this last time. I'm talking about earlier. Back when the Markses were living on the family farm."

"I don't understand. I thought . . . of course, I don't believe it for a moment, but I'd heard that Signe was supposed to have poisoned her mother."

"Heavens, no. That girl was just a child. Everyone knew that the problem in that house was the mother. Everyone in town knew."

"Really?" Susan leaned forward, hoping the other woman would continue.

But the movement apparently distracted Constance Twigg. She shook her head and laughed a bit self-consciously. "I'm sorry. It's all gossip. Ancient gossip, if you will. I know you'll excuse me for not passing it on."

"Of course, but sometimes there's a kernel of truth . . ."

"And sometimes not." For Constance Twigg that apparently ended the subject. "But I brought you in here for a reason, Mrs. Henshaw."

"What?"

"I really must ask you not to speak openly about your friend's murder in the inn."

"But—"

"Quite simply, it is not good for business. No one wants to sleep in a bed where a corpse has lain." She grimaced and corrected herself. "No one normal wants to, anyway. You would be shocked by the perverted requests we have been subjected to in the last few days."

Now that was something interesting! "Really?"

"Really."

Damn, that seemed to close the subject for Constance Twigg. Susan had been hoping for some salacious details. "I'm sorry if we were overheard. I certainly didn't mean to upset anyone. Ah . . . were you forced to throw away the mattress in our room?"

"No, we certainly were not. Ashley Marks was not the first person to die in this inn, and she won't be the last. Our guests are given immaculate rooms, which they enjoy during their stay with us. They do not need to be given details of everything that happened in the room prior to their arrival. Don't you agree?"

"I . . . I guess." The truth was that she had never thought of this before. Had other people died in that room? That bed? And how had they died? But apparently she was not going to be allowed to ask any other questions. Constance Twigg stood up and turned off the CD player. "I am needed to greet guests this afternoon. My sister has chosen this inconvenient moment to take some time off. And you, of course, have your guest waiting in the restaurant, don't you?"

"Yes, I do. And we'll be careful what we speak about."

"I would appreciate that."

Susan left the room, feeling that she had been dismissed. It was unfortunate that Alvena Twigg wasn't available. Susan suspected she would have learned much more talking with her than with her sister.

Jinx was waiting in the restaurant. "I asked for a table separate from the other diners so we wouldn't have to worry about being overheard," she explained, stirring cream into her iced coffee. "I haven't ordered yet, but I was out late last night, and frankly I need the caffeine."

"But did you learn anything?" Susan got straight to the point.

"Besides the fact that the *Oxford Democrat* has one sexy editor?"

"Jinx! Is that why you're sleepy today?"

"We were out late last night. We went to dinner and then just started talking and forgot the time."

Susan grinned. "Sounds very romantic."

"Not really. Well, not what I always think of as romantic. Not wine and candlelight. More tea and fortune cookies. We went to a Chinese restaurant."

"Good food?"

"Only okay."

"It was the company that made it special."

"Yes, and that company is going to pick me up here in less than an hour, so we'd better get a move on if we want to talk privately."

"Does this mean another dinner date?"

"This means that while Sam Redman is a sweetheart, his newspaper's files are a mess. You would not believe the work it takes to find anything. I'm having a terrible time resisting trying to organize him."

"Men don't like that," Susan said, picking up the menu.

A smile spread across Jinx's face. "I know. So, what are you going to have to eat?"

"Green gazpacho and the avocado salad with grilled shrimp. I'm told it's excellent."

Jinx tossed aside the menu. "Then I'll have the same. Where is the waiter?"

By the time the food had arrived, the two women had caught up on their personal lives and Jinx was ready to start reporting what she had learned. She started with Peter Konowitz because he was easy to talk about. "I learned next to nothing," she said. "I mean, I know he was born in the area, went to school here, started in the local police department, traveled from department to department, and then returned to his old hometown as chief of police about three weeks ago. That's his bio. That's it. Sam says most of the crime around is petty and there isn't a whole lot of police news." She shrugged. "It sort of fills a column here and there between school events and the 4-H Club."

"Oh."

"But I'm in the middle of learning a whole lot about the Markses. And I think there's some information about accusations of murder while they were living on what is always referred to as the family farm."

Susan bit a shrimp off her fork and leaned forward. "Really?" she muttered, chewing.

"I don't have all the details yet. I thought I could work forward from the beginning, but that doesn't seem to be possible. Sam turned the sixties and seventies files over to a group of high school students who were doing a project on the history of team sports in the country. I don't know how their research went, but they put nothing back where they found it. Sam promised to spend the morning trying to get things in order, but I don't think organizational skills are his forte, frankly."

Susan speared a tempting chunk of avocado and wondered how important organizational skills were to Jinx when she was considering a romantic entanglement. "So what have you learned?"

"Well, first the Markses—Doug's parents—were very important people in this area. Their farm was huge and one of the largest growers of tobacco in the state. They also bred Jersey cows and were major milk producers. This, Sam pointed out, made them not only important people in the farming community, but important employers. Sam says that if Doug had stayed in the area, he would have been a very important man."

"Really?"

"Why are you surprised?"

"Doug has never struck me that way. Of course, the more I learn about Doug, the more I realize I've never really known him at all."

"Well, I've been reading about him for the last twenty-four hours, and I don't know that much." Jinx put down her fork and looked up at Susan. "But I do know one thing. He's either a very unlucky man or else someone's been trying to kill him for decades."

TWENTY-FIVE

"WHAT?"

"Let me give you a little background on the family first. It won't take long."

"Okay." Susan glanced down at her watch. "Just as long as you finish before Sam gets here."

"I will. I don't know that much yet. As far as I can tell, there have been Markses in the area almost as long as this inn's been around. I actually found an article about the history of the family. Doug's great-great-grandfather was a member of the local militia during the Revolutionary War. And his great-uncle led a company from Oxford Landing at the Battle of Gettysburg."

"Sounds like Doug's affection for guns may be a family trait." Susan poured artificial sweetener into her iced coffee.

"What?"

"Nothing. Go on. I don't suppose the *Oxford Democrat* owns a copy machine?"

"No. But I've got a pile of papers ready to go to Kinko's."

"This afternoon?"

"Sure. Do you want me to go on?"

"Yes, yes, yes."

"Well, as I was saying, by the time the family got down to Doug's parents, they were very important landowners around here. Doug is an only child, and my impression is that his minor achievements received a disproportionate amount of attention."

Susan smiled. "Are you saying Sam Redman can be influenced by the movers and shakers of Oxford Landing?"

"No, I'm saying his father could be. Sam seemed to be mostly amused by the entire thing, to be honest." Jinx looked up at Susan. "Do you want to hear more about this, or do you want to talk about Sam and me?"

"I'd rather talk about you and Sam, but that's not what we're here for. Go on. I'll stop interrupting."

"You'd better, or we're not going to get done. Well, the paper recorded all the ordinary things: Doug and his heifer calf at the county fair were featured on the front page in August when he was eleven or twelve. And his various science projects in high school. But those might have been featured because he won, not because of his family. Doug actually won the state science fair two years in a row."

"Clean water?"

Jinx looked up from her food, surprised. "Yes, how did you know?"

"He's apparently become an international authority on the subject."

"Well, he got an early start. But he went to college in California, and there's a break of four years when, except for a few announcements about his mother's circle meetings at the Presbyterian church, the Markses weren't mentioned much. Then, of course, there was the wedding."

Susan leaned forward. "Whose wedding?"

"Ashley and Doug's."

"Of course. Did they meet in California?"

"No. Ashley grew up here. In Oxford Landing. You didn't know that?"

"No. It wasn't mentioned in the paper."

"Well, of course she didn't get the same press attention as Doug did."

"Does that mean she isn't from an important family?"

"Definitely not. The only thing I know about her background came from their wedding announcement. You know how those things are—at least, how they were thirty years ago. Most of the emphasis was put on the bride."

"And what did you learn about Ashley?"

"Her father and mother ran the Texaco station out on the highway. I asked Sam if it's still there, and he said he thinks it's become that big truck stop. He vaguely remembers when it was known as Hurley's Texaco."

"I gather Ashley was Ashley Hurley before her marriage?"

"Nope. Ann Hurley—not even an e on the end of Ann. Apparently she changed her name after she got married."

"So Doug and Ashley grew up together. I had no idea."

"I don't know how together they were when they were growing up. Doug had just completed his second year in a Ph.D. program at Stanford the spring before their wedding. Ashley had her high school degree and had been studying acting in New York City, according to their wedding announcement There was no mention of any professional acting school."

"So she could have been doing almost anything at all in the city."

"Yes, but with her looks, she could have gotten some small jobs here and there."

"She was good-looking?"

"You should see her bridal photo. I don't remember her

at your party, but when she was young, she was beautiful. In a rather conventional way."

"I shouldn't be surprised. Ashley was a very attractive woman. Very well groomed and benefiting, maybe, from a bit of plastic surgery. But you could say that about lots of women in their fifties."

"That's true." Jinx pushed her hair off her forehead. "I've been thinking of having my eyes done myself."

"Hmm." Susan didn't respond. She knew that women of a certain age—as she and Jinx were—could talk about this subject for hours on end, and she had other things on her mind now. "Well, I don't know about Ashley when she was young, but she's nothing spectacular now."

"And, apparently, neither well educated nor particularly affluent."

"And Doug was both."

Jinx nodded. "It sounds like it."

"According to Signe they didn't live around here after their marriage."

"No, the paper didn't mention much. There was a society reporter in the fifties and sixties, but Sam thought the column she wrote caused a lot of hard feelings. So when she retired, he didn't replace her. But in the early sixties photos began to appear of Signe—she was in a play that her Girl Scout troop took to nursing homes in the area, things like that."

"No mention of her parents?"

"Nope. Well, I don't think so. As I said, it's difficult to locate all the issues from that period."

"So you didn't find information about the first reports of poisoning."

"Yes. And no."

"No?"

"I didn't see anything that was published about it in the newspaper, but Sam knows a lot—a whole lot—about it. That's what . . . well, that's one of the things we were talking about last night."

"And what did he tell you?"

"It upsets him to talk about it. I hated to upset him."

"Jinx!"

"Look, I'll try to explain, although to tell the truth, I hate to—but you'll understand about that when I finish. I'll try to start at the beginning."

"Good idea."

Jinx took a deep breath and began. "Sam used to date one of the nurses who worked in the emergency room of the local hospital. And he says she told him about the poisoning first. To begin with, he says, everyone thought it was just a rather odd accident."

"Why odd?"

"Because it happened to people who lived on the farm but who didn't actually work in the fields."

"What does that have to do with it?"

"I didn't understand that, either, but Sam says that's because I didn't grow up in a farm community. Remember, a lot of the regulations concerning insecticides are fairly recent. Farmers used to use many more dangerous chemicals than they do now. And farmworkers, mostly migrant workers, frequently came down with baffling illnesses that doctors assumed had to do with the chemicals they were exposed to. But apparently everyone was surprised when Doug and Ashley became ill."

"Both of them at the same time?" This was news to Susan.

"Yes. Sam says he's sure that the first thing he heard about any poisoning was that the two of them had been admitted to the hospital with severe stomach problems. Of course, no one thought it was poisoning then. Food poisoning or the flu was the diagnosis."

"Really?"

"Yes. As Sam said, who would have suspected poison? A couple is admitted to the emergency room with severe diarrhea, nausea, and stomach cramps, and the doctor will work to stabilize them and send them home. If a group of unrelated people come to the emergency room with the same problem, authorities may be called in to attempt to track down the source of food poisoning, but a married couple with the same symptoms . . ." Jinx shrugged. "According to Sam, no one paid any attention. At least not the first two times."

"Two times?"

"Yes, but then the third time Doug almost died."

"Doug? Just Doug?"

"Yes. Sam thinks they were both poisoned, only Doug became deathly ill. At least, he says that's how he remembers it."

"Was it reported in the paper?"

Jinx frowned. "That's one of the problems. Sam says it was kept quiet. He knew about it, but . . . Well, he didn't say this, but I got the impression that it wasn't reported on because of how important the Markses were in the community. Sam seemed a bit upset and embarrassed about that, so I didn't push him."

"Someone was being poisoned, and it was kept quiet?"

"No, that's what I'm telling you. At first, no one had any idea it wasn't all just a terrible accident. The assumption was that Ashley and Doug had accidentally ingested some of the insecticide used on the farm."

"Isn't that a little odd?"

"Yes, but Sam says it's not unheard of. The Markses checked out the storage of all insecticides and decided that no matter how the poisons had gotten into their food in the past, it couldn't happen again."

"But how did they explain the first two times?"

"Apparently the theory was that someone had delivered groceries and insecticide at the same time and the insecticide had somehow contaminated the food. But then Ashley got well and Doug continued getting sick." Jinx yawned and took another sip of her coffee. "According to Sam, that's when the police were called in."

"By who . . . whom?"

"By the emergency room doctors. Tests had been done on Doug to attempt to track down the source of the poison, but when he continued to be ill, the doctors decided something odd was going on."

"And?"

"And the police decided that the poison was being administered intentionally by what Sam called a person or persons unknown." Jinx blushed. "I think he watches a lot of cop shows on TV."

"Like most men," Susan said. "And who did the police suspect?"

"Sam says Signe."

"How does he know that? Who told him?"

"He didn't tell me who told him. He did say that he'd make a few calls this morning and try to learn more."

"But Signe wasn't arrested, right?"

"No. Sam says a story went around town that Ashley had claimed responsibility for misplacing the poison or something like that. He said it was all very odd and that he probably should have investigated further, but—"

"But he didn't want to upset a prominent family unless he absolutely had to."

"He's embarrassed about it, but he said the poisoning stopped and everyone got well. Ashley and Doug went back overseas, and Signe graduated from high school and moved to New York City to attend college. Sam says he thought that was the end of it. Most people who had been involved assumed the whole thing was an accident. And then, of course, he heard about Ashley being arrested for poisoning Doug."

"That sort of changes everything, doesn't it?"

"Yes, but . . ."

"But what?"

"Sam doesn't know if the police in Hancock were informed about the first poisoning. I think that's what's worrying him most of all. Especially now that Ashley has been murdered."

"Wait. I don't understand. Ashley's arrest for poisoning Doug was front-page news all over Connecticut. It even made the New York City TV stations. Are you telling me that Brett and the police in Hancock weren't notified about the earlier poisoning?"

"Not as far as Sam knows."

"He didn't call?"

"No, and he says he's pretty sure no one else did, either."

"No one?"

"He says the man who was chief of police back then retired to Florida years ago and may even be dead. The doctor who was in the emergency room left the area and now lives and works in Boulder, Colorado, and may not even have heard about Ashley's arrest. And . . . well, Sam says this is not a cosmopolitan area and people tend to distrust the wealthy suburbs to the south."

"It might have made a big difference," Susan said slowly.

"Yes."

"Ashley might never have been arrested if the story of the first poisonings had come to light."

"Yes. That's possible."

"On the other hand, Signe might have been considered the major suspect instead of her mother," Susan continued.

"Yes." Jinx was fiddling with her knife and fork and didn't look up at Susan. "But that's not what's worrying Sam."

"What is?"

"Sam is worried that if the police had known about the first poisoning, they might have found and convicted whoever was poisoning Doug this last time. And, of course, Ashley might not have been poisoned. She might be alive today. That's what's worrying Sam. That's why he's so upset. He feels partially responsible for her death."

TWENTY-SIX

That's when Sam Redman walked into the restaurant of the Landing Inn. His smile, which appeared when he spied Jinx, changed to a frown when he realized who was sitting across the table from her. Ignoring a waiter who was trying to seat him, Sam strode across the room, grabbed an empty chair, pulled it up to their table, and sat down.

"Greetings, ladies."

They responded politely, but apparently Sam Redman wasn't interested in polite chitchat. "I've been up since five A.M. going though what I've been stupidly referring to as the morgue down at the office. Can't believe what a mess I've let it become. And I'm paying for it now."

"Did you find more information about the insecticide poisoning?"

Susan and Jinx both leaned forward to hear the answer—and were both disappointed.

"Nope. If a file about that event ever did exist, it's gone now."

"You're sure?" Jinx asked.

"Yup. I pulled everything that related to police activity. Nothing. There's a big hole in the files in the beginning of the seventies. Guess this should be a lesson for me. I'll never let loose a bunch of high school kids in my files again."

"That's probably smart." Jinx reached over and touched his hand.

"Well, I have to get going." Susan stood up.

"Don't you have anything to ask Sam?" Jinx protested.

"You know what I'm looking for. And I really should get going," Susan repeated.

"Well, I'll call you this evening," Jinx said, jumping to her feet.

"That's great. Bye, Sam. Thanks for helping out."

"No problem." Sam said the words to Susan's back.

She knew she was being rather abrupt. But she had just seen Alvena Twigg in the hallway. She hoped Alvena had answers to some of the questions that were beginning to crowd her mind. And the first question she was going to ask was about Sam Redman's character.

Alvena was sitting in the bar, a large frosted glass of lemonade on the table before her. "Why, Mrs. Henshaw, I guess you just can't stay away from our wonderful inn."

"It is beautiful here, and I was . . . in the area," Susan explained. "Are you . . . Do you have a few minutes to talk to me?"

"Yes, of course. I'm just enjoying a nice tart homemade lemonade. So difficult to get properly made, and I'm afraid the chef at the inn stops making them after Labor Day. I sometimes think his quest to be seasonal is carried to an extreme. Last year he was offering mulled cranberry juice when the temperature was in the eighties. It was October, but still. I shouldn't bore you with my babbling. My sister is always complaining about that. And dear Constance just mentioned that you still have some questions about our most recent tragedy. Perhaps that's why you were so anxious to see me that you interrupted your lunch."

"I . . . I was finished with lunch." Susan, as always, was

confused by Alvena's combination of old-world manners and directness.

"But you do have some questions."

"Yes . . ."

Alvena leaned closer to Susan and lowered her voice. "I promised Constance that no one would overhear any talk about the murder. Perhaps you would accompany me to the housekeeping room. I don't believe anyone will be there this time of the day." She stood up.

"That's very nice of you."

"Do you know anything about the running of an inn, Mrs. Henshaw?" Alvena asked, leaving her frosted glass on the table and heading toward the back stairway Susan and Kathleen had used a few days ago.

"No, I don't. I used to think I'd like to own an inn—or a bed-and-breakfast, actually—but the opportunity never came up."

"Many people think that and a few of them actually do it, but I don't believe most of them have any idea how much work is involved."

Susan felt as though she had offended Alvena. "Certainly providing all the meals as you do . . ."

"Oh, anyone can run an excellent restaurant. Just hire an excellent chef and a competent kitchen manager. It's the rest of the inn that is so difficult to get under control. So many rooms to clean, linens to launder, pillows to fluff. It's the little things like the bottles of Crabtree and Evelyn toiletries that our guests have come to expect. Constance doesn't always realize just how important these things are."

"So you two divide up the work?" Susan guessed.

"We have since my retirement from the school district. While I was working, I could only do my part in the summertime. The rest of the year, Constance struggled on with only local help. Things were not always as one would have wished," Alvena explained, looking over her shoulder to make sure they weren't being overheard—by Constance rather than a guest, was Susan's guess.

"It's in here." Alvena opened a door on their right, and Susan followed her inside. The housekeeper's room appeared to have been a guest room at one time. But now, instead of a bed, two large tables dominated the center of the room. They were piled high with laundered sheets and towels. Raw pine shelves lined the walls, providing storage for blankets, cases of tissues, toilet paper, and those little bottles of shampoo and cream rinse that Alvena thought so important. The spicy scent of carnations emanated from a large box of soap tablets. Susan breathed deeply.

"Wonderful, isn't it, dear? I do so love my potpourri. I make it up fresh each summer."

Susan realized Alvena was pointing to a large bowl of blue-and-white export china sitting on a table in the small bay window. "You make it? I didn't know." Susan remembered that the bowl in her room had smelled like a mixture of sage, cloves, and old socks; she had stashed it in an unused drawer in the dresser and prayed no fumes would escape.

"Yes." Alvena smiled the wan smile of those who believe themselves to be chronically unappreciated. "I wanted to sell little packets of potpourri at the front desk, but . . . alas."

"One of those ideas that your sister vetoed?"

"Yes. But I could sell you some—privately, so to speak."

"That would be very nice," Susan lied.

"But before business—pleasure. That's what my dear father always said." And slipping a hand under a pile of fluffy white Egyptian cotton towels, Alvena pulled out a bottle of dark amber liquid. "There are glasses in the bathroom," she explained, her eyes widening at the coming treat.

"It's a little early. . . . Well, just a small glass," Susan said, hoping the alcohol would make Alvena indiscreet. But there were only standard water glasses in the bathroom, and Alvena filled both to the rim and handed Susan one. "Chin. Chin. Drink up."

Susan put her lips to the rim of the glass expecting sweet sherry or possibly a homemade concoction of elderberry wine, so the explosion of eighty-proof alcohol came as a shock. "Oh. You didn't make this, did you?"

"Not unless my name is Jack Daniels, dear." Alvena beamed and sat down on a straight-backed chair by the window. "Now sit down." She pointed to an equally uncomfortable perch for Susan. "And tell me what you want to know."

Susan coughed a few times. "Sam Redman . . . Did you know him when you were young? I was just wondering."

"Of course, the young lad who runs the *Oxford Democrat*. He grew up in Oxford Landing, but I'm afraid his parents sent him away to a private school somewhere in New Hampshire. So unfortunate I thought at the time. Our school would have benefited from the ink in his blood. The newspaper is an inherited business, you know. His father ran it before Sam. And I suppose Sam's son will run it after Sam is gone."

"I thought . . . Didn't he say . . . Isn't he single?"

"Divorced. His wife lives in New York City. She's a decorator. Her name comes up in those fancy shelter magazines from time to time. But Sam's kids—he has two, a boy and a girl—visit their father from time to time. He sometimes brings them here for dinner."

"Oh."

"What were you wondering about him, dear?" Alvena asked, taking another delicate sip of whiskey.

Susan decided the direct approach was best. "Is he honest?"

"As the day is long. Mind you, he's a little bit odd. He uses the profits from that sporting goods place to keep his paper running because he says every town in the country deserves something better than CNN and Fox News. I believe that's become a minority view in this day and age. My dear father would call Sam Redman a crackpot, but he's honest. Yes, he's honest."

"Oh." Well, that was one theory shot to hell. "I was wondering . . . also wondering . . . about Doug and Ashley. I hadn't realized they both grew up around here. I don't want you to think I'm being nosy."

"Please, Mrs. Henshaw, don't apologize. I'm thrilled that you would ask for my help in your investigations."

Susan smiled. "Then tell me everything you remember about Ashley . . . or I guess I should say Ann."

Alvena smiled. "So you learned that already, did you? She always hated it that anyone knew she didn't have a fancy name. Ann Hurley she was born. Only daughter of the owners of the local gas station. Her parents were lovely people. Hardworking. Intelligent. Members of the Methodist church. They must have been real surprised to wake up one day and discover that they'd created Ann. She was a little spitfire right from the first. Cute as a button. Bright as a pin. And determined to get her own way in the world. Unfortunately, her parents adored her; and sensible as they were about most things, they spoiled their daughter. By the time she was eight or nine, Ann ruled her family. And she went on from there. Power," Alvena advised Susan ominously, "corrupts."

"Yes, I've heard that. So, tell me what happened as Ashley—or Ann—got older."

"Just what any sensible person would expect. She got her own way at home, and she expected to get it everywhere else. By the time she arrived at our school, she'd learned to wrap the teachers and the students around her manicured fingers. She was the most popular girl in her class, starred in all our little theatrical productions, got excellent grades, and cared about nothing and no one except herself. Dreadful girl. Of course, I'm afraid that was something of a minority opinion."

"But that's what you thought."

The habitual smile on Alvena's face had disappeared. "I disliked her from the moment she walked in the door of my office."

"Why?"

"She always wanted something. Oh, I know what you're thinking. Teenagers are frequently self-absorbed and self-centered. But Ann was different. She actually thought she could boss me around! I put a stop to that immediately, I can assure you."

"How did she feel about that?" Susan leaned forward.

"She didn't like it at all. But I had never had a student lord it over me, and I assure you, little Ann Hurley wasn't going to be the first. I cannot be ordered about, and I cannot be manipulated."

Susan thought of Constance and made an effort to resist smiling. "What did you do?"

"I chose to ignore her. I didn't give her the time of day. Ann was accustomed to a lot of attention, but I can tell you that she didn't get it from me. Oh, she acted as though she didn't mind, but I believe she was hiding the hurt. She would come into my office, giggling and chattering like a magpie with one of her friends, and she would make the most outrageous requests. I felt it behooved me to nip this sort of thing in the bud. I would refuse to comply with her requests, and then she and her cohorts would scream with laughter and run out of the office. I have always thought that I made my point."

Susan doubted it. "Was she friendly with Doug back then?"

"Not in school. They must have been over four years apart. My memory is that Doug graduated before Ann came on the scene. They were as different as night and day. I can't imagine how they ever came to get married. Although there were rumors," she added darkly. "I would prefer not to pass them on, though."

"What was Doug like?"

"A very nice young man. He caused no trouble at all. He cared deeply about his science classes and immersed himself in the labs. We had a very able science teacher in those days, Mr. Daviet, who was pleased to take young Doug under his wing. You may not know this, but Doug won the state science fair two years in a row. Unheard of! We were all pleased as punch, I can tell you. His parents rented the inn and gave Doug the most incredible graduation party. And then he went off to someplace in California, and we thought we might never see him in Oxford Landing again. And wouldn't it have been better if that had been true."

"Why?"

"Hitching up with Ann—or Ashley as she was calling herself by then—was the worst thing he could have done."

"Why?"

"Well, just think about it. If he hadn't married her, he wouldn't have killed her now, would he?"

Susan reached for her glass and took a rather too large

sip of the liquor. "How do you know he killed her? Did you see something at the inn that night?"

"Oh, please. How could anyone doubt it? He lived for years with that awful woman. Of course he killed her. I can't imagine that the police even have any other suspects."

"I think . . ." Susan decided she wasn't going to get the information she needed unless she leveled with Alvena. "I think the police are convinced Signe did it," she continued.

"Signe? How could she possibly have done it? She had left the inn long before her mother died."

"You saw Signe at the inn that night? At the party the night her mother died?"

"Not at the party itself. I gather you didn't invite her. But I know I spied her earlier in the day. It was almost evening, but you and your guests hadn't arrived. She was delivering one of your gifts from that fancy shop in Hancock."

"Twigs and Stems?" Susan asked weakly.

"The very place. I saw her put the package on the buffet in the foyer. She just came in and dropped it off and dashed out the back door. She didn't say anything to anyone. I just happened to be passing by and saw her. I assure you, Mrs. Hancock, Signe Marks was far away from the inn when her mother was poisoned."

TWENTY-SEVEN

SUSAN HAD RETURNED HOME AND FOUND KATHLEEN AND Erika sitting in her living room, having been welcomed—then abandoned—by Chrissy and Stephen.

"Signe was at the inn right before your party?" Kathleen asked, putting down her knitting.

"Yes."

"And she came and went through the back door? By the kitchen? Right by the area where the food was set up waiting to be served?" Erika asked.

"Yes."

"And she didn't say anything to anyone?" Kathleen followed up.

"Not that I know of. Alvena told me she scooted along—that's the phrase she used—into the foyer after Signe left, and read the envelope of the attached card; otherwise she wouldn't have realized the gift was for us."

"But she said Signe came and went through the back entrance—that she was near the kitchen where much of the food must have already been laid out for the party."

"Yes," Susan agreed. "And, of course, that's the significant thing, because poison, as we all know, is an excellent way to kill someone without actually being present at the time of death." Susan looked from Kathleen to Erika. They were both frowning. "I've really screwed things up, haven't I?"

"Well . . ." Kathleen answered slowly. "It does sound as though you've done a better job of proving that Signe might be guilty than proving her to be innocent."

Susan sighed. "That's what I thought."

"But maybe not," Erika protested. "Look, Alvena apparently didn't like Ashley—Ashley doesn't, for that matter, sound terribly likable even when she was young. So doesn't it stand to reason that a lot of people might not have liked her and maybe even enough to want to kill her?"

"Everyone says that," Susan cried. "I thought that same thing!"

"And?"

"I asked her about other suspects. Although, of course, I didn't call them suspects. Anyway, she tried but she couldn't come up with anyone else. To be honest, taking Alvena's judgments at face value just might be a mistake. She seems to have two opinions—perfect or awful. Doug was perfect. Ashley was awful. Thinking about it on the drive home, I began to wonder if sex wasn't involved. Alvena loves Doug, Peter Konowitz, and Sam Redman. But she hated Ashley. It could be a coincidence. There might be dozens of men she didn't like and lots of women that she did, but so far it looks like boys are good, girls aren't."

"You could go back and ask her about other women," Kathleen suggested. "You know, to kind of test that theory."

"No, thank you. It takes Alvena forever to answer a simple question. Besides, she's probably napping right now. She must have consumed at least six ounces of pure whiskey while I was there. And she was still sitting at that table in the housekeeping room with her glass and an almost half-full bottle by her side when I made my escape."

"That sweet old lady drinks?" Kathleen asked.

"She sure did today," Susan assured her.

"I feel terrible," Erika spoke up.

"Why?"

"Signe was helping out at the store. But being at the inn right before her mother died as well as being around the food . . . Well, it's just one more reason why she's a suspect."

Kathleen picked at a knot that had formed in her yarn. "There are, however, lots of ways poison could have been put in Ashley's food or drink."

"Yes, there were! I mean, there was," Susan cried. "Jed and I found an empty bottle of wine—Italian wine. We gave it to Chief Konowitz!"

"Why?" Erika asked.

"He was going to have it tested for poison. And when I saw him this morning, he didn't say a thing about it!"

"Perhaps the report isn't in yet," Kathleen suggested.

"That might be true. On the other hand, maybe it is." Susan stood up again. "I'll be right back. I'm going to give him a call." She hurried back to the study.

It wasn't easy getting through to Chief Konowitz. She had to call three times. The first time, the phone was answered by a young woman. Susan had identified herself, asked to speak with Chief Konowitz, and then waited expectantly for him to come on the line, rearranging the bits and pieces on Jed's desk to occupy her time. She was lining up paper clips when the woman came back on the line to assure Susan that Chief Konowitz was very busy, he had spoken with her already that day, and he could not be bothered to speak with her again. Susan was stunned with the abrupt good-bye followed by the unmistakable click of the receiver being replaced.

Susan dialed again immediately, unwilling to let this go by. This time the young woman refused even to pass on her message.

Susan sat at the desk, furious, trying to figure out what to do. A few minutes later there wasn't a paper clip capable of clipping anything to anything, but she'd come up with an idea that might work. She reached for the phone and dialed the police station. The same woman answered, but this time, instead of identifying herself, Susan lowered her voice an octave and claimed to be Ingrid Anderson, reporter for a New York City network affiliate.

"I know how busy Chief Konowitz must be, but I just have a few questions to ask him. We go on the air in—" Susan glanced at the grandfather clock Jed had, as it happened, inherited from his own father. It kept perfect time. "—in fifty-seven minutes, and we're doing a big story on the chief and your police department. If you could just tell him that I'll take up less than fifteen minutes of his time, I'd appreciate it."

The phone was picked up in less than fifty-seven seconds. "Chief Peter Konowitz here."

Susan smiled. She wasn't the only person on this phone line who had lowered her voice. "Hello, Chief, I—"

"Ms. Anderson, I understand you have some questions for me, but I should tell you first that I'm running the investigation into the death of Ashley Marks by myself. Everything goes through my office. I'm frequently in the field collecting information. This is a small town, but this is not the first time we have had a case of poisoning, nor is it the first time I've been involved. Years ago, when I was just a fledgling police officer, right out of the state police academy, I was involved in—"

"I just have one question, Chief Konowitz. I understand a wine bottle was turned in by your office to a laboratory to be tested for possible poison content. I need to know if that lab has issued a report and whether it was positive or negative. I mean, if there was poison in the bottle or not," Susan added after he did not reply immediately. "If you received the report," she added into the lengthening silence.

"Who the hell? You're not a reporter. There is no way a reporter could know about that test! Mrs. Henshaw! Do you know anything at all about the laws concerning fraud?" He hung up the phone without giving her an opportunity to reply.

Susan swept the pile of ruined paper clips into a nearby wastebasket and stood up to return to her waiting friends.

"Well? Did they get the results of the tests?" Erika asked as she joined them.

"I don't know. Chief Konowitz refused to talk to me. And then, when I pretended to be someone else, he caught on before I found out anything." Susan sat down in the place she had vacated just a few minutes ago. "Is it illegal to tell a police officer that you are someone you're not?" she asked.

"It's not a good idea to lie to the police, but it's not necessarily illegal," Kathleen replied.

"Good," Susan said. "So what do we do now?"

"I suppose going back to Oxford Landing in person and asking to see Signe would be a waste of time?" Erika suggested.

"I don't think Chief Konowitz would let us see her.

Maybe Brett . . ." Susan didn't even want to ask the question.

Erika took a deep breath. "I suppose I could ask Brett if he'd help, but—"

"But your marriage is too important. You shouldn't have to do that," Kathleen interrupted. "If we decide to contact Brett, Susan can do it. He's used to turning her down."

Susan couldn't do anything but agree. "I think the only way one of us is going to get to see Signe is to go to law school and volunteer to represent her. Hey, why don't we hire a lawyer for her?"

Erika spoke up. "I did get an answer from Brett about that. He says not to worry. She's represented."

"Is he sure?"

"Yes. He says—has said over and over, in fact—that there is no reason at all to worry about Signe." She brushed her bangs off her forehead. "That's why I hate to ask him anything. I think he's getting tired of hearing the same worried questions. I know I'm tired of the same damn answer."

"You know, there is another way to approach this," Kathleen said. "Maybe we should talk to Doug—"

She was interrupted by the phone. Susan got up to answer it, and when she returned to her friends, she had a frown on her face. "That was Doug," she explained.

"What luck!" Erika said. "And we were just thinking about contacting him!"

"Why did he call?" Kathleen asked.

"You won't believe this. He asked me to speak at Ashley's funeral service tomorrow."

Kathleen leaned forward. "And what did you say?"

"That I was honored and would be proud to speak." She took a deep breath. "Well, what else could I do?"

"No, you did the right thing," Kathleen agreed.

"What am I going to say? I didn't like Ashley."

"Not many people in town did," Erika reminded her.

"Then maybe not many people will show up for the funeral."

TWENTY-EIGHT

It was standing-room only at Ashley Marks's funeral. Susan, as one of the speakers, had been ushered to a pew at the front of the Hancock First Methodist Church and then seated next to an overweight woman wearing a hideous teal blue polyester suit over an equally unattractive flowered print blouse. She also wore an excessive amount of large jewelry. But she smiled broadly when Susan introduced herself.

"Fanny Hurley. Ashley's cousin." She took both of Susan's hands in her own ring-studded ones. "And how did you know Ashley?"

"We . . . she moved in next door to me last year."

"Lord in heaven, you must be the woman who is so famous for solving mysteries. And I know you and your husband have a charming big old house as well as a place on an island up in Maine that you go to in the summer. And doesn't one of your children attend Cornell?"

"I . . . yes, my son is in his third year there," Susan answered, surprised to hear so much information about her life coming from a stranger. "I'm sorry, but have we met?"

"Oh, I don't think so. This is my first visit to Hancock. I live in Fostoria, Ohio. Have you ever been there?"

"I don't believe so."

"Well, you might not remember us. We're pretty small, but I like to tell people we have everything you could want. We have a wonderful library, some interesting antique shops, and an absolutely fascinating museum of glass. I'm one of the docents."

"It sounds charming," Susan said, still a bit confused.

"It is. But I don't want you to think we're country bumpkins. I've been on-line for years and years. Ashley and I used to e-mail each other all the time." Her wide smile faded. "I'll miss hearing from her."

"Really?" Susan blurted out and then hoped she didn't sound too surprised.

"Yes. Ashley kept me up-to-date on her life, and she told me all about your lovely town. I know she was unhappy when Doug decided it was time to retire and come back to the States, but I think your charming community had helped make up for the loss of their exciting life overseas. She wrote me about such fun goings-on—parties at the Hancock Field Club, shopping trips to those luxury stores in New York City. I can tell you, sometimes when I was reading those messages, I just wanted to hop in my car and come out and visit."

"You should have," Susan said sincerely.

"My cousin kept putting me off. You know Ashley. She wanted everything to be perfect before I saw the house. And now she's dead and the first time I'll be seeing the things I've heard so much about, I'll be alone." A tear slid down the woman's cheek.

Susan reached out and squeezed Ashley's cousin's hand. "I'm sure Doug is pleased you're here," she whispered.

"I suppose you're right. But it's so difficult to know what

that man is thinking. He seems sad, but . . . Oh, dear, here's the minister. We'd better be quiet. We'll have an opportunity to talk back at the house after the service."

You bet we will, Susan thought as the organist slammed out three loud chords and the congregation struggled to their feet.

A tall young man dressed as a minister jogged up the steps leading to the pulpit, grasped the sides of the lectern with red, beefy hands, and stared down at his congregation. "We are gathered together to celebrate the life of a wife, a mother, and a friend. A woman whose impact on her community can perhaps best be demonstrated by the immense number of mourners here today, joined in our grief to find comfort and solace in reflecting on her life and remembering the unique part she played in each of our lives.

"The Markses—Doug and Annette—moved to Hancock only recently. Too recently, alas, for me to have been given the opportunity to become personally acquainted with them. But, in the few days that have passed since her untimely death, I've spoken with Ann's family and friends, and I've learned just how important a place Annie had—in a short time—found in the hearts of many in Hancock. Known for her generous and giving spirit, she had been involved in various community affairs . . ."

If it hadn't been most unlikely in this solemn place, Susan would have thought the sound she heard coming from the pews behind her was laughter. A neighbor she barely knew, sitting by her side, leaned over and whispered in her ear, "Are you sure we're at the right funeral?"

Susan nodded, suppressing a nervous giggle as the minister continued, enumerating a remarkably long list of Ashley's imagined virtues.

Taking a deep breath, he changed the subject—and, once again, Ashley's name. "It would be remiss of me to ignore the recent tragic event in Abby's life, but despite the unfortunate mistake made by some local officials . . ."

Susan looked over her shoulder and saw that Brett and Erika were seated right beside Peter Konowitz. Peter was smiling. Brett was not.

"Angie's husband reported her to be in good spirits the day of her death, happy to be celebrating the anniversary of a dear friend's nuptials."

Susan was aware of the curious glances of those seated nearby.

"Is it really surprising to those of us—of you, who knew the dear departed more intimately than I—that she chose to celebrate with friends rather than mull over the injustices of her life away from the prying eyes of . . . uh . . ." Apparently realizing that many of the people to whom those prying eyes belonged were now seated before him, the minister struggled to continue. ". . . uh, of the justifiably curious. No, of course not!" He finished that thought with a flourish before going on.

"Just this morning, speaking with a member of Annie's family, a woman who had flown many, many miles to be here for this occasion, I learned a bit about Ann's youth. She grew up not far from here, as the crow flies, in the same town where her future husband was born. Now that's a rare thing in these mobile days, and they were a rare couple, traveling the world together because Abby chose to follow her husband to whereever his job took him. And besides wifely support, she brought along style and taste, maintaining standards that can be missing in the less developed parts of our world. Ann . . . Abby . . . A . . ."

Apparently realizing for the first time that he had no idea

what the woman was called, the minister sorted through his pages of notes. Unfortunately they all slid onto the floor beside the pulpit. So, gathering up his courage, he ended with a flourish. "One and all, we will miss her.

"And now a few words from . . . uh . . . her dear friend, Susan Henshaw. And before Miss Henshaw speaks, I'd like to extend an invitation to the congregation from Doug Marks, who wishes to invite each and every one of you back to his house right after this service is ended. Mrs. Henshaw."

Susan stood up and walked up to the lectern, her statement held firmly in her hand. When Doug had asked her to speak, she hadn't realized she was going to be the only speaker. She had taken an entire year of speech classes in college. The only thing she remembered now was her professor's two words of advice: Breathe deeply. She did that now, climbing the steps to the pulpit. At the top, she stopped and gasped. She hadn't realized that not only were all the pews filled, but the back aisles were crowded and the balcony as well. And not just with those friends and neighbors the minister had been speaking of. The press corps was also well represented.

Susan decided another deep breath was called for, then looked down at her notes and began. She had spent most of the night trying to write nice things about a woman she disliked, only to realize as she watched the sun come up that sometimes funerals weren't as much about the person who died as about all the people we've known and lost. Once she saw that, she had been able to sincerely mourn Ashley, and she'd written a short, sincere speech. Reading it now, she had no idea whether she was touching anyone listening. If she had been completely honest, she would have admitted that all she wanted was for these few minutes to come to an end.

They did. And after another hymn and the benediction, so did the service. Susan hurried back to the narthex, looking for a shortcut to the ladies' room. She and Jed were going to meet back at his car, but first things first!

Maybe it was its location, but miracle of miracles, the room was completely deserted. Susan had slipped into a booth and locked the door behind her before anyone else even entered the room. Her promptness was rewarded by overhearing herself complimented almost immediately.

"Susan did a wonderful job, didn't she?" came the voice from the stall next to her.

"She did!" The agreement came from a woman standing by the sink. "I was so impressed. You don't think she actually liked Ashley, do you?"

"I doubt it. But you never know with Susan. She's not one to trash people. Unlike you and me. So what did you think of the minister?"

"What an idiot. I couldn't believe he couldn't get her name right!"

"I know. He mentioned every woman's name starting with an *A* that I could think of! And I thought I'd die when he mentioned affairs."

"Me too! Did you think he might ask one of her lovers to come up and speak?"

"That's exactly what I was thinking. Hey, look who's been in the toilet stall! Susan, have you been listening to everything we were saying?"

"Yes," Susan said, smiling at the two women. They'd all known each other since their children played on the same soccer league. She knew they would answer her next question. "What affairs?"

"Susan, don't tell me you lived next door to Ashley and

didn't know she was sleeping with every available man in town?"

Susan walked over to the sink and began to wash her hands. "Really?"

"Really. She flirted with half of the husbands at that party you and Jed gave when they first moved in, and while I don't know if she actually reeled in any of them right away, I've heard rumors about her and Malcolm Freedman."

"No! I heard that she and Johnny Kovacs were spending long afternoons upstairs at the Hancock Inn."

"You're kidding! I thought Johnny had better taste."

"He probably does usually, but you know how Ashley could be."

"What? Did she tell men that they had two choices? They could either sleep with her or else she'd poison them?"

"Wait a second." Susan broke into the frivolity. "Are you sure about these men, or is this just gossip?"

"Yes, we're sure."

"It's not just gossip."

"Why didn't I know?" Susan asked. "Why didn't anyone say anything to me?"

The two women exchanged glances. "I guess everyone thought you knew. Ashley was always telling people how close you and she had become," Maggie explained reluctantly.

"We didn't believe it for a moment!" Betsy added quickly. "None of your friends did."

"We were just neighbors. In fact, I've spent the week realizing that I knew almost nothing about Ashley or Doug!" Susan protested.

"We're only telling you what Ashley said. She thought you and Jed were a big deal in town, I guess, and she wanted everyone to think you were close," Maggie continued.

"And you were the only speaker at her funeral," Betsy reminded her.

Susan was becoming more and more confused; but Jed was waiting for her, so she decided to return to her primary interest. "Do you think Doug knew about Ashley and other men?"

"I don't see how he could have missed it. According to what I heard, they'd had an open marriage for years. I mean, it's strange that he didn't say anything at her funeral, isn't it?"

"Maybe he was too distraught," Susan suggested. "I was sitting nearby, and I can tell you, he looked dreadful."

"You're kidding!"

"Why are you so sure he didn't sincerely care about his wife?"

"Susan, she'd been trying to kill him for the past few months. If Doug was feeling anything at all this morning, I would think it was relief."

"Yes, he can finally sit down to a meal and feel confident that he'll be able to get up when he's finished," Maggie agreed.

"Do you . . ." Susan stopped speaking as the door opened and Ashley's cousin wandered into the room.

"You know Ashley—" Betsy began.

"This is Ashley's cousin, from Ohio," Susan interrupted before said cousin might hear something hurtful. "I'm sorry, I don't remember your name," she apologized.

"Fanny. Fanny Hurley. I'm so glad to see you. I thought

that talk you gave was wonderful. I know Ashley would have been touched."

"I'm glad you liked it. I didn't have a very long time to write it. Doug just called and asked me to speak last night."

Fanny frowned at the mention of Doug's name. But her good manners prevailed, and she exchanged polite chitchat with the women for a few minutes before excusing herself and entering one of the stalls.

"We'd better head out. We'll see you at Doug's, right?" Maggie asked as Betsy pushed open the swinging door.

"Of course." Susan was rummaging around her large, black Italian leather bag when Fanny rejoined her. "I know there's a lipstick in here somewhere," she explained.

"Your friends left?"

"Yes, I'm sure you'll see them at the house later."

"I followed you here." Fanny said, turning on the water. "I have a favor to ask you. In fact, a few favors."

"I told you: anything I can do to help." Susan repeated the standard offer, hoping she wasn't getting herself into anything onerous.

"First, I need a ride back to the house. I told Doug to go on without me."

"Of course," Susan said, relieved. "Jed is waiting outside. We can leave right away."

"But I'd like to talk to you, just for a moment. Privately."

"Sure."

"You are investigating Ashley's murder, aren't you?"

"Well . . ."

"Of course you are. I know my cousin tended to exaggerate." Fanny chuckled. "She always knew how to tell a good story. I used to tell her that she should write books. And I was right. She could have made her fictional characters do just what she wanted without resorting to more drastic measures."

"What do you mean?" Susan asked, mystified.

"This is the church where my cousin's memorial service took place. I don't want you to think I'm hopelessly old-fashioned, but there must be more appropriate places for this conversation to take place."

The bathroom door swung open, and three more women surged in.

"Why don't we stop at my house for a bit before we go over to see Doug?" Susan suggested.

"I'd like that," Fanny said, sounding relieved.

TWENTY-NINE

"IT'S SO GOOD TO HAVE A GLASS OF DECENT ICED TEA. ICED tea with lots and lots of fresh mint just means summer to me."

Fanny Hurley leaned deeper into the cushion of the chaise lounge on Susan's awning-covered brick patio. "It's really lovely back here." She looked around at the large green lawn surrounded by wide perennial borders leading down to the brook that marked the back of the Henshaws' property.

"Thank you. We have a very good landscaping company," Susan explained, wondering how she might encourage Fanny to "get on with it."

"Of course, Ashley talked about all that in her e-mails— her decorator, her landscape designer, her cleaning service, her house painter, her personal trainer. So many people seem to be necessary to maintain a lifestyle like this."

"I suppose that's true. But this garden wasn't really designed by anyone. It just sort of developed over the years, and although I dream about a personal trainer, I've never had one. And Jed and I have always painted our own house—well, the inside at least," she added, feeling obliged to be honest.

"So it was all just another of Ashley's fantasies."

"You mentioned that earlier," Susan said, putting a plate of coconut shortbread cookies on a table close to her guest.

"You must think I'm crazy."

"No, but I am a bit confused," Susan admitted.

"I came here determined not to say anything negative about my cousin. After all, she's dead and I didn't ever confront her while she was alive."

"What do you mean?" Susan asked, picking up a cookie and biting it in half.

"I'm not sure where to start—yes, I am. You know Ashley's real name was Ann. At least that's the name her parents gave her."

"Yes."

"Well, that's just it. She was always trying to be something—or someone—that she wasn't born to be."

"I had heard that her childhood wasn't a lot like her adult life," Susan said tactfully.

"Please don't misunderstand me. Ashley was my only cousin. Signe is my only . . . well, I call her my niece, but of course, she isn't really."

Susan nodded, thinking that while Fanny had mentioned Signe twice in the short time they'd spoken, she hadn't asked where that young woman was. It was a subject Susan certainly was not going to bring up. "I understand that you didn't travel all this way just to trash your cousin."

"Thank you. I must admit that there was always a kernel of truth in Ashley's stories. She said she had moved into a town made up of very rich and very kind people. I don't know about the rich part, but everyone is being very kind."

"There are a lot of good people in Hancock."

"Despite what the priest said this afternoon, I don't believe Ashley would have been included if you were making a list of them. But please do not misunderstand me.

Ashley did not deserve all the things that had happened to her."

"No one deserves to be murdered," Susan said, thinking she was agreeing with Fanny's sentiments.

"No one deserves to be arrested for attempted murder, either. Not if they're innocent."

"You don't think she did it?" Susan realized immediately how dreadful that sounded. "I mean . . ."

"You mean that you—and everyone else in Hancock—believe she poisoned her husband. Your local paper is online, you know. I followed the story. But, no, I don't believe Ashley poisoned anyone—not knowingly, at any rate. That's what I want to talk to you about."

Susan's hand stopped on the way to picking up another cookie. Some things were even more interesting than food. "Why do you say that?" she asked.

"You're thinking that I hadn't seen my cousin in years. And that's right. And you're thinking that Ashley wasn't a very nice person. And that's right, too. But she's not a murderer."

"I . . . I don't know how to say this politely."

"Just blurt it right out."

"How do you know?" Susan asked.

"Makes sense. Ashley didn't care much about anything but Ashley. Never did. She was like that when she was growing up, and nothing she wrote, did, or that I heard about her led me to believe she had changed."

"So?"

"So why would she poison anyone? She had what she wanted. Money. Time to play around. Status. What did she have to gain if Doug died?"

"I don't know. Wasn't she his heir?"

"Nope. Signe was. The money—and there is a whole

lot of money—was settled on Doug for his lifetime. But Doug's parents weren't real fond of Ashley, so if Doug had died first, the money was to go straight to Signe. I think Signe is a lovely lady with a good head on her shoulders, and she just might not be all that amenable to sharing her inheritance with a mother who was not at all interested in raising her. Signe's a smart young thing, and I'm sure she's managed to accept the fact that she's alive because her mother had to trap a man with money into marrying her."

"Oh, I didn't realize that."

"No doubt about it." Fanny took another sip from her glass and peered at Susan. "So, am I making sense?"

"Yes, but you know so much more about Ashley than I do. For instance, I had no idea that she and Doug got married because she was pregnant."

"Yup. Those were the days when few women chose to raise children alone. Besides, Doug had to stay in the good graces of his parents, and his parents certainly did not want their grandchild to be born out of wedlock. They offered to help out with the rearing of the child."

"I did know that Signe was raised by them."

"Yes, she was. Although I don't know if either of them expected that when Ashley came to them with the news. But Doug's parents were good people, real good people, and they did a good job of raising Doug's daughter. Better, I daresay, than he or Ashley would have done."

"You don't think much of Doug, do you?"

Fanny sighed. "I know that in his field he's considered something of a genius. And I know that he's used his parents' money to get where he is."

"I thought he was employed by various agencies and governments to work on water . . . uh, water issues."

"Yes, I don't know very much about his field, either, but I can tell you a few things you might not know."

Susan leaned forward. "Please."

"Doug is famous for his knowledge—both practical and theoretical—concerning fresh, I guess I should say drinkable, water."

"Potable," Susan said.

"Excuse me?"

"The word is *potable*."

"Oh, well, whatever it is, Doug is an international authority on it. But he has used his parents' money to become that. He's taken dozens of jobs all over the world without even considering whether or not they pay an adequate salary or provide any amenities like family housing or medical insurance. I know this because Ashley's written me about it—*and* because I've done a bit of checking these things out on the Internet."

"You're saying that part of the reason Doug moved to the top of his field was because he didn't have to worry about making a living."

"Exactly!"

Susan thought for a moment. Fanny really didn't seem to be the type of woman who would trash her cousin's husband for no reason at all. "But Ashley wasn't faithful to him," she finally blurted out.

"How do you know he was faithful to her?"

"I . . ." Susan stopped and took a deep breath. "Maybe you'd better tell me what you know."

"Not all that much. I do know that Ashley loved her life with Doug, although I very much doubt if she cared about Doug himself particularly. As I said, she was not a very nice woman. And Doug? Well, I don't know him all that well."

"He doesn't talk that much about himself," Susan said. "But I gather he's done some things that are very important. I mean, even I know that clean water is a requirement for life."

"In my experience many men—and women, I suppose—who are successful and contribute to society are less-than-admirable characters when it comes to their private lives."

"Of course, that's true. But who do you think was poisoning Doug if Ashley wasn't?"

The answer was prompt and surprising. "Doug."

"You think he was poisoning himself? How?"

"Well, I don't know how exactly, but I think it would be easy for him to mix up something that would make him ill, but not kill him. After all, he is a scientist."

"I guess. But why?"

"I've thought and thought about that, and the only thing I've come up with is that he wanted Ashley in prison—out of his life—for some reason. I've wondered if he's involved with another woman or if he just got tired of putting up with her and wanted to be alone."

"I suppose either could be true. I hate to admit this, but I've lived next door to Ashley and Doug for a year, and in the past few days I've come to realize how little I know about them."

"But you are investigating Ashley's murder?"

"Yes. But I don't seem to be getting anywhere."

"Perhaps we should go next door," Fanny suggested reluctantly. "I need to express my condolences to Doug, and maybe you can talk to the guests and learn something that will help your investigation. That is how you work, isn't it?"

"Yes," Susan answered, but she didn't add that this time her investigation was going nowhere.

It looked as though everyone who had attended Ashley's funeral service had come to the reception afterward. Fortunately the weather was fine, and the guests had spilled out into the backyard. Susan was almost immediately swept away by her friends commenting on her tribute to Ashley. Looking over her shoulder, she saw Fanny heading toward the living room.

"Susan, we've all been wondering where you were," Jerry Gordon greeted her.

"Just over the fence," she answered, pointing in the direction of her yard. "Where's Kathleen?"

"Sitting down out back," he answered. "She looked tired. I made her promise to rest for a while."

"I'll go find her," Susan said, smiling at friends as she passed through the house into a large Victorian conservatory and then out into the yard. Kathleen was sitting on a teak bench, a glass of yellow liquid by her side.

"Lemonade? Isn't there any wine?" Susan asked.

"There is, but for some reason Jerry brought me this." Kathleen grimaced. "He's been acting a little strange lately."

"He's just trying to take care of you. He told me you looked tired."

"I feel tired. I was hoping a glass of wine would perk me up."

"I'll get us each one in a minute. But listen first. You'll never guess who I've been talking to!" Susan explained what she had just heard.

Kathleen sat quietly, nodding once or twice. "You know, this Fanny had some good points. Doug certainly could have been poisoning himself. And he also had ample opportunity to poison Ashley's food or drink at your party."

"He has all those guns," Susan mused. "If he wanted to kill someone, wouldn't he just shoot them?"

"No, too obvious," Kathleen said. "He's too smart to do that."

"Probably. And you know if he had been poisoning himself, it would explain one thing."

"What?"

"Why he was such a supportive husband during the trial. He was the only person who really did know that Ashley was innocent."

"That's true." Kathleen looked around the yard. "Do you know who does this lawn? There's not a weed in sight."

"That's funny," Susan said. "Just the other day Doug was asking me what lawn service I used. . . . Kathleen, that's it! Weeds! I saw Doug weeding the day after Ashley was killed. I didn't think anything about it at the time. I mean, who knows what a person will do when they're in shock. But what if it wasn't shock? What if Doug was pulling up poisonous plants to get rid of the evidence? What if he used those poisonous plants to kill Ashley!"

"I suppose that's possible," Kathleen said. "But wasn't Doug being poisoned with insecticides, and wasn't insecticide what had been used years ago back in Oxford Landing?"

"Yes, but . . ."

"But that doesn't mean something else wasn't used to kill Ashley last weekend," Kathleen continued.

"That's what I was going to say! We must get hold of the autopsy results. Then, once we know the type of poison, we can find out where to get it—and if it's something that might be or might have been growing in this yard," Susan ended enthusiastically. "And that would help clear Signe, don't you think?"

"I suppose." Kathleen paused. "I never even considered

the possibility that Doug was poisoning himself. I did consider the possibility that he killed Ashley, though—and I'd bet that thought has at least crossed the mind of every single person here."

"That's true."

"So tell me, if your theory is that Doug poisoned himself so that Ashley would be blamed and sent to prison, why, when that didn't happen, would he kill her? Do you think he just became fed up with her, and once she was acquitted, he decided he couldn't live with her one second more and he poisoned her?"

"Ah . . . I suppose that's a possibility. Unlikely, but a possibility. But there is another possibility that would fit in with what we're saying. Suppose Doug did poison himself—with whatever poison—and suppose Ashley was accidentally poisoned with . . . well, with whatever Doug was using before she was arrested."

Kathleen pursed her lips and thought about Susan's idea. "To tell the truth, I don't think that's much of a possibility. Remember that Doug was poisoned over a long period of time. A few weeks, right? It doesn't make sense that he would do that and then be so careless with the poison that Ashley could accidentally take a lethal dose the night of your party."

"The trouble is, we need the results of the autopsy done on Ashley. And for that, we're going to have to go see Chief Peter Konowitz."

"Well, here are two of the best-looking women in Hancock, sitting all alone and without drinks." Dan Hallard walked up, grinning, hands behind his back. "What are you two talking about?"

"Poison," Susan answered.

"Can't help you with that. But I do happen to have this."

He brought out a bottle of Chardonnay and four wine-glasses.

The women smiled. "Just what we were looking for," Kathleen said.

"Yes," Susan agreed. "Wine and a man who graduated from medical school."

THIRTY

"I GATHER YOUR ACCEPTANCE OF THIS WINE MEANS YOU'RE not pregnant," Dan said, handing a full glass to Kathleen.

"Pregnant?" Kathleen glanced down at her completely flat stomach. "Why would you think I'm pregnant?"

"I don't. But your husband does. He's been asking me questions about the OB/GYN man who bought my practice. Things like is he competent and whether he believes in natural childbirth. I assumed he was asking because he was worried about you."

Kathleen looked at Susan. "Why would Jerry think I'm pregnant?"

"How would I know? Oh, Kathleen! Your knitting! He probably assumed—"

"—that I was working on that baby blanket again because we were going to have another baby. Oh, I hope he's not disappointed when he finds out it's Chrissy who—"

"Chrissy is going to have a baby?" Dan interrupted. "You and Jed are going to be grandparents! Well, well, well. Congratulations. I should have stolen a bottle of champagne from the bar instead of wine!"

"No one knows yet," Susan said quickly. "You won't tell anyone . . ."

"Susan, as one of the best gynecologists in Hancock, I've kept more secrets than you'll ever know. You can count on me."

"Thanks, Dan."

"So I hear that Ashley's only daughter is so broken up by her mother's murder that she didn't make it to the funeral."

"That's the story you heard?" Susan asked.

"Is that what everyone here believes?" Kathleen said, her eyes running over the large crowd.

"Don't know what they believe. I, myself, think it's mighty odd for a daughter not to come to her mother's funeral. Of course, it was a mighty odd funeral."

Kathleen smiled. "That's true. It's the first time I've been to a funeral where the minister couldn't decide what to call the deceased."

"You did a nice job, though, Susan. Anyone listening would have thought you were close friends with Ashley."

Susan frowned. "You know, I've just learned that more than a few people in town think that very thing."

"Why?" Kathleen asked, sipping her wine.

"Apparently that's what Ashley had been telling people."

"How weird!" Kathleen said.

"Not so weird. I know Martha thinks I'm nuts, but I got the impression that having you as a next-door neighbor was a real selling point for the house," Dan said.

"Why?"

"Well, there was a lot of publicity about how you solved the murder of that woman killed out at the discount mall— I don't remember her name. I do remember there was a front-page article about it in the *Hancock Herald* the weekend we had the open house. And you know Martha—she didn't become the biggest realtor in the area without learning to use every single advantage she could find to sell a home. That issue of the *Herald* was on more than one coffee table—just sort of casually flung there."

"You mean it really is true that Ashley and Doug might have bought your house just to be our next-door neighbors?" Susan asked, wondering what this could mean.

"Well, not just to be your neighbors. I like to think that our home had something to do with it," Dan suggested, smiling.

"Of course, but . . . but why?"

"Maybe it made someone—either Ashley or Doug—feel safer to have you living nearby. You know, if there's a murder in the area, you're bound to investigate," Kathleen said.

"And you do find the murderer," Dan Hallard added.

Susan frowned. "Yes, usually," she said.

"On the other hand, everything I've heard about Ashley Marks indicates that she sure was one status-conscious individual. Maybe she just wanted to shmooze with one of Hancock's local celebrities."

"That is possible. You just told us that she had been bragging about being good friends with you," Kathleen reminded her.

"I know, but it still doesn't make sense. There are lots of truly famous people living in Hancock. If Ashley had been interested in status conferral, she could have bought a house near one of our local celebrities, not next to me. Or she could have run around town lying about being friends with them instead of with me."

"That's probably true," Dan Hallard agreed cheerfully. "She could have snuggled up with that morning talk show host. I hear he's not too choosy about who he hangs out with. Oh, there's Doug. I'd better go offer my condolences. See you later, ladies."

"Bye, Dan. Thanks for the wine."

"Yeah, thanks," Susan muttered, putting her almost-full glass down on the bench by her side.

"Doesn't make a lot of sense, does it?" Kathleen asked.

"No, it sure doesn't. I wish I knew more about that first poisoning case."

"Didn't you say that woman you went to school with was investigating that?"

"Jinx Jensen? Yes. She probably still is."

"Not unless she's looking through church records. She was at the funeral with a very good-looking gentleman."

"Is she here? Did she come back to the house?" Susan asked quickly.

"I may have seen her companion when Jerry and I came in. But that was a while ago."

Susan stood up. "Let's try to find them. It could be important. I'll go into the house, and you look around out here. And if you find Jinx or Sam Redman—that's the man she's probably with—um, bring them back here. This is as good a place to talk as any."

"Fine, but . . ." Kathleen looked down at her watch. "Let's meet here in ten minutes even if we don't find them. Otherwise we could end up wandering around until we're the last people here."

"Good idea," Susan said, starting back toward the house. The crowd had thinned out, and she ran into Sam almost immediately, his height making him easy to find.

"Very nice speech, Mrs. Henshaw. I was wondering if I could have a copy of it to print in the paper."

"Oh, of course." Susan looked around. "Didn't you come here with Jinx?"

"Yup. She's around here somewhere. Jinx Jensen is one very independent woman. She said she needed to find someone and took off."

"Oh, well, I need to find her, too. If you see her . . ."

"I'll let her know you're looking for her. She had a whole pile of stuff in her purse to show you."

Susan smiled broadly. "That is good news."

Jinx was sitting on a hideous crushed velvet chaise lounge in the living room, peering at the crowd. She waved when she spied Susan, spilling her glass of wine on her seat. "Damn, I didn't mean to do that. Do you have a napkin?"

"No, but I wouldn't worry. It would take more than a little wine to damage that ugly thing." Susan sat down beside Jinx. "I've been looking all over for you. I found Sam, and he said you have some papers."

"Yes! You don't want to know how much work it took, but I finally found a few articles about the Markses, and even a mention of the first poisoning." Jinx looked around the crowded room. "Maybe this isn't the best place to look at them."

"We could go next door, but I haven't seen Doug yet and I wouldn't want him to think I'd leave without talking to him. Why don't we go upstairs?" Susan suggested. "If anyone wonders what we're doing, we can claim to be looking for an empty bathroom."

"Lead the way."

There turned out to be an unoccupied bathroom conveniently located at the top of the stairs. Susan and Jinx slipped in and carefully locked the door behind them. "I can't tell you how glad I am that you copied the articles," Susan said, holding out her hand.

"Where do you think that came from?" Jinx asked, staring at a hideous oak toilet surround.

"Who knows? Where are the papers?"

"Here. Sam said it was okay if I circled the relevant bits.

He said I'm only the third person interested in searching through the morgue since he's been editor of the paper, so there's no reason to be too fussy. They're not in any order."

But Susan didn't care. She sat down on the closed toilet seat lid and picked up the top issue of the *Oxford Democrat*. She'd been waiting so long.

She looked up five minutes later. "I just remembered. I told Kathleen I'd be back in ten minutes."

"Where is she?"

"In the backyard by the rose garden. She's sitting on a bench."

"You go ahead and finish reading, and I'll go tell her what's going on," Jinx offered.

"I didn't know you two knew each other."

"I know who she is. It was her husband who offered the toast at your party, right? And they both ate dinner with you."

"Exactly. Tell her I'll be out as soon as possible."

"No problem." Jinx opened the door. Susan, hearing her explain to someone that the bathroom was still occupied, returned to her reading.

The articles about the Marks family were on top of the pile. Susan learned that not only had Doug been active in Scouts and 4-H, but that he had won the egg toss at the annual July Fourth picnic held in the Oxford Landing town square. There was a charming photograph of him as an eleven-year-old, dripping raw egg on the ground and grinning proudly. She skimmed articles about his science fair wins and studied in detail the article announcing his wedding to Ashley. As Jinx had said, Ashley had been a beautiful bride. Susan found herself staring at the black-and-white photograph, wondering whether the young

woman there had had any inkling of what the future held
for her and her new husband.

Signe's birth was announced properly, but there was little more of note until Susan found three clippings concerning the untimely illnesses of the owners of the Marks
farm. Jinx had implied that Sam's father was intimidated
by the important citizens of Oxford Landing, and the short-
ness of these articles attested to her belief. Poison, as a
possible reason for the family's continuing illness, wasn't
even mentioned until the final article, when it was stated
that authorities had sent samples of various bodily fluids
off to state forensic experts for identification. What the
samples revealed had either gone unreported or else that
article was still hidden away in one of the *Oxford Democrat's* filing cabinets.

There were four more articles clipped together underneath those she had already studied. Susan picked them up
and removed the paper clip, frowning until she recognized
the photograph accompanying the top article. The Twigg
sisters, years younger but still recognizable, stood together
on the steps leading to the front door of the Landing Inn.
Alvena was smiling broadly; Constance's expression was
more reserved. The women's arms were outstretched in a
gesture Susan didn't understand until she read the article.
They were supposed to be welcoming guests to the Landing Inn after what the article called "a major remodeling"
of the inn. The article went on to enumerate the various
improvements, many of which, it claimed, had been suggested by the inn's guests. The next article concerned a
crime wave that had "held Oxford Landing in its grip"—
Jinx had added red exclamation marks after this phrase—
seven years ago. Among the various problems, cars in the

inn's parking lot had been broken into and various personal items stolen. Alvena was quoted, confirming her belief that Peter Konowitz, a local boy she had known for years and who was now attending the state police academy and had been hired as a security officer for the inn, would easily catch the perpetrators of these horrors. There was no mention of whether or not that had happened.

The last article concerned the hiring of Peter Konowitz by the Oxford Landing police force. The new Officer Konowitz was described as good-looking, young, and enthusiastic. The accompanying photograph confirmed the first two qualities. Alvena Twigg confirmed the last. "I've known Peter since he was in ninth grade," Miss Twigg was quoted as saying. "He's smart, ambitious, and hardworking. He will be a real asset to the Oxford Landing Police Department. I, for one," she ended, "will sleep better knowing Officer Konowitz is on the job." Susan read the story once again. Then she put the articles in calendar order and reviewed what she'd just read. Why, she wondered, had no one bothered to mention the fact that the first poisonings had taken place only a few months after Peter Konowitz had been hired?

Susan stood up. Time to return to her family and friends. She opened the bathroom door and found herself face-to-face with Doug Marks.

"Doug . . . I didn't mean to be in here so long," she said, stuffing the clippings into her purse.

"Some of my guests were concerned about the length of time this bathroom has been in use. I just came up to make sure everything was okay. But now that I've found you, I can tell you how much I appreciate your participation in Ashley's service. I know she would have felt the same way I do."

"I was happy to be asked," Susan lied, following her host downstairs. "I was looking for you earlier. I haven't had an opportunity to express my condolences. We'll all miss Ashley."

The tears that suddenly appeared in Doug's eyes came as a complete surprise. He took both her hands and squeezed them. "Not everyone will miss her. I know how she could be. But I will, and I believe Signe will. And that might just be enough, don't you think?"

"I . . . Yes, of course." Susan didn't know what else to say. It was a relief when another neighbor appeared to offer condolences. Susan hurried off to the backyard and found Kathleen and Jinx chatting together. She collapsed onto the spot they cleared for her on the bench and sighed. "He loved her. Doug Marks really loved that awful woman."

Jinx looked up, obviously surprised. "Why are you surprised? That's the way it seemed throughout her trial. The papers said that he was there every day."

"I know. I can't believe how stupid I've been. I didn't like Ashley. She was certainly not the type of person I wanted to move in next door. I guess I just assumed everyone else felt the way I did."

Kathleen reached for the bottle of wine Dan Hallard had left, poured out a glass, and handed it to her. "Here. This might help."

"Nothing helps. I want to find out who killed Ashley. I ask dozens of questions, and I still don't know anything. No one seems to know anything. I go from one police station to the inn to the other police station. And I don't learn anything new. I find a bottle that could be evidence, but I still don't know if it is or if—" Susan stopped speaking and reached into her purse.

"What's wrong?" Jinx asked.

"Wasn't there something about evidence in those newspaper articles you just gave me?" Susan flipped through the newsprint as she spoke. "See, that's what I'm saying! I just read those articles, and I'm not sure what's important and what's not. I just can't get a handle on this investigation. Alvena tells me about the Markses' past, and Jinx finds a bunch of information in the local newspapers, but I can't fit it all together. I know I'm missing something. Hell, I know I'm missing a lot. There must be lots of people I haven't talked to. I just don't know who they are. As far as I know, Ashley and Doug didn't have any real friends in Hancock. They may have moved into this house because I was living next door. But neither Doug nor Ashley ever made any serious attempt to get to know Jed or me. Of course, Ashley didn't need to. She ran around town claiming to be my friend without ever worrying about whether she was or not." Susan picked up her full wineglass and drained it. "That's bothering me, too. I seem to have been set up here. I feel like the Markses invaded my town, my neighborhood, and then, damn it, my party and my life, and I don't have any idea why!" She stood up.

"Where are you going?" Kathleen asked.

"Home. I'm going to . . . I don't know. Maybe I'll go finish my thank-you notes."

There were only a dozen or so more notes to write, and Susan got down to work immediately. She'd had a rotten day, she was tired, and she certainly shouldn't have inhaled that last glass of wine. But, for some reason, the combination of anger, fatigue, and alcohol did the trick, and she dashed off the last of the notes in record time.

"There you are, Clue," she said to the dog who was lying

on her dog bed, underneath Jed's desk. "Want to take a walk to the mailbox with me?"

Clue jumped up, putting her front paws on the desk and toppling the pile of stamped notes Susan had left near the edge. She grabbed for them and came up with yet another of the Landing Inn Guest Questionnaire forms that Alvena was always after her to fill out. Clue sat back down, an eager expression on her furry face. Susan glanced at the sheet of paper and tossed it on Jed's desk.

And then picked it up. She had promised to fill this out. If she did it now, she could put it in the mail with her thank-you notes and she wouldn't have to think about it again. It would take very little time. The first question was standard: How did you hear about the Landing Inn?

Susan thought for a minute before realizing that the answer to this question was at least part of the answer to all the other more serious questions she'd been asking for the last week. In a way, it was the key that held everything together.

THIRTY-ONE

"ASHLEY MARKS PLANNED HER OWN MURDER!"

"Susan, you know how these cell phones are! It sounds like you said that Ashley Marks planned her own murder," Kathleen responded.

"You heard me just fine. Ashley planned her own murder. I called Brett and he's on his way over here, but I wanted to tell you first."

"So tell me! And start from the beginning," Kathleen insisted.

"Remember the party we gave for the Markses right after they arrived in town?"

"Of course. I learned that Doug was a clean-water expert who loved guns, and you were busy elsewhere."

"I was busy talking with Ashley. About our upcoming anniversary party. That's when she did it. She suggested the Landing Inn."

"Really?"

"Yes, I got so involved in the planning and all that I forgot where the original idea came from until a few minutes ago. But the idea was Ashley's. I remember thinking that it was a brilliant idea—having the party where we spent the first night of our marriage. I didn't know about the food and all, but she assured me that the inn had changed over the years and would be a perfect place for a party. And of course it was.

"Kath, that's the doorbell. It must be Brett."

"Don't you dare go on until I get there! I'm only three blocks away! It will take less than two minutes! I want to hear everything!" Kathleen hung up without bothering to say good-bye.

Erika and Brett were at the door, still in the clothes they'd worn to the funeral. Jed, who had come home to find Susan excited and Clue desperate for a walk, strolled up the sidewalk behind them. Susan glanced next door. There were three cars in the driveway and about a dozen parked on the street. It looked like Doug was still entertaining funeral guests.

"Kathleen's on the way over. I caught her on her cell phone in her car. She had just left Doug's house," Susan explained, leading them all into the living room. "Although maybe I should have called Jinx. She did a lot of the research." But a quick glance at Brett's face and she stopped chattering. "You know," she said quietly, sitting down on the arm of the chair where Jed was sitting.

Brett nodded. "Yes, I've tried to think of anyone else who would fit, and I can't." He leaned against the mantel and frowned. "Erika and I were at the service. But after we left the church, we headed straight for the police station. We decided not to go next door. I was worried that our presence at the service might have been disrupting enough, so Erika went to the station with me."

"I saw Signe. She's fine," Erika spoke up.

"I should have realized that you had Signe," Susan said to Brett.

"Protective custody. Signe agreed because she was scared. She refused to talk about it, but I think she believed her father had killed her mother. And that he just might be dangerous."

"Poor Signe."

"She'll be okay now," Erika said. "Brett told her that her father was no longer a suspect, and when we left, she was packing her things. One of Brett's officers will drop her off at her home after the rest of Doug's guests leave. She didn't want to run into a lot of people and feel obliged to explain where she's been—and why."

"But where's Peter Konowitz?" Susan asked.

"We're not sure. I've been calling around, and apparently Peter has disappeared. He must have known we were getting close."

"Then he won't be arrested?" Susan asked.

"Oh, he will be," Brett assured her, a grim expression on his face. "Everyone involved is making the assumption that he's left the state already. The FBI's been called in. They'll find him. Don't worry. Peter Konowitz is going to pay for killing Ashley Marks."

"But will he pay for doing so much damage to their lives over the years?" Susan wondered.

Kathleen appeared in the doorway of the room. "Wait a second," she insisted. "Before you get philosophical, I need to know the details. Who? What? When? And all that."

"I'm completely in the dark, too, hon," Jed spoke up.

"I'm not sure I know where to start," Susan said.

"Susan, less than fifteen minutes ago you were saying you didn't have the information you needed to solve this case. What changed?" Kathleen asked, sitting down on the couch and petting Clue.

"I realized what not having the information meant," Susan said.

"That's not an explanation," Jed protested.

"It is! You see, I thought I didn't know anything because I was used to Brett being in charge of a case. I thought that was what was wrong. But it wasn't what Brett wasn't doing. It was what Peter Konowitz wasn't doing."

"He didn't pass on information like Brett would have done," Kathleen guessed.

"I doubt if he even bothered to get the information." Susan looked up at Brett.

"You're right." Brett answered her unspoken question. "There's no record of him turning in an empty wine bottle to determine if there was poison in it. Either he knew that there was—and I suspect that's the truth—or he knew there wasn't because he had used some other method to poison Ashley. Either way, he didn't want anyone else knowing."

"What about the first time?" Susan asked "One of the newspaper articles Jinx found reported that Peter Konowitz was sending samples of various foods and what the reporter referred to as bodily fluids out to the labs. Did he do it then?"

"We're going to have to find that out. There were records kept. We'll know all of this eventually. But I suspect he didn't."

"This is somewhat confusing," Jed said.

"But that was the point!" Susan cried. "The confusion was intentional. And it was created by Peter Konowitz. Once I realized that, I began to understand what was going on."

"What do you mean?" Kathleen asked.

"Right from the first, Chief Konowitz had everyone running in circles. Well, not right from the first. He actually asked Jed and me a few intelligent questions when Brett reported the body to him. But that was only because Brett was present and would pick up on any unprofessional behavior on the part of a colleague." She glanced over at Brett. "Right?"

"Probably."

"But that was the only time," Susan continued. "There were no follow-up questions. No interview later to get all the little details he might have missed the first time. Nothing. After that initial meeting, all Chief . . . Would anyone mind if I called him Peter? It would be easier."

"It would be more appropriate, too," Brett said. "Peter Konowitz should never have been made police chief. He shouldn't have been a cop at all. I should have . . . could have . . . stopped his career years ago. But . . ."

Erika was up and by her husband's side immediately. "It isn't . . . It wasn't your fault," she insisted, taking his hand in hers. "There was no way you could have known this was going to happen."

"No, you're right about that. And I had no idea he'd screwed up his first big investigation back when I hired him to work here in Hancock. But I knew he didn't get along well with the people he worked with. And I gave him the benefit of the doubt and didn't even put that in his permanent record. You can't get around the fact that I made some bad judgment calls when it came to Peter Konowitz. To tell the truth, I was so glad he was leaving the force that I didn't care about too much else."

"You know, I think he used the fact that he irritated people," Susan spoke up. "He kept popping up here and there and making life difficult for me. Instead of going to him for help, I began to avoid him. And, of course, that was just what he wanted. He didn't want me around. He didn't want me looking too carefully at Ashley's murder, so he was happy that I was running around looking for Signe in the wrong place, being offered opinion as fact by Alvena

Twigg. I was busy, busy, busy, and I didn't accomplish a damn thing."

"So Peter Konowitz killed Ashley," Jed said. "Why?"

"Because she knew he screwed up his very first big investigation as rookie police officer back in Oxford Landing."

"The first poisoning case?" Jed asked for clarification.

Susan nodded vigorously. "Exactly."

"Who . . . ?"

Susan didn't have to wait for him to ask the question to answer. "Ashley. Ashley poisoned Doug both times."

"For God's sake! Why? And why was she so incompetent that he lived—twice?"

"Because she didn't want him to die. She wanted him to move to a place where she could live the type of life she wanted to live."

"You're saying Ashley used poison as some sort of lifestyle change incentive?"

"Sure. The first time she didn't want to live on the farm with Doug's mother. So she placed insecticide in the food she and Doug ate. My guess is that she thought Doug would think it was all a tragic accident and take the family away from the farm. But I think Doug may have known what she was doing."

"But didn't he just encourage her by moving? I mean, she did get what she wanted, right?" Erika asked.

"Yes, but he also protected everyone. Ashley may have gotten the result she wanted, but he also protected Signe from prosecution. There's no doubt that he loves his daughter. I'm sure that was important to him, too."

"So you don't think Ashley loved Hancock, either," Kathleen said.

"Even I know Hancock isn't Paris," Susan explained. "But Ashley saw a way out at the same time Doug was falling in love with the house where he would have his shooting range. She saw the articles about me. I doubt if Ashley thought I was Hancock's Nancy Drew. She probably thought I was a meddling busybody who would investigate in an incompetent manner—which would mean she wouldn't be caught. She waited until she'd lived here long enough to make it look as though the two families were friendly, and then she began the poisoning again. And that upset Peter Konowitz."

"Why?"

Susan looked at Brett. "Because he screwed up the first investigation, right?"

"Right. Peter probably thought he'd gotten off scot-free when Ashley was arrested and the first poisoning wasn't reported. But then she was freed, and Brett started to investigate again. This time there was no way the first poisoning was going to remain in the past. It wouldn't have taken my guys long to realize that Peter screwed up the first time, and that would have ruined his fading career."

"So moving to Oxford Landing—even as chief of police—wasn't much of a promotion," Erika suggested.

"Damn right." Brett looked angry, and Susan finished off the sad tale.

"So Ashley was freed and decided going to our party was just the thing to perk her up after the weeks in jail and the trial. And Peter knew you wouldn't just let the question of who poisoned Doug die. Unfortunately, Ashley had suggested the Landing Inn, and I had thought it was a great suggestion. But Oxford Landing is a small community. Peter probably heard about my party. And he could assume I'd invite my next-door neighbors. Ashley was in place when Peter offered her a glass of wine and killed her.

"And then he put her in our bedroom. He knew about my

reputation, and he knew I wouldn't be able to resist investigating. And he couldn't resist sending me off on the wrong track again and again."

"He might have gotten away with it," Jed said slowly. "Everyone was so sure that Doug was the killer. Of course, Peter Konowitz didn't know that you're not exactly a linear thinker. You did what you always do. You looked in all directions until you found what you were looking for—the man who poisoned Ashley Marks."

THIRTY-TWO

●

A WEEK LATER, KATHLEEN AND SUSAN WERE ROCKING together on an old-fashioned outdoor swing placed in the shade in the Henshaws' backyard.

"Kathleen, this is the best anniversary present we were given," Susan said.

"I'm glad you like it. It was really Jerry's idea. I shopped and shopped and couldn't find anything I thought you and Jed would both like. Then Jerry came home from the garden center with one of these things for us, and I sent him back to get this one for you and Jed."

"It's sensational. Thank you."

"You're very welcome." Kathleen looked closely at her friend. "You seem a bit tired."

"I am. Chrissy and Stephen and their dogs left early this morning."

"And you miss them already."

"Not yet. But we were all up late last night talking and making plans for the upcoming blessed event."

"You must have been terribly disappointed when Chrissy told you that it was one of the dogs who is expecting, not her."

"I was, but she and Stephen are young. There's lots of time for them to have children. And last night Stephen said

●

that he's being wooed by three different brokerage houses, and two of them are located in New York City!"

"Susan, that's sensational!"

"You know, Kathleen, you've been asking all the questions. Now I have one for you."

"What?"

"Are you pregnant?"

"Heavens, no! You know I'd tell you if that were true."

"Then why are you still working on that baby afghan?" Susan asked, pointing at the knitting bag slung on the ground by Kathleen's feet.

Kathleen grinned. "Oh, Susan! I'm really enjoying this. Do you have any idea how rare it is that I know something about one of our friends before you do?"

"Someone we know is pregnant?"

Kathleen's grin grew wider. "Yes. Erika."

"Erika and Brett are going to have a baby? Are you sure? How do you know? When? That's the most fantastic news!"

"It is," Kathleen agreed. "I ran into them at the Hancock Inn last night. When Brett left here last week, I thought he'd never cheer up. He was really blaming himself for a lot of bad things happening to a lot of people. But last night he was drinking champagne and laughing. I stopped by their table to say hello, and they told me the big news."

"Wow. A new baby. What great news!" Susan thought for a minute. "You know what else?"

"What?"

"We should give Erika a baby shower! We can have it here—or at the Hancock Inn!"

"That's a great idea! Do you think we should have a meal?"

"How about just a late-afternoon tea?" Susan suggested.

"We could do it sometime in late January or February, and we can decorate with spring flowers. We'll all be dying for a reminder that warm weather is coming by then."

"How about a guest list."

"And a theme."

Ten minutes later Jed and his son were standing by the back door, watching the two women.

"I can't believe this," Chad said. "After what happened two weeks ago, they're busy planning another party! I would have thought they'd be afraid of bad luck following them from party to party."

Jed smiled at his son. "I can't say that I understand women, but I do know one thing."

"What?"

"Your mother always looks at the future with optimism, no matter what has happened. And you know what else? That's just one of the many reasons I'm very glad I married her thirty years ago."

Chad rolled his eyes and headed inside to check out the refrigerator.

Susan, having overheard, looked up at her husband and smiled before getting down to work on yet another guest list.